# UNEASY LIES
# THE HEAD

## CEDI ALI RAJAH

Uneasy Lies the Head

Published by Night Fire Publishing, a division of Night Fire Media

Cover Design: Debbie Bright, The Cover Collection

Digital ISBN-13: 978 1-7365293-2-4

Print ISBN-13: 978 1-7365293-0-0

Printed in the United States of America

*To Chris, my special one.  I will love you forever.*

# PROLOGUE

The term "tent" was generous; the entire structure was an assortment of threadbare fabrics upheld by wooden beams and dead branches. While it offered shade it did nothing to protect from the brutal sandstorms that ravaged the area. The old man greeted the sight of it with a grunt; it was hardly fit for human life.

But he doubted what resided here was human.

Wrapped in a flowing robe, the old man plodded across the Sahara. He carried only a satchel. His guides, local men, were happy to stay with the camels and not come within fifty yards of the place. While most of his Arabic had long deserted him, he still recognized "cursed" when he told them their destination.

As he neared the tent he saw a thin figure seated on a cinderblock beneath the shade. The figure stood as he approached; the old man could almost feel the thing smiling at him.

With his heart pounding from anticipation, he stepped inside. His vision darkened in the shade, and although he blinked several times to adjust his eyes nothing changed. How could he forget? The last time he saw this apparition, now decades past, it had been around a fire that inexplicably failed to illuminate the figure's face. Then, as now, its face remained obscured in shadow, regardless that it stood an arm's length away. In these unholy places even the laws of physics could be disregarded.

"You tempt death by returning." The figure's voice hadn't aged in three decades: same unplaceable accent, same eerie quality.

"I've been dead for thirty years," the old man replied. "I'm here to live again." He saw the glint of teeth. A smile?

"The one who brought you before—what became of him?" The old man kept silent. "I see. How?"

"Drug overdose."

"They always die first," the figure chuckled. "The consorts, the ones who bring. Greedy enough to thirst for power, weak enough to be killed by it quickly. Always." The old man shifted, uncomfortable. The figure's grin widened. "Surely you didn't think you were the first. Or that you'll be the last."

"It's over."

The figure didn't answer. Instead, it retrieved a small tin container from the sandy floor.

"This is for your vessel."

The old man took the tin and opened it; inside was a sheet of ancient white parchment that pulsed like a slow-beating heart. The old man closed the tin with a gulp and placed it into his satchel.

"What do I do with it?"

"Place it over the face of your vessel and activate it."

"How do I do that?"

The figure now held a small wooden box. Inside was a small white porcelain bowl.

With it was a tiny stake, black as night.

"The same way you open the portal for your champion." The figure was smiling again. "Under the light of a full moon. And with a bit of the other stuff."

The old man stared.

"You can't mean...why would they need—"

The figure giggled; it sounded like small birds being killed.

"It's ironic, is it not? Blood is life. No matter what side you're on."

The old man breathed through gritted teeth. He then stuffed the tin into his satchel alongside the box.

"Forty-eight hours?"

"And not a moment more," the figure replied. "One word of caution. Once the portal is open, it's open to all. If the darkness is given a vessel it will use it."

"That won't happen." The satchel was unnaturally warm against the old man's side. "When it's over I won't be able to return any of this."

"These things always find their way back to me. They'll be ready the next time one of you comes to make a deal."

The old man's mouth tightened.

"I said it's over. I'm ending this." Anger fueled his certainty. But this time the figure didn't smile.

"No, you're not," it said. "You're praying your champion will."

Then it smiled again.

Furious, the old man stomped back into the scathing sun.

\*     \*     \*

# CHAPTER ONE

## Sunday Night

For all its luxury, the snow-covered cabin was a mere 6,000 feet above sea level, and Dominick Reinhart knew that was well-shy of "top the world" status. But Wrightwood, California was much closer to LA than the Himalayas, and looming over the city was an indulgence too delicious to forgo—even if the San Gabriel mountains had nothing on Mount Everest. The words of his grandmother came to mind: "Boy, sometimes you just gotta use what you got."

Dominick sipped his hot cider. He and his mentor had been sitting in silence for nearly five minutes, with only the moonlight between them. What words could capture the moment? Victory—tangible, heart-pounding, life-affirming victory—defied description. Talking about it would be like trying to paint a portrait with hues that had escaped the color wheel.

The metaphor was poignant. Color—specifically the

pigmentation of his skin—had long fed conversations about him. He had been a *black* MBA, then a *black* businessman, and was now a *black* executive. It was as if his race was a herald who traveled ahead to inform all in earshot that *a Black man* approaches. But now, with victory upon him, even his herald had gone silent. The only color anyone cared about now was green.

Satisfied, Dominick absorbed every nuance of now. The cabin's front porch, where they sat, afforded them a commanding view of the forest hills around them. The log in the fire pit popped beside them. The wind, crisp and gentle, wafted across his cheek. It was tranquil, beautiful, and most of all, quiet.

"What happened to Miller?" Mr. Wellington's voice cut through the silence with surprising urgency.

Dominick spared him a glance. Mr. Wellington knew what happened to Miller—the part that mattered anyway.

"I mean how did you do it?" the old man added. "How far did you go?"

"The circumstances preceding Miller's resignation— his *voluntary* resignation—are best kept between the parties present at the time." Admittedly, it was perhaps the sweetest corporate kill of Dominick's career. But given this "corporate kill" had almost become literal and could have resulted in the *involuntary* ending of Carson Miller's life, pride would defer to prudence.

"I don't need deniability. I need to know I'm right about you, even if it's too late."

Dominick's jaw tightened in confusion, but he saw only resolve on the older man's face. Dominick leaned in close and spoke softly.

"Oppo found something. Illegal gambling. Dog-fights, cock-fights, bare-knuckle cage matches."

"You blackmailed him?"

"Not exactly."

The investigating firm had warned against it; besides being dangerous, it could be construed as an obstruction of justice. But Miller—pompous, well-connected, and son of a former United States Congressman—would never withdraw from consideration over dirty laundry. His proud Kentucky family had once owned people who looked like Dominick; so rolling over under threat of blackmail and ceding the corporate throne to Dominick, a *black man,* was more than Miller's ego would bear. So Dominick took the risk.

"The gambling ring is on the FBI's radar," Dominick continued. "They had Miller under surveillance. I let the criminals know."

"You told them he was an informant."

"They arrived at that possibility themselves."

"You could have gotten him killed."

It was true. Hours earlier, when Dominick watched two career criminals climb into the chauffeured Town Car carrying him and Miller, he knew the already-high stakes had escalated to that of life or death. He was proven correct about this in short order. How much should he tell the old man?

That afternoon Dominick and Miller were exiting the Johnathan Club, LA's posh gathering place for the city's power-brokers, with Miller delighting in what he believed was his countdown to victory. His hubris made setting the trap both easy and gratifying.

"There's a car outside taking me back to the office," Dominick told him. "If you want to come along."

"Sure," Miller said, his voice loud from the night's whiskey. "Given that you're about to be one of my direct reports, I'm happy to give you some of my time." He laid a condescending hand on Dominick's shoulder. "Make sure you have the support you need."

Dominick smiled back. "Get your hand off me."

Miller withdrew his hand with an easy, arrogant laugh. "I'm going to enjoy this," he said to no one.

Minutes later, with Dominick and Miller in the backseat, the driver of the Town Car made a special stop under the freeway. There, lurking like wraiths in the darkness, were two mob men. The first was an enforcer who squeezed his bulk next to Miller; as he did the butt of his pistol became visible under his sport coat. The second, the apparent mob lieutenant, looked more like a CPA with his small stature, balding head, and glasses. The driver, who'd been hired by the criminals and was likely one himself, rolled up the tinted windows and cruised along.

"Carsie, baby!" the small bespectacled man announced as he got in the passenger's seat. "How the heck are you?"

As expected, Miller was confused at the presence of his mobster friends, but he was unaware of any federal investigation and thus more annoyed Dominick had been digging into his dirty secrets than anything else.

That was when the "CPA" pulled out a pistol.

"Check him," he told the enforcer.

"Fellas, what the hell?" With the enforcer's rough hands on him, Miller's voice was loud and higher-pitched.

"You mind not yelling, Carsie?" The bespectacled man motioned with the pistol. "My ears, yeah?"

Miller's mouth slammed shut. The enforcer concluded his

search.

"Clean. Except for this." The enforcer held up a tiny ziplock bag containing white powder.

"Let it snow." The balding man's voice was humorless.

Miller, attempting calm despite the perspiration beading on his forehead, gave the bespectacled man a nervous smile.

"Listen, I don't know what dickhead here told you, but—"

"Carsie?" the balding man cocked the pistol and aimed it at Miller. "Shut. The fuck. Up."

Miller's breath seized in his throat and his head rocked back, as if increasing distance from the gun's barrel might provide additional safety.

With his gun angled in Miller's direction, the balding man turned to Dominick. "You expect me to believe this pencil-neck fucktard doesn't know anything about the feds being up his ass?"

"He doesn't know what state's evidence even means." Dominick kept his voice neutral in spite of his elevated heart rate.

"Fair point," the bespectacled man nodded. Then, ever-so-slightly, the barrel of the gun edged towards Dominick. "Problem is, there's another possibility, yeah? You could be a better actor, sent to save his ass. And both of you are working with the feds."

Dominick's eyes shifted to the barrel of the gun and then to the two eyes behind it. Anger lumped into his throat. The past refused to stay dead.

Dominick laughed, but it wasn't the nervous laughter of the fearful. Lord knows he'd seen that received badly, both on the streets and in the boardroom. His was hard, defiant laughter. He couldn't get himself killed, not now, not when he was this close.

"I say something funny?" The bespectacled man's voice was low, dangerous, and the enforcer shifted. Heedless, Dominick kept his eyes drilled on the bespectacled man's own.

"You compared me to this asshole. That's the best joke I've heard all day." Dominick leaned forward, his face in a snarl. "Let's get something straight, gangster-man. I don't care about you. I don't care about Miller. I don't care about feds, dog-fights, cage-fights, or whatever the hell else you got going. I care about the job I'm getting tomorrow. It's already taken more from me than you ever could."

It had gotten too personal. He needed to distract himself, so he glanced over at Miller. He was sweating so much he looked like he was melting.

"Me save Miller's ass?" Dominick continued, turning back the gunman. "If you put a bullet through his thick skull right now, my life would move the fuck on." A small whine escaped Miller. "Would it be inconvenient? Yes. Worth the heat you'd get for killing a former congressman's son? Probably not. The end of the world? Please."

His heart throbbed so hard he felt it in his face, but Dominick kept his eyes on the balding man and away from the insistent black hole of the gun. The balding man considered. Then he shrugged.

"One way to find out." He pointed the gun at Miller's head. Miller instantly squealed and cowered, his hands raised to protect his head.

Dominick didn't blink, or even look Miller's way. When the bespectacled man held the gun steady but didn't fire, Dominick remained still. After a moment the small man smiled and lowered his weapon; Dominick wasn't surprised.

The tactics of the street never changed.

Miller was hyperventilating. The bespectacled man chuckled as he put away his pistol.

"Carsie, Carsie, you wet noodle! Relax, your buddy here saved your life." He patted Miller's cheek good-naturedly. "Had to make sure. Business, yeah? We'll drop him off and then grab a drink."

They pulled over to drop off Dominick a few blocks later. He was grateful to keep his lunch down in the interim. Before getting out of the car he turned to Miller.

"Withdraw from consideration," Dominick said. Thankfully, his voice didn't crack. Miller, his shell-shocked face as grey as a winter sky, didn't respond. He could have passed for a corpse. Later he resigned from the company altogether.

"A couple parting words." The bespectacled man, his voice cheery, rolled down the window as Dominick got out. "If the boys come around, this never happened."

"Obviously."

"And congrats on the job. Honestly. But it's just a fucking job. There's more important things in life, yeah?"

He motioned to the driver and away they went. Dominick caught a glimpse of Miller's pallid face before it vanished into the night, and with it went Dominick's final obstacle. He'd won.

He puked on the sidewalk. He laughed between spasms, even as he tried to avoid getting vomit on his $2,000 Oxfords. He'd done it, at last.

"Got change?"

A gaunt toothless man lumbered his way like an extra off the set of The Walking Dead. Wiping vomit from his lips and still grinning, Dominick gave him three twenties and patted him on the shoulder before walking on.

Remembering all of this, Dominick rocked back in his seat and considered. With a decided shrug he related the story to Mr. Wellington. The old man shook his head.

"You could've been killed. Both of you."

"It was the riskiest play I'll ever make. But if I'm not strong enough to ignore a gun in my face and tell a killer to kiss my ass, how could I ever run this company?"

"This isn't Detroit."

"And yet, the same games persist. You think Miller could have done that?"

They both knew that answer. Miller had involved himself with criminals, but he would always be a member of American aristocracy. His backbone would always be fortified by personal wealth and family privilege—not character. He would never be a leader who could relate or inspire.

He would never be Dominick.

Dominick settled into his seat and smirked. He'd earned it, goddammit.

"You want to tell me why you needed to know? And what you meant about being right about me even if it's too late?"

Ignoring the question, Mr. Wellington searched Dominick's face.

"You want this more than life itself." It sounded like an accusation.

A stab of buried pain wiped the smirk off Dominick's face. He stifled it, but it left an angry aftertaste in his voice. "At this point what else is there?"

"Then it has to be you. I'm sorry in advance."

"Sorry? For me having my dream?"

"Nightmare," the older man whispered, as if to himself.

Dominick cocked his head. "I don't follow."

"No. In one sense I'm counting on that." Disgusted, the older man tossed his mug off the porch and into the night. His lined face now looked pained, and his bright green eyes studied the darkness like those of a restless panther. "What exactly do you think is happening tomorrow?"

Dominick resisted the impulse to blink. What he *thought* was happening? Miller's resignation guaranteed it.

Dominick faced his mentor to look him in the eye, but the older man kept his eyes on the darkness. Nonetheless, Dominick let his words be undergirded by the steel of all the sleepless nights, all the strategizing and glad-handing, all the sacrifices and compromises and defeats.

"Tomorrow I take the reins of TJ&D. I accept what it is, and I then guide it toward what it can, will, and should be. As only I can, as taught by you."

Mr. Wellington's eyes hardened further.

"'What is' is the grandest lie of all creation," Mr. Wellington said loudly, as if his audience extended beyond the porch. "It is the greatest shame of my life." He turned to Dominick with burning, urgent eyes. "The company is a liar and a killer. It killed me. In two days it'll kill you too."

Dominick was stupefied. "You're kidding."

With a grimace, Mr. Wellington left his chair and went to the porch railing; as he turned his face skyward, the light of the full moon gave him an eerie glow.

"What is your greatest weakness, in my eyes?"

"Arthur, you've lost me. What happens in two—"

"We're running out of time!" Mr. Wellington spat. "You're smart, you're determined, you're ambitious, and yet you still have a sense of humanity. You are my champion, my dream made flesh in every regard but one. What is it?"

Dominick was aghast. What was all this?

"You mean your view of me being narrow-minded?"

"You lack faith in things unseen," Mr. Wellington almost yelled as he turned towards Dominick. "And now I fear..."

His mouth snapped shut. Even as he glared at Dominick with blistering urgency, it was clear whatever words completed that sentence would remain unsaid. Mr. Wellington's gaze returned to the moon.

Dominick's exasperation waned. There it was, at last: cold feet.

"Point taken." Dominick knew the first step was to validate his mentor's feelings. "And it's true, I'm more inclined to read profit pools than read auras. Much to Antoinette's dismay of late." His disarming smile was ignored. "But I'll still make you proud. And if you're concerned the board might—"

Mr. Wellington laughed with a bitterness Dominick hadn't often heard during their two-decades together.

"The board may be a nest of vipers, but after a time one learns to wear proper gloves and gaiters when handling them."

Dominick's understanding of the moment evaporated. Nest of vipers?

"How are they a nest of vipers? You appointed them." Dominick imagined them on a tennis court, and himself executing an impressive backhand stroke.

"Tell me what you know of Wallace Purdie."

This was an odd return (a moonball maybe?) but Dominick prepared for his return volley nonetheless.

Wallace Purdie was a larger man than Dominick, both in stature and influence, and older by ten years. Wharton-educated and with a laugh that paralleled his girth, he was a major player in the telecommunications industry. As a deal-maker, he'd brokered agreements that lined the pockets of shareholders and executives from Beijing to Silicon Valley to Wall Street.

On a personal level, Wallace was almost larger-than-life itself. He ate enough for two men (sometimes three), but he prided himself on the size of his tip equaling the size of his plate. He was quick to laugh and often made jokes at his own expense. Dominick had met Wallace's high school sweetheart-turned-wife Janice at two different fundraisers for community causes.

He'd been on the board of TJ&D for nearly six years. Often loud and never subtle, some chafed at his Fred-Flintstone-in-a-Brioni suit presentation. Nonetheless, he was an affable man and a consistent ally, and by no criteria of which Dominick was aware did Wallace Purdie merit the designation "viper."

He related all this to Mr. Wellington. Dominick thought his thorough description of Wallace would soften the strange, calloused expression his mentor now wore.

It did not.

When Mr. Wellington replied it was with a dull, measured tone. Dominick tried to identify the type of stroke his mentor employed to retain the tennis metaphor, but the more Mr. Wellington spoke the more the tennis court melted away.

"Wallace Purdie currently possesses thirteen, yes, *thirteen* pre-paid multi-year memberships to extreme pornographic websites on the very edge of legality. Each of these thirteen is bundled with additional sites, so the true total is exponentially higher. One site he frequents features women who are defecated upon and then forced to gag on men's genitalia until they vomit. African-American women. From it he has downloaded nearly a terabyte of material. Last year he spent over five hundred thousand dollars in strip clubs in Las Vegas and New York, and he purchased more than alcohol and table dances. Two of the dancers who privately entertained him— one of whom was underaged—have since gone missing. Two months ago he became an angel investor in a company that advertises itself as 'the leader in facial humiliation.' And then there's the pedophilia."

Mr. Wellington's eyes remained on the darkness as he continued.

"Wallace Purdie is a racist, a pervert, a misogynist, and a predator. I suspect he's a murderer. He hates you. Yet he presents himself as your friend and a 'good ol' boy' who made it rich. That he is capable of this duality is proof that he is capable of anything, and thus he should be trusted as far as he can be thrown. And at his size that isn't far at all, is it?"

It wasn't until Dominick exhaled that he realized that he'd been holding his breath. He recoiled. If any of this was true, the resulting implications far outweighed the condemnation of a big, fat, jovial, wealthy, intelligent, fun-loving, racist, perverted board member.

The questions spilled over each other. How could Mr. Wellington, even with all his resources, come to know such private information about another powerful businessman? Even if he could legally discover this, which itself was unlikely, why would he want to invade Wallace's privacy? In what universe was that in-line with TJ&D's "Principles in Action," which Mr. Wellington had extolled for decades? How long had he known? Why mention it tonight, when Dominick would go before the board in less than twenty-four hours for their approval?

These questions clamored over one another, screamed, waved their hands for attention. But the most potent question lingered behind. This silent lingerer was also the most undeniable, the most insightful, and the most likely to shatter Dominick's world.

What had been spoken flew in the face of everything he'd known Mr. Wellington to represent. For it to have been said with seriousness and sincerity, then it was not by the man he'd come to know as intimately as a son might his father. So the most important question was the most simple: who was the man before him?

How long he stared at Mr. Wellington in open-mouthed silence, he'd never know. But at some point Dominick's awareness of his vision returned, and he saw the greying man staring at him with hard, despairing eyes that now looked satisfied.

"Now you've begun to understand how much of a lie it all is. Be careful." Stuffing his hands into the pockets of his coat, Mr. Wellington left the railing and re-approached Dominick. "We're out of time. Take off one of your gloves and give me your hand. And close your eyes."

Dominick didn't move. He wanted to seize control of the moment, *his moment*, his night. He would demand answers; he would make it clear that now he was the one in charge, and as such he would put TJ&D onto his back and carry it to dizzying new heights no matter how delusional the old man's mind or cold his feet.

Yet when he looked into his mentor's aging eyes the desperation there stole Dominick's indignance right out of him. Dominick opened his mouth to ask what was wrong, but before he could speak Mr. Wellington shook his head.

After a dumbfounded moment, Dominick set down his cider mug and did as he was asked.

With his eyes closed, Dominick's sense of hearing sharpened. He heard rustling from Mr. Wellington's coat, then the snap of something opening. There was more rustling, and then silence.

He felt Mr. Wellington take his hand, then heard the old man take a breath.

A prick at the tip his pointing finger yanked Dominick's eyes open and he instinctively tried to pull his hand away. But Mr. Wellington held it firm. The older man held a tiny black stake, presumably what he'd used to stab Dominick's finger, and now wiped a dimple of blood from his fingertip into a small white bowl.

The inside of the bowl started to pop and sparkle.

"What the hell?" Dominick cried. Mr. Wellington released Dominick's hand and closed his own around the bowl as he stuffed it into his coat. With grim eyes he met Dominick's confused gaze.

"You have forty-eight hours to right the ship, or you'll go down with it. I pray I haven't just killed you. Or worse." A tear left Mr. Wellington's eye. "Find my granddaughter and tell her I'm sorry. Vincent was my fault."

Heat rushed to Dominick's face and his jaw unhinged.

The man wearing Mr. Wellington's skin walked into the cabin without another word. The oak door closed behind him with a thud.

Dominick's heart throbbed in his throat. Something rattled; his hand was shaking and thus tapping against the arm of his now-forgotten chair. He stilled it and took several deep breaths.

The outcome of this battle wasn't in doubt. He would gain control, stand, enter the cabin, and calmly quote one of his favorite films and ask Mr. Wellington what in the *blue fuck* was that. He would get to the bottom of this. In the end, even in the paralyzing haze of outrage, he was clear he would win.

Until it happened for the first time.

A voice spoke as clearly as Mr. Wellington's own.

*He's lost his mind,* it said.

Dominick jumped to his feet.

"Who's there?"

His voice was ragged, but no one answered.

Furious, he circled the chairs and peered around the porch. Spies? Now? Here? Having overheard that? Had they been recorded? Panic bloomed in his chest at the thought of their conversation going public.

He left the porch and searched the snow-covered front lawn. He found no one, nor found any footprints. He returned to the porch and searched overhead for a speaker. There must be a source somewhere. The voice sounded close enough to touch.

Then a new question occurred to him, and with it came a strange stab of uncertainty: was he sure that he heard that voice with his ears?

A loud crash from inside pulled his eyes to the cabin. Within a breath he was running to the door.

*         *         *

On television being air-lifted to a hospital is an expeditious, even exotic event. But an hour after Dominick had found Mr. Wellington unconscious on the living room floor of the cabin, his aging mentor had barely made it onto the gurney. The helicopter thundered on the cabin's expansive front lawn as the medical team made their final preparations to get him moving. As the paramedic and the nurse made their adjustments, their leader (the "retrieval physician" Dominick had been told) came his way.

"He's stable now, but in a comatose condition. His heart attack has been confirmed." The man had a shockingly pink face. "We'll move him now."

Dominick, having retrieved his cider mug, now gripped it with both his hands. Its smooth hardness helped remind him that this unfathomable night was still, in fact, reality.

The doctor (retrieval physician!) continued speaking and Dominick heard himself replying. His mouth explained how Mr. Wellington was famously healthy in his habits, but Dominick's mind had frozen on what the doctor said.

Heart attack. Comatose.

Mr. Wellington didn't smoke, rarely drank, ate little red meat, and saw his doctor regularly; he hadn't taken a sick day in at least two years.

And yet...

Comatose.

The word sent a tremble through him as if whispered by an abusive lover. It was an awful word from the same nightmare Mr. Wellington inexplicably mentioned; it was a word Dominick had forced from his mind. Yet here was another doctor in his face, using it again.

The doctor (retrieval physician!) rejoined his team as they pushed the gurney through the cabin's front door. Dominick followed them as if dreaming on his feet. Like an actor on a proscenium stage, he had a vague awareness of what his next lines were supposed to be. He knew highly effective people / leaders / winners / guys-who-did-important-stuff-and-should-be-respected-accordingly recovered quickly from seeming adversity. But this was different. "Seeming adversity" looked like a major investor pulling out at the last moment, or negotiations taking an unexpected turn, or the FTC moving to block a previously-approved acquisition. It didn't include encountering the impossible mere hours before the most important meeting of his career.

His mind drifted to what Mr. Wellington had said; it was a mad string of mysteries looping around like rope about a dead man's throat.

*'What is' is the grandest lie of all creation.*

*The company is a liar and a killer. It killed me. In two days it'll kill you too.*

*Now you've begun to understand how much of a lie it all is. Be careful.*

Dominick shook his head. Be careful?

*We're out of time. Take off one of your gloves and give me your hand.*

Dominick reflexively looked at his finger, as if it could explain its part in this bizarre evening. Already there was no sign of the prick, but Dominick's confusion didn't need one. Yes, that happened. His mentor stabbed the tip of his finger and extracted blood.

He looked around at nothing in particular while his mind grappled with the growing list of questions. The little white bowl was part of the mystery. What substance popped and sparkled when mixed with blood? What the hell did Mr.

Wellington do?

Dominick was outside now; he trailed the medical team as they wheeled Mr. Wellington towards their majestic blood-hued helicopter on the front lawn. They were halfway to the helicopter when a pair of headlights pulled onto the lawn. The black Range Rover crunched to a halt and a thin woman in a silver coat and furry cap hopped out and trotted towards them.

Without pause she ran to the gurney. The nurse (retrieval nurse?) turned to keep the new arrival from interfering, but upon reaching them the thin woman stopped, stared at Mr. Wellington's unconscious form, and let them pass without a word. Dominick walked to her side and they both watched the medical team meticulously load him into the helicopter.

The rotor blades thundered, and both Dominick and the woman turned away as the snow-tipped wind howled around them. The helicopter soon lifted into the air and plunged into the darkness; within moments only a blinking light marked its path. Agitated silence soon enveloped them.

He turned to her. She was almost silhouetted by the Rover's headlights, with only the light from the cabin to illuminate her tight face. As numb as he was, he knew he should say something supportive; god only knew what she felt.

"What did he say? Before he collapsed, what did he say?" she pre-empted him. She had her father's brilliant green eyes, but now they looked at him in a flat, dull fashion. He'd come to hate that look.

"He wasn't himself." Dominick suspected that was the understatement of the year.

"Don't dance. What did he say?"

"It's private, I'm sorry." He didn't have the faintest idea of how to retell the conversation even if he could. He replayed another one of Mr. Wellington's mysterious proclamations in his head: *Wallace Purdie is a racist, a pervert, a misogynist, and a predator. I suspect he's a murderer.* "But he wasn't acting like himself."

He knew he should tell her Mr. Wellington had mentioned the kids. But he couldn't. Not yet. Instead, he reached out to cup her body into his; if she wouldn't offer a hug he'd take one.

"Don't." She brushed his hand aside. Surprise-turned-outrage spiked in his chest.

"What the hell is your—"

"I'm moving out."

"What?"

"I want a divorce."

The entire moment around him, and all of his bodily functions, froze.

"What?"

Time took a moment off. The wind still blew the golden strands of her hair; her thin, gloss-coated lips were still pressed tight with little lines of tension at their edges; her defiant eyes still stared into his; his heart still pounded at an alarming rate.

And yet nothing moved at all.

"What are you talking about?"

"I'm done pretending. With him gone there's no point."

"Pretending? What do you—"

"You only married me to be his son."

This stabbed into him like a butcher knife; before he could gather a response, she began backing away.

"My lawyer will call you," she said. "We need to find Violet and tell her."

She turned and stomped towards the Range Rover—the Range Rover he bought her, his mind recalled.

"Antoinette!"    He followed.    Without thinking he grabbed her arm. "Antoinette!"

"Back off!"  Again she batted away his hand—this time harder.  Nearing delirium, words flew from his mouth.

"You can't do this!  Not now!  There are expectations!  Expectations!"

"Oh, expectations, poor you!" she screamed. "I have some new expectations for you.  Expect me to live my life again!  Expect me to be with someone that will touch me!  Expect me to stop being the solution to your daddy issues!"

Of their own will his hands shot out to grip her shoulders, as if to shake some sense into her.  But as he made contact she slapped him.

The brief flash of white and warm sting on his cheek induced a daze; disconnected, he watched her eyes blaze and nostrils flare.  Neither of them spoke.

She held his stare for a moment and then jumped into the SUV.  Within moments she was gone.

The stillness of the moment somehow sharpened his senses.  The darkness was a cloak he felt on his skin.  The air bit at his face.  His stomach was alive with emotion.

And then it happened again.

*Bitch!  We'll make her pay.*

He jumped in surprise.  It wasn't a thought—it was an audible, independent, and unfamiliar *voice.*  And even though he instinctively looked around for a speaker, there was no doubt it had come from inside his head.

"We?"

Yes, it said "we," plural, as in "he and another."  Except he was deep in the snowy woods with no one else.  Maybe it was he who was losing his mind.

"Bullshit."

He strode towards the cabin, his determination now engaged. He pulled his phone from his pocket and dialed. A crisp female voice answered on the first ring.

"Yes, sir?"

Normalcy, at last.

"Relay to Dr. Roth and the board that he's comatose and being air-lifted to Cedars-Sinai. Heart attack per the retrieval physician. I'm en route to there in less than ten. Also, tell Baxter to sweep the hospital room. Immediately."

"Yes, sir."

He pushed through the cabin's front door and entered the front room. In moments he'd gathered his clothes.

"And send someone for the rest of his things here."

"Of course. Are you all right, sir?" Her bright, familiar voice with its slight Virginia twang was touched with concern.

He stopped and looked into the mirror. The gray dissenters in his beard were poking out of his face, and his deep brown eyes were touched with the pink of bloodshot. But he was still himself.

Antoinette's voice in his head made him wince: *Back off!*

"I'm fine. Thank you. And get Terrance on the phone for me, as soon as humanly possible."

"Absolutely, sir. Is there anything else I can do?"

"That'll be all." He disconnected the line. Bags in hand, he strode for the door—then stopped.

Dropping the bags, he rushed to the living room, where he'd found Mr. Wellington. He checked the coffee table, the end tables, in between the cushions of the couch. Nothing. His anxiousness rising, he strode to Mr. Wellington's bedroom, unzipped his bag, then searched his belongings. Had Dominick's moment of distracted shock cost him? Did Mr. Wellington still have them on his person? But then he unzipped a side pocket of one of Mr. Wellington's bags and spotted a small wooden box. Dominick pulled on his leather gloves and opened it with a snap; sure enough, inside was the white bowl and tiny black stake Mr. Wellington used on the porch. Both were clean.

Dominick wrapped them into a pocket square and headed for the door.

*          *          *

By the time he reached the front porch, he had a plan. The tiny bowl and blade had come from somewhere, and Dominick was confident modern forensic science could uncover their origin. That could shed light upon Mr. Wellington's riddles.

When Dominick reached the rented Town Car, his other plans were taking shape. Antoinette, ever the attention-hungry performer, needed reassurance. In a way her outburst made sense; with succession looming he'd been neglecting her. Add Violet's absence and the tension of their marriage, of course she would go stir-crazy alone in their big house. Of course she would overreact.

He would schedule a trip to St. Lucia, to the resort she adored with en-suite infinity pools overlooking the Caribbean. They couldn't go immediately, not with her father comatose and things in tumult. But he would get it scheduled. That would help.

When he started the car, he could already envision her begrudging smile as he handed her the plane tickets and a lavish bouquet of white roses. Warmth returned to his face.

But then—

*Bitch!*

He shuddered at the uninvited memory of the word, and his visualization faltered. Obviously, the stress of the bizarre night had taken a surprisingly quick toll on his mind. But it didn't change anything. He was no one's victim, least of all some mental traitor temporarily loosed by tragedy.

He shifted the car into gear and sped onto the road.

He again focused, but discomfort lingered around the fact that she'd hit him. That was a new low. He shook his head and accelerated.

He started down the mountain. There were two fronts to the surprising new war. His deteriorating relationship with Antoinette was the first. The second war front was farther-reaching and more complex: the vacuum of leadership left by Mr. Wellington's sudden ill-health. He built TJ&D and had served at its face for more than three decades. For many in the company he was a father-figure, and they would react badly to his heart attack. Reassuring them would be one of Dominick's first actions as *de facto* CEO.

Further, other details of Mr. Wellington's exit strategy hadn't been outlined—at least not outside of Mr. Wellington's head. How would they deal with the accelerated time frame? That question needed an answer immediately; key members of the board needed to be consulted.

What had Mr. Wellington called them? A "nest of vipers?"

Maybe there was a third war front: solving the mystery behind what Mr. Wellington said. Was there a brain disorder preceding a heart attack that could bring on nonsensical speech?

Mr. Wellington hadn't been loopy in the slightest, though.

At the end he was as intense as ever, as if his words danced on a razor's edge. What he said about Wallace was shockingly specific. And for him to mention the kids…

An ache bloomed in Dominick's head as he remembered his mentor's parting words: *please find my granddaughter and tell her I'm sorry. Vincent was my fault.*

Dominick dismissed the thought. He'd handle that mystery in time; the corporate family came first.

He'd taken one hand from the wheel to initiate a call when motion on the street caught his eye. Lightning fast, a dull brown figure leaped into his path. He jammed on the brakes, and the ABS brought him to a smooth stop bare inches before impact.

The deer turned its majestically-horned head his way.

Dominick's exasperation swelled as he breathed down the adrenaline. He jammed the horn. The deer didn't budge. Dominick banged the wheel, then jammed his horn again.

"Move! Move! Move!"

He punctuated each syllable with a blast of his horn. Despite the staccato bleating, the deer only stared at him and flicked its ears.

"Dammit!"

Dominick got out of the car. He raised his arms and waved them at the beast, but the deer stood its ground. Dominick had long enough to wonder how he'd get it to move before there was an *explosion* of light in his head.

The deer, its huge black eyes swallowing his own, slanted before him. The earth pitched. The Town Car's hood rushed towards him. He tried to put out his right arm to catch himself, but it felt limp, powerless. There was a thump a moment later, and before the black came Dominick thought it all proof he was dreaming.

\*　　　　　\*　　　　　\*

*He sees only white. Engulfing, consuming, suffocating white.*
*"I pray you do not die in vain," a female voice says.*
*The contours of a face emerge from the white abyss. A little*
*girl. Red hair. Familiar. She looms above Dominick like a ghostly*
*giant framed in brilliant, blinding white. But she's not looking at*
*him. So familiar.*
*"It's not my death that concerns me," a man replies. "It's his."*
*The red head looks down at Dominick with her lips a thin*
*line of worry. She then looks away again with a shake of her head.*
*Wait—is that Sherrill McKinnen? Then something changes.*
*Something inside. Dominick sees her with new eyes.*
*Yes. That's Sherrill McKinnen.*
*She's in Mr. Honor's homeroom class too. Her and Evan Ward*
*are the only two white kids in fourth grade. Dominick didn't*
*like her; in second grade she took Carlos Bautista's pencil box and*
*blamed it on a kindergartener. What second grader tries to get*
*kindergarteners in trouble?*
*"The vessel you selected does not easily assist our cause," Sherrill*
*McKinnen said. "They have history. I fear madness may take him*
*in short order."*
*"That's why you have to succeed." The man's voice was insistent.*
*"You can't fail him."*
*"My commitment is absolute," she replied. "My faith in his*
*ability to retain his sanity is not."*
*"He'll adapt. And he's strong. You'll see."*

29

*Dominick tried to sit up, but it was hard. Why was he feeling so heavy? What happened?*

*Shapes and colors materialized as the blinding white loosened its grip. His BMX bike was in the grass. Its red knobby wheels were upside down in Mrs. Larrimore's lawn. Ma said Mrs. Larrimore didn't cut her grass like she was supposed to. Her husband had run away, Ma said. Dominick didn't know grownups ran away. Dogs did that.*

*"He will soon reconnect the memory," Sherrill McKinnen said. "When he does their forces will be upon him, far sooner than I can arrive. His strength will be tested."*

*"He was never safe. But now he has a chance. Now we all have a chance."*

*Dominick was sitting up in the grass now. There was a man there, facing Sherrill McKinnen; that's who she was talking to. It was funny; Dominick couldn't see the man's face because of all the light, but he somehow seemed nice. He looked at Dominick and offered his hand. Blinking in the sun—wow, it was bright— Dominick took it and stood.*

*"I can't see you," Dominick said to the man. He blinked stars from his eyes; he must have fallen off the bike pretty hard.*

*Both Sherrill McKinnen and the man he couldn't see looked up sharply. Within seconds, the all-consuming white decayed to a dead grey.*

*The man turned towards Dominick. Now his face was shrouded in growing darkness.*

*"We're out of time. Again. Good luck, son. I'm—"*

*His voice trailed off, even as his lips continued to move; voiceless, the man was now fading away.*

*Sherrill McKinnen spoke from behind him.*

*"Go in peace."*

30

*In a breath the man was gone—faded from view like smoke in the night.*

*Confused, Dominick turned to Sherrill McKinnen.*

*"What's going on?" Dominick's voice was touched with fear.*

*"It has begun."*

*The moment the words left her lips, the scene changed. Dominick was walking now, and Sherrill McKinnen was with him. They were on Monica, the street she lived on. But they weren't really walking together; she was ahead of him, stomping through the snow and swinging her arms in stiff anger.*

*Then he remembered what was going on. She was being stupid. She was always being stupid. That's why he didn't like her.*

*Another Sherrill McKinnen stood on the corner across the street watching them with a look of concern. But she was dream-like, hazy. The real Sherrill McKinnen was up ahead; she was walking fast to make him mad.*

*He stopped and scooped up some snow and packed it. It wasn't slushy enough to make a real snowball, but it would do. He chucked it and it sailed past her shoulder.*

*She spun around with her face a livid pink.*

*"You are so stupid!" she screamed. "I hate everything about you!"*

*"Girl, if I wanted to hit you, I woulda hit you! Stop walking so fast!"*

*"If you want it back you have to walk fast, you stupid idiot." She resumed her almost-run. "We have to get there 'fore my step-daddy gets back."*

*Dominick trotted to catch up. He didn't want to get too close to her, though; the last thing he wanted was for people to think they were friends. He kicked the snow in frustration. He would never trade with Tavares Ford ever again. This was all his fault.*

*"Wait here." She left him on the sidewalk and ran into her house. Why hadn't they shoveled their sidewalk? It was already freezing over.*

*A moment later she came out with his Nintendo cartridge— the one he'd given to Tavares Ford, the one she should have never had. She was handing it to him when a green Buick slid to a halt in front of them and she looked at it in horror. Dominick turned around and was roughly pushed aside. Sherrill McKinnen screamed.*

*"You bringing boys to my house now? Like a little ho?" The man grabbed her by her hood, yanking her red hair in the process.*

*"No, it's not like that!" she shrieked. "We're not even friends! Tell him!"*

*The man, his cheeks red with liquor, stared at Dominick with uncut hatred. Dominick tried to speak, but the blaze in the man's eyes held him in mute horror.*

*"Tell him!" Her voice was shrill, desperate.*

*Dominick's mouth worked in a futile attempt to say something, anything, when the man snarled.*

*"Not like that, huh?" In a deft motion the man backhanded Sherrill McKinnen. Dominick watched her spin like a rag doll into the snow; the man then turned to Dominick and pulled a small black pistol from his coat. "You get outta here. And if I see your little ass around here again, I'll kill you. You understand me?"*

*Dominick, panting, crying, still couldn't speak.*

*"I said do you understand?" The man took a step towards Dominick.*

*In an instant Dominick was off running at full speed, his face wet with tears. Sherrill McKinnen screamed again, but he didn't dare look back.*

*Again he saw the other Sherrill McKinnen, the dream-like one, standing on the corner with her face a hazy look of worry.*

*Much closer, however, was something else. It was heavy, dark. And even though he was running, it wrapped itself around his neck and drew beside his ear.*

*"Coward," it sneered.*

\*                    \*                    \*

# CHAPTER TWO

## Sunday Night

Dominick's eyes flew open and he scrambled to his feet. Freezing rain pelted his face. His fingers tingled. The Town Car still ran and the driver's side door hung open. His right shoulder stung.

Had he *fainted?*

He ran a heavy hand over his head. A deer had jumped into the road. He got out of the car to wave it away. And then…what?

Like whispers on an autumn wind, recent memories breathed through his awareness

*(coward)*

as he tried to reassemble the pieces. He remembered being home, being a kid again, and walking with…Sherrill McKinnen?

"What the hell?" He squinted against the rain as the memory emerged. He hadn't recalled the moment; he'd relived it. He felt the ice beneath him as he stood on her un-shoveled walkway. He smelled the alcohol and cigarettes on her stepfather's breath. He was there.

"Mr. Wellington," he said.

That got him moving. He checked his watch as he walked towards the car. How long had he been face-up on the pavement like over-sized roadkill?

"One of America's top executives, ladies and gentlemen," he muttered as he climbed inside.

He must not have been out long, as no passerby had seen him and stopped to assist. That was a lucky break. Imagine the headlines tomorrow had both he and Mr. Wellington been rushed to the emergency room on the same night! Their stock price would have nose-dived.

He again started down the mountain with a shake of his head. Snoozing in the road at a time like this? *Have mercy,* Grandma might have said. Her ability to show displeasure in economical fashion was impressive.

He started to touch a button on the steering wheel when he caught sight of his finger. When Mr. Wellington pricked him—could something have been on the blade? A psychotropic, or maybe a hallucinogen?

He shook the thought away and pushed the button.

"Call Gerald Higgins."

His phone's automated voice assured him it was doing just that, and while the phone rang he visualized the edge of a katana blade. Time being as it was, an abbreviated version of this focus exercise would have to do.

"Hello, Dominick."

Higgins often over-enunciated when he spoke. Dominick was convinced it was a tactic Higgins used to slow his speech to keep his listener waiting for him (to gain a psychological advantage) and to give himself more time to consider his own words (to gain a strategic advantage). Still, Dominick was surprised to hear him speaking in leisurely fashion now, given the circumstances.

"Gerald, glad you answered. I wanted you to be the first I spoke with one-on-one."

"That's considerate of you. But unneeded. I'm sure you have your own needs to attend to at this time."

This was the first red flag. Not at the words themselves—they were the same posturing ass-smoke blown in board rooms across the globe. What struck Dominick was the sense that Higgins meant them.

"The company's needs are my needs," Dominick said. *You know that*, he wanted to add, but that would come out sounding coarse. If he was now in a more traditional tennis match, this was the time to feel out his opponent and not yet try to smash the ball at him.

"Nonetheless, the hour is late and the times are indeed singular. How can I be of assistance?"

Then again, maybe ball-smashing wasn't a bad idea.

"Are you in shock, Gerald?"

"Excuse me?"

"Are you in shock?"

"Do I sound like I'm in shock?"

"If you're in shock at the sudden enormity of this situation, and then compensating for that shock, then I would fully understand your seeming lack of urgency."

"I should sound more surprised our 78-year-old friend has encountered some health challenges?" Neither Higgins' tone nor his pace of speech had wavered.

Dominick's jaw tensed. Not only was Higgins not sounding alarmed, he wasn't pretending to not sound alarmed. Time to switch tracks.

"Surprised or otherwise, can you meet me at the hospital? I'm having it swept for privacy, and there are some key points about succession I'd like to—"

"I'm afraid that won't be possible. We'll have time enough to discuss succession tomorrow. Collectively."

Higgins drew out the final word. His refusal joined the sea of red flags this conversation had produced. Sill, Dominick persisted.

"If we don't jump on this thing, you and I, tonight, we're looking at a potential free-for-all starting at opening bell. You realize that, yes?"

"I realize things a bit differently. I realize people will need to know leadership hasn't deserted them. And they will. Tomorrow."

Silence fell between them as Dominick grappled with his newest surprise. He was about to conclude the conversation when Higgins spoke again.

"By the way, how was he before the heart attack? How were his spirits?"

Heat pulsed in Dominick's face. *Nest of vipers,* he remembered Mr. Wellington saying.

"He was fine. Why?"

"A terrible thing like that. What moods and what thoughts bring it about? Poisons, I would think." The smile in his voice was unmistakable.

"Good night, Gerald."

"Good night, Dominick."

Dominick accelerated as the line disconnected. Higgins

was up to something and had no qualms about showing it. He'd long been the least-predictable member of the board, but an open refusal to cooperate now was stunning.

And his last question—Antoinette had asked something similar, but hers had been an honest inquiry. Higgins was prodding him. Had Higgins bugged the lodge and/or Mr. Wellington? Why? And why would Higgins *want* Dominick to know? Was that a warning? A threat?

"What the hell is going on?" Dominick muttered.

The voice in his head answered him:

*Whatever it is, it's bad. Get away while you can.*

He was so startled he jerked the wheel and lurched into the other lane. Correcting himself, he looked around the empty car.

He glanced at his finger once more. How quickly could he have blood work done? And get something to stop this madness? He again touched the steering wheel to initiate a call. To hell with the katana blade.

"Call Christian Leftwich."

Within moments it rang. He focused on the sound as a way to steady his thoughts. It was working; his heart rate began to slow and his grip on the wheel relaxed as his mind fell into a familiar sweet spot of relaxation.

Leftwich's voice, thickened by age and cigars, reached out of the phone.

"What the hell did you do to him?"

Leftwich was notoriously cavalier in his speech. Others lost their openness as they ascended the corporate ladder, but Leftwich had reveled in it. As one of Mr. Wellington's longest friends, Dominick considered Leftwich like a somewhat-volatile uncle.

38

"Send your prayers," Dominick said. "He could use them right now."

"So could we all. What are you planning to do?"

The newest red flag didn't go up the pole at this question, but it was unpacked with gloved hands and unfurled.

"My only plan is to do the best I can with one hell of a curveball." Dominick broadcast his honesty in his voice; he was coming to Leftwich as a friend, and he wanted him to know it. "But after talking with Gerald I think he's got plans he's not sharing until the meeting. Heard anything?"

A fractional pause ensued.

"Forget Gerald. He's in his own shit storm at the university."

The red flag in Dominick's mind was knotted to the pole and drawn to the sky. Leftwich's customary response to a direct question was either a direct answer or a direct invitation to go to hell. He rarely dodged questions and had never dodged Dominick's—until now.

Again the voice chimed in:

*They're playing you for a fool! And you're letting them!*

Again Dominick jumped. It sounded so *real*, like someone sitting beside him. This could not continue.

"I need to ask you about something in the briefs," Leftwich continued. "Maybe it's what Gerald saw."

"What is it?" The dry lump in Dominick's throat had swelled in bare moments. Hadn't he just been in his sweet spot?

"Electronics in Asia cut ties with the principle contracted supplier?"

"And?"

"Why?"

"A conflict-free supply chain for the micro-processors is why," Dominick said, confused. "So what?"

"The claims named against them were never verified."

"Armed factions in the Congo funding themselves through metal sales aren't known for their bookkeeping. Why are we talking about this?"

"Because you're making a mistake!" Leftwich shouted. "You want to do something for the children of Africa? Make the money and then use it to fund a foundation. Profit and PR simultaneously."

"It's a PR home-run as is. But connect the dots for me. Why are we talking about this when Mr. Wellington—"

"Damn him. He's asleep with a tube on his prick. We have real problems right here and right now."

"How is this a problem?" Had the entire world gone mad? Silence on the line. Had it dropped? "Christian?"

"What were you doing before his heart attack?"

That question. Again. Dominick slowed the car and pulled to the shoulder.

"Talking. Why? And you didn't answer my question. Why are we discussing suppliers when—"

"What were you talking about?"

"Why is everyone asking me that?"

Mr. Wellington's warning about the board wafted into Dominick's awareness: *after a time one learns to wear proper gloves and gaiters when handling them.*

After a pause, Leftwich spoke.

"Maybe we can talk after the meeting."

With three beeps the line went dead.

Dominick stared at the phone display as if it would tell him something different from what he already knew. No luck.

Leftwich had hung up on him.

Anger washed over him. But before he could form a thought of his own, again someone else inside his head did the talking.

*You're a coward now? You're going to take this?*

Even his anger could not withstand the surprise of the intrusion.

He closed his eyes and took a breath. If ever a forked road lay before him, it was now. Would he retreat? His mentor fallen, his wife acting out, his board untrustworthy and now his mind exhibiting signs of

*(madness)*

some strange psychosis—were these not all excellent reasons to withdraw? Shouldn't he seek tactical refuge and employ the "wait-and-see" strategy?

Or did he dare to push onward anyway?

His heartbeat quickened. Their faces, like smoke from a dying fire, floated before his mind's eye. Leonard. Little Mike. Robert. Poncho. Antonio. Rock. Mark. Sean. And how many others? How many childhood buddies, classmates, neighbors, friends? How many fatherless young men like him were now dead or imprisoned, drug-addicted, or derelict? Could he estimate the amount of potential snuffed out by those unforgiving streets? Could he count off those who didn't make it out?

No. But he could count off the one who did.

"'Wait-and-see' my ass."

He shifted the car into gear and accelerated down the mountain.

\*                    \*                    \*

Hospitals always smelled like death. Granted, the air in the intensive care unit in the VIP wing of Cedars-Sinai was treated with the greatest filtration technology available on the planet. And yet the moment the silver elevator doors parted, the smell of death slithered its way into Dominick's nose.

The impeccably dressed bulk of Roderick Baxter was Dominick's first sight upon entering the wing.

"This way, sir." Baxter's voice was always steady. "The doctor will join us momentarily."

"Is the room clean?"

"Yes, sir. And the rooms above and below as well."

"And you're certain the cabin was clean? The front porch in particular?"

Baxter looked surprised.

"The cabin was swept. But certain devices have a greater range in the open air, as we've discussed. Was there a problem?"

Dominick had developed a theory, and it could explain why Higgins was coy during their call. But his motives for listening in on them remained a mystery. Equally mystifying was why Mr. Wellington had spoken louder than necessary, as if he knew and wanted to be overheard.

"We'll discuss it later. Where is he?"

Baxter extended a beefy hand down the hallway, and Dominick got moving. Baxter, whose fluidity of movement still surprised Dominick, effortlessly fell in step beside him.

"And sir? Mrs. Reinhart, her associates, and Rachel have already arrived."

The pause before "associates" made Dominick turn

towards him.

"Associates."

"The Kelleys. They're here."

Dominick couldn't stop himself from sighing. Baxter, ever the polished professional, didn't react. They continued without another word.

One of Baxter's men opened the door for them. Inside the expansive corner room, which offered a panoramic view of the LA skyline, was a single bed. At the foot of the bed stood Antoinette, still dressed in her silver coat, with her back towards him. Beside her, flanking her like faithful bookends, were Bill (right side) and Esther (left side) Kelley.

*Blood-sucking assholes!*

Dominick's heart-rate spiked at this latest outburst from the interloper in his mind. The fact he concurred with the voice on this point didn't mitigate the surprise.

Both of the Kelleys turned his way upon entering. Esther's lips pressed together into a vaguely sympathetic smile, and Bill offered him a grim nod. Antoinette's back remained as inviting as a glacial wall.

Mr. Wellington, somehow now smaller, lay in the large bed beneath an array of tubes, scopes, and wires. With eyes closed and mouth parted, only the subtle rise and fall of his chest indicated he was alive at all.

Rachel, wearing large red-rimmed glasses that made her caffeinated eyes look even larger, bounced out of her nearby chair and thumped his way.

"Hi, sir. Can I get you something? I was about to order food." She already had her tablet in hand and was tapping away.

"No, thank you. Where's the doc—"

"Mr. Reinhart?"

He turned to see a tall man in a white coat walking towards them. He extended his hand.

"Dr. Saltzman. Mr. Wellington suffered a heart attack, which in turn produced the current comatose state. He was stabilized on-site and appears beyond the window of immediate danger. We're running tests to assess possible damage to his neural system."

"Doctor," Dominick fought the urge to hold his temple as if to contain the throbbing there. "How could this happen?"

"When the heart is momentarily disabled and the central nervous system is deprived of oxygen—"

"Not the biology lesson. How does a man ski all day on Saturday then have a heart attack and fall into a coma on Sunday?"

"Dominick." Antoinette sounded far away.

"I understand your confusion, Mr. Reinhart—"

"No, I don't think you do. He was in *perfect health,* doctor. He was cleared to ski four days ago. Have you spoken with Dr. Roth? How the hell—"

"Dominick!" Antoinette yelled. "Don't make a scene."

He blinked dumbly. Was he more upset about her father's condition than her? He opened his mouth to vent his anger, not knowing what he would say, when she again pre-empted him.

"He knew it was coming."

Exasperation slapped Dominick across the face.

"I have test results to check on," Dr. Saltzman said. "Excuse me."

He pattered away. Dominick forced his jaw to relax.

"Everyone, can you excuse us?" he said.

Rachel turned on her heels and Baxter followed her towards the door, but Antoinette put her hands on each of the bookends beside her.

"They stay," she declared.

Bam-bam-bam, Dominick's head went as the door closed behind Rachel and Baxter.

Esther Kelley put her hand on Antoinette's own, and the familiarity of the gesture further irked Dominick.

"It's okay, hon," Esther said.

"I know it's okay. It's okay you stay." Antoinette stared at Dominick. Did she have to act like a petulant child now, of all times?

"No offense intended," Dominick said, keeping his voice calm. "But this is a personal family matter."

"They are family."

He started to ask what that was supposed to mean, but the change in her eyes stopped him. It wasn't stubbornness anymore, but something more aggressive.

"Not now," Bill Kelley said, speaking for the first time. The authority of his tone also fanned Dominick's ire. Who the hell was Bill Kelley to tell his wife what to do?

"It's nothing they haven't already heard," Antoinette said.

"And what's that?" Dominick asked.

"Dad called me yesterday, when you got off the mountain. He wanted to say goodbye."

Don't patronize, Dominick thought. He forced his hands to stay at his sides.

"Are we speaking metaphorically?"

"Don't patronize me. I know when my father is trying to tell me something."

"What did he actually say, is what I mean."

She cocked her head.

"He asked me to stay with you. He said you'd have a lot to deal with and a divorce now could destroy you."

Astonishment.

"You told him before you told me?"

"I didn't have to," she spat.

Keep calm, he told himself.

"He said I'd have a lot to deal with," Dominick repeated. "That doesn't mean he knew he'd have a heart attack. He was probably referring to tomorrow."

She shook her head.

"At the end he said 'Goodbye, angel. Your daddy loves you.' He hasn't talked to me like that since I was nine. He knew."

Dominick rolled his eyes, but then her tone shifted.

"He didn't say goodbye to you too?"

Her eyes were plaintive, almost shimmering. Her eyes had always been expressive; it was one of her sparkling traits that made him fall for her.

Maybe it was the slight look of vulnerability, the wall coming down a bit, that had him reflect. The memory of Mr. Wellington's voice wafted into his mind again.

*The company is a liar and a killer. It killed me.*

*Be careful.*

*We're out of time.*

Dominick blinked. She was right.

"He did." Her eyes were hardening again. "I knew he did."

This time Dominick didn't fight the urge to wipe his head as he cast a glance at Mr. Wellington's comatose form. In all the craziness in his head, Dominick had missed the obvious:

the old man knew it was coming.

Despair rose within him as he looked to Antoinette. The night's mystery had deepened, but that didn't change what he needed to tell her: Mr. Wellington's goodbye was but a piece of his parting message. The rest of it spoke directly to their family's greatest pain.

*Please find my granddaughter and tell her I'm sorry. Vincent was my fault.*

The mere memory of those words nearly brought a tear to his eye. But he would die a thousand deaths before he'd let one fall in view of Bill-and-Esther-goddamned-Kelley.

"Can we go home?" Dominick blurted more vulnerably than he'd intended.

Nineteen years together, some of it good, came down to this moment. The soft beep of a heart monitor was its only soundtrack; the audience of this pivotal scene featured their fallen patriarch and two granola-loving friends welded to each hip of his wife. It was before this bizarre ensemble that the next defining moment of his marriage would arrive.

Bill and Esther Kelley, bookends-turned-inappropriate witnesses, looked at Antoinette as the room awaited her answer. The symmetry of their equally-turned heads would have been comical under other circumstances.

"I'm sorry," Antoinette said.

The voice inside him screamed again:

*Bitch!*

He closed his eyes. He didn't move, didn't speak, didn't breathe.

She turned away (with her bookends affixed to each side) and headed towards the door. He resisted the impulse to see how they would navigate leaving; he imagined them side-stepping through the doorway like a disoriented chorus line.

After they exited he went to the door and motioned to Baxter. He spoke softly into Baxter's ear.

"Have her followed and notify me when she's in."

"Yes, sir." Baxter glided away and spoke softly into the device on his wrist. As Dominick closed the door he again pulled out his phone and dialed.

"Yes, sir?" Linda answered.

"Still nothing from Terrance?"

"No, sir."

At this hour there was likely a woman behind his lack of availability.

"Keep me posted. While I'm here I want my blood drawn. Tell Dr. Lockhart I want a full panel and complete toxicology report as soon as humanly possible."

"Yes, sir."

He disconnected the line and returned to Mr. Wellington's bedside. Not trusting the sweep, Dominick leaned in close and whispered into his ear.

"I'm going to use your last line about the kids to bring her back to me."

He would win her over. Granted, he wished she had agreed to go home; working together to decipher Mr. Wellington's cryptic words would bring them together. But her delay wouldn't change the outcome. "For better or for worse" was still the guiding order of it all.

Succession, however, seemed to be losing more "guiding order" by the minute. If they'd been listened to at the cabin, what Mr. Wellington said about Wallace could leak. Late-night TV would have a field day with that information, even if it wasn't true. A sex scandal involving a board member of one of the world's largest conglomerates? Tabloid editors would wet themselves. Hell, TJ&D's own media holdings would have to cover it.

Maybe Mr. Wellington's comments could be spun as pre-event dementia; that might soften the scandal and reassure the market. But what about Higgins? Why would Higgins spy on them? Had a competitor gotten to him? Shocking, but not technically impossible. And Leftwich, what was his angle? Why would he give two shits about a contracted supplier at a time like this? Should Dominick contact other board members, even at this hour, to again gauge the field of play?

*Call Dai.*

He flinched. He couldn't blame the voice in his head for that one; it was merely a bad idea he had on his own. Still, he fought the desire to glance about to check if anyone else had heard.

Ah, Dai. In an instant he was with her again. He could feel her fingertips on the back of his neck, the warmth of her face inches away from his, the wonder of her amber eyes as they drank of his soul.

*Ay papi,* she'd breathed into his ear.

He massaged his temples, but not for the benefit of the cameras he still suspected might be spying on him. There were many things to reflect upon at this moment. The woman whose legs he'd had no business being between was not among them.

He smiled to himself. Then again, might not sex with Dai be helpful right now, if she were open to it? It would clear his head, relax his body, and remind him of how powerful he was. Are these not good things? Why should he accept Antoinette's rejection when he could have Dai's embrace?

Occasionally he allowed himself to enjoy the fact that he was, in truth, partially insane. Having more sex with the woman he should have never had sex with in the first place, tonight of all nights, would be disastrous. Wasn't he just talking about sex scandals? It was good to laugh at such ruinous ideas.

Yes, further infidelity was out of the question. He was still married, regardless of how maddening Antoinette could be.

*Icy bitch,* the voice in his head commented.

His smile died. He gulped down the surprise and waited for the adrenaline surge to pass. Where was the phlebotomist? The sooner he gave blood (voluntarily this time) the sooner he could end this part of the nightmare. Amusing partial-insanity was one thing; having something independently share its opinions inside his head was another.

He briefly considered returning to the nurse's station to find a phlebotomist himself, but he knew better than to risk the privacy breach. If Higgins was now working for a competitor—unthinkable hours ago, but now a possibility—imagine what he'd do with medical records suggesting Dominick was unfit to lead. No, he'd let Linda do her job. She had earned his trust and was under a strict non-disclosure agreement.

Dominick stared at his mentor, whose face was barely visible through the ventilator mask. Of all the times to keel over, did it have to be right now? And what the hell was with his last line?

*Please find my granddaughter and tell her I'm sorry. Vincent was my fault.*

Nausea tap-danced in Dominick's stomach. Yes, Mr. Wellington had mentioned the unspeakable as well.

Suddenly fatigued, Dominick slumped in the chair. This was such a stupid, ill-timed mess. What he wouldn't give for a piano right about now. Pianos always brought him to himself—his deepest, oldest, truest self.

He could still smell the dank but reassuring wood of the old upright piano of his youth. Where Ma had gotten it, or even why, he never knew. But it had appeared in their living room one day as if by magic. And in sixth grade, when their lights had been turned off and he'd gotten tired of pretending to watch TV, he turned his attention to the strange-looking piece of furniture that somehow made noise. He ran his fingers over its dusty surface, opened it, started plinking away at it, and then the damndest thing happened: it started to speak to him.

It often spoke in colors, but at times in feelings as well. Some days it laughed. More often it moaned. It sang of vibrant reds and somber blues. It lamented better days since passed, but sometimes it dared to hope for a brighter spring ahead. Somehow they formed an agreement; if he sat there long enough with its cool stiffness beneath the pads of his fingers, it would pour its heart out to him and take him on journeys he could scarcely imagine.

The first summer with it was amazing. It was a friend like none other. It didn't curse at him, it didn't fight, it didn't steal candy from the corner store and incense the Chaldeans. It didn't try to get him to look at musty Playboy magazines, it didn't throw rocks at the crackheads. It only wanted to share its soul.

Now he had a Steinway baby grand at the house. But while he played semi-regularly, it was to avoid completely losing his hard-fought dexterity. Pianos had stopped sharing their souls with him long ago.

*Except when you played for Dai, you fuck!*

With a choked scream he didn't recognize as his own, Dominick jerked upwards. To his amazement, he was on the linoleum floor. He scrambled up again and self-consciously wiped off his clothes. He was still next to Mr. Wellington's bed, but the chair he'd been sitting in was now on its side a few feet behind him.

Fear clawed at his chest. Had he fainted again? Did he fall out of his chair and not even know it? He looked at his fallen mentor and his cryptic warning again came to Dominick's mind:

*Be careful.*

With Mr. Wellington beside him, remembering his words now felt like hearing a ghost. The woody smell of his once-best friend, that first piano, which had been peddled for drug money decades ago by his mother's then-boyfriend, was in his nose; as with the dream with Sherrill McKinnen, he hadn't merely recalled a memory—he'd revisited it.

Vibration in his pocket startled him. Without thinking he pulled out his phone and answered the unlisted number.

"Yes?"

"I'm walking out of the Short Stop with a new friend about to enjoy a lovely double-D cup sandwich when I get an 'urgent' message," Terrance said. "This had better be damn important."

As if on cue, a woman pushing a phlebotomy station entered the room with a polite smile.

*       *       *

# CHAPTER THREE

## Sunday Night

Dominick chose Swingers Diner. Admittedly, it was better suited for an after-club debrief than a business meeting; with dim lighting, a festive atmosphere, and a high concentration of the young and beautiful, it was a cherished icon of LA nightlife. But practicality won out over pertinence. Swingers was open late, a mile from the hospital, and—most importantly to Dominick—it didn't smell like silent death.

True to form, the atmosphere was lively. A group of bearded young men in snug-but-sagging designer jeans joked nearby; a table of fifty-something men with greasy hair and pinky rings ranted across the room; a gaggle of attractive young women laughed as they posed for one group selfie after another. When still new in town, Dominick had been awed by such places. Did no one in this city have work in the morning?

He was met by a hostess with a disinterested smile and a silver hoop through her left eyebrow; she seated him in the back of the restaurant, as if aware that he was not one of the cool kids who should be easily seen near the front. He was grateful for the isolation. Once seated, he checked his phone and ran through the mobile sites of Forbes, the Wall Street Journal, and Bloomberg. Public Relations was already working on the official release regarding tonight's events, but with Higgins off-script Dominick was on the lookout for an alternate version of the story leaking prematurely.

Earlier, after his impromptu nap on the hospital floor, a text message alerted him of Antoinette's whereabouts; she'd returned to the two-bedroom Koreatown apartment of the Kelleys. Dominick bought them a five-thousand square foot house in Brentwood—a neighborhood that was home to movie stars and the former governor—but Antoinette now spent most of her nights in an apartment not much larger than their kitchen. That she found their second-hand couch more comfortable than their own pillow-top California king-sized bed was obscene.

But such were the times.

"You look like shit," Terrance announced as he sat opposite Dominick. No hello or handshake, as was customary between them.

"You gaining weight?" Dominick responded. Terrance smirked as Ms. Pierced Eyebrow came over.

"I'll have a red-eye," Terrance told her. "From the looks of my buddy here, it's going to be a long night. And actually, he's paying. So make it two."

"Of course." For him, her smile was genuine. Terrance got a lot of those from women. She turned to Dominick. "And you?"

"Iced tea."

Off she went, and Terrance regarded Dominick with hazel eyes still bloodshot from whatever alcohol he'd consumed earlier that evening. With a biracial Black-and-French father and a full-blooded Yaqui Indian mother, Terrance was the definition of "ethnically ambiguous." As a younger man he'd been approached by a modeling agency for possible representation. Even earlier, soon after they'd first met in middle school, Dominick was horrified to learn a girl had dated him merely to try to get Terrance's attention. Terrance teased him about that to this day.

"So?" Terrance asked.

Dominick almost smiled. Despite his casual demeanor, Terrance didn't pussy-foot around when it mattered.

Dominick took a breath, leaned forward, and told him almost everything.

Included was the heart attack, the bizarre statements Mr. Wellington made about the board, Antoinette's divorce declaration, Higgins' flat refusal to cooperate, and the fruitless conversation with Leftwich.

Excluded was the finger prick, the voice in his head, his two fainting spells, and Mr. Wellington's actual last words.

Terrance listened without a word. By the time Dominick finished they had plates of food before them. Dominick's remained mostly untouched but Terrance was almost finished with his plate of jerk chicken.

With the silence now between them, Dominick became aware of how long he'd been speaking. The cast of characters around them had changed from when he'd arrived. He sat back and sipped his now-watery tea.

"'What is' is the grandest lie of all creation,'" Terrance quoted. "'It is the greatest shame of my life.' Is there a line in the one-percenter rule-book that says 'always speak dramatically?'"

Dominick's face cracked a smile. There was nothing on God's green earth like an old friend.

"What do you think?" Dominick asked. Terrance sipped a red-eye, his third.

"Hell of a coincidence that the old man talks shit about the board, promptly has a heart attack, and then the board starts stonewalling you. The night before the vote, no less."

"Some timing, huh?"

"Clearly a play."

"Clearly."

"And nothing unusual before now?"

Dominick shook his head.

"And the thing about the computer chips," Terrance mused. "Fearless Leader does a face-plant and Leftwich is worried about hardware? Doesn't pass the smell test."

"Thanks for the penetrating analysis."

"You having the hospital run toxicology on the old man?"

"Poison?" Dominick scoffed. "They're opportunistic business people. Not the mob."

"Keep thinking like that."

Dominick waved it away. They were running toxicology tests anyway, of course, but he doubted they'd yield any results.

"Speaking of toxicology, I need an important favor." Dominick retrieved from his pocket the white box and tiny stake he'd wrapped in a pocket square. He leaned closer to Terrance and explained what Mr. Wellington did with them in the lowest voice possible. Terrance momentarily forgot his food.

"You're shitting me. You saw it sparkling?"

"I did."

"WTF." Terrance leaned forward to look at them more closely.

"I haven't told you the strangest part. And you cannot repeat this, ever. Bro code."

"Bro code, I got it," Terrance said. "But you can't confess—"

"No, not like that."

Dominick tried to lean even closer. He explained about fainting in the street and re-living that terrifying day in front of Sherrill McKinnen's home, then about doing so again and revisiting the piano of his youth.

Still he left out the voice in his head.

The look of incredulity on Terrance's face convinced Dominick that he'd said enough.

"You want it traced," Terrance said finally.

"Of course I want it traced. We find out where he got it from, it may give us a clue of what he was talking about." Dominick's excitement about having answers accelerated his speech.

"That's not all that you want," Terrance said with a smile. "You want the stake tested for substances."

"Wouldn't you? A psychotropic or hallucinogen would explain—"

Terrance chuckled and returned to eating.

"Not necessarily. As one with experience with certain substances, they don't typically work that way. They induce a state, usually over time, and then you have the experience. And then it ends. Afterward the body purges while it re-calibrates. But the experience doesn't flick on and off again like a light switch."

Equal parts anger and fear rose within Dominick. The

piece he'd left out—the voice—he experienced exactly like a light switch. Terrance continued.

"A finger prick isn't a great way to introduce anything into the bloodstream anyway. But it's good for getting blood, so I'm damn curious what was in the bowl that would react like that. I'll get them into the lab."

"How long for the results?"

"A few days."

Dominick tried not to roll his eyes. Terrance shrugged and continued.

"Like I said, happy to do it. But I advise you explore alternatives to the 'my mentor and father-in-law poisoned me with a finger prick before my biggest meeting' theory."

Dominick's annoyance was now in full bloom.

"Then what do you think?"

Terrance burped, touched his chest.

"I think you need a blowjob."

Dominick looked at him for a moment and then laughed. When was the last time he laughed?

"That's a fantastic idea."

"I'm serious. If you're fainting in the street you're even more uptight than usual."

"I'm important," Dominick protested. "I'm supposed to take myself seriously. If I'm not a little uptight I'm not paying attention."

"Hence eating asphalt in front of Bambi, because that's a good sign. Did I mention a blowjob?"

"Remember that whole 'I'm moving out' conversation? Doing me sexual favors isn't high on Antoinette's to-do list right now."

"Was it ever?"

"Here's where I remind you that your less-than-favorable opinion of my wife has adversely affected opportunities for us to spend time together."

"And here's where I remind you that I told you marrying an Ice Queen was going to suck donkey balls. Even if she was his daughter."

"Only you could work 'donkey balls' into a serious—"

"Vincent! Vincent!" one of the greasy-haired pinky-ring men yelled. His audience, another man entering the diner, came over and hugged him drunkenly.

Dominick was frozen only a moment before he caught himself and turned back to Terrance. But seeing his friend's knowing eyes meeting his own told Dominick that avoiding it would be pointless.

Still, he tried anyway.

"Been that kind of night," Dominick conceded. Maybe it could be left at that.

"What else are you not telling me? Cagey bastard."

Or maybe not.

Dominick looked in the direction of a group of young men in black t-shirts and eyeliner. But he saw nothing. Visual acuity was superseded by the implications of Terrance's question. Dominick's fingers tapped the indifferent surface of the table as he considered his reply.

The answer could be furnished by the mere utterance of a few words. That sounded simple enough. But could he speak of it? Could he say it here, of all places—a dark, loud fine-dining restaurant that masqueraded as a hip-and-cool diner? What a peculiar setting this would be to lay plain the most painful experience of his life. It had cut through his family's collective existence like a gleeful executioner. And yet Mr.

Wellington mentioned it as if commenting on the weather.

*Please find my granddaughter. Tell her I'm sorry. Vincent was my fault.*

Dominick's eyes burned. Twelve words. Three sentences; two imperative, one shockingly declarative. Simple. Horrible.

Dare he repeat it?

A single tear fell before he noticed. He wiped it away. Keeping his view on the nothingness occupied by strangers, he opened his mouth to answer—but then his phone, which had been sitting innocuously on the table, rang.

With a mirthless smile Dominick glanced at it. His face tightened at the name on screen: Wallace Purdie. He showed it to Terrance.

"What a coincidence," Terrance said.

Dominick answered. "Hello, Wallace."

"Dominick!" Wallace's voice bellowed into his ear. "I'm almost to the hospital now, not even five minutes out. You're still there, right?"

Mr. Wellington's words came to Dominick's mind: *Wallace Purdie is a racist, a pervert, a misogynist, and a predator. I suspect he's a murderer.*

Dominick closed his eyes and kept his voice even.

"I'm down the street at Swingers, with my god-brother. Come join us."

"That's a negative, compadre," Wallace replied. "We need some alone time."

Dominick raised an eyebrow. The image of a rabbit sniffing a baited trap came to mind.

"How much time?" he asked.

The pause on the line, while momentary, was dense. That Wallace was openly calculating while continuing to be casual set off any remaining alarms within Dominick that weren't already blaring. This was doing nothing to help pass the smell test.

"A couple minutes," was the reply. "Meet me outside. We can talk in the car and go in after if you want."

*If I want?* Dominick thought.

"Sounds good," Dominick said without hesitation. In truth it sounded very *not* good and he was full of hesitation, but it was advantageous to pretend otherwise. Perhaps Wallace would tip his hand sooner.

"Great," Wallace thundered. "You said Swingers, right?"

"Yes."

"I'll be there in a couple."

"See you then."

Shaking his head, Dominick disconnected. He looked at Terrance and started to speak, except—

*Goddamn if that fat pig-fucker isn't up to something too! What the fuck?*

—he then had to close his eyes and again breathe down the adrenaline surge from the surprise of the voice screaming in his head.

"You alright?" Terrance asked.

"Yeah. Headache."

His head did hurt. Surprising, disorienting, and now painful, these explosive mental blurts were now officially worrisome.

"Blowjob. Just saying."

"What, are you offering? Is this your way out of the closet?

Terrance smiled. "Asshole."

"I'm meeting Wallace outside for some alone time," Dominick said with casual ease he didn't feel.

"It's cool. I'll be here, ordering dessert that you're paying for."

Terrance was thinking more than that and they both knew it. Dominick nodded. Inwardly he thanked himself for recognizing that whatever was happening, experiencing it with his best friend made it easier.

His phone lit up with a text message.

"Outside." From Wallace. Dominick stood.

"Be right back."

Dominick headed towards the door and pondered the trap that lie ahead. Given his last two interactions with board members, he was certain some version of "what were you and Mr. Wellington talking about?" would soon be asked of him. After what Mr. Wellington had said about Wallace

*(pervert)*

hearing him ask it would be a special irony. But this time Dominick would have questions of his own. This time the game would be a bit different.

*                        *                        *

He walked out into the night and spotted the immense S-Class Mercedes poised near the curb like a giant bird of prey. He strode to the passenger's side and got in.

Dominick immediately noted that Wallace's expression didn't fit the circumstances. He looked something between embarrassed and amused. Dominick's mouth tightened for the curveball.

"Hey there, buddy," Wallace said as the two shook hands—

or rather, as Dominick's hand disappeared into Wallace's meaty grasp. "No disrespect to your god-brother, but this is something to be shared in private."

Wallace fished out a manila envelope and offered it to Dominick. The curveball, apparently.

"This is going to seem out of left field," Wallace added. "But I'm sure it's not."

Adrenaline pumping, Dominick took the envelope and opened it. In spite of his wall of impassivity, for the third time this impossible night he was shocked.

Inside the envelope were surveillance pictures of Dominick with a woman—a woman who wasn't his wife. They were pictures of him with Dai.

They were pictures of his affair.

In one picture they were holding hands over dinner. In another they were entering the bed-and-breakfast together. In yet another she was kissing his face in the way he loved, in the way he still sometimes missed.

God-fucking-dammit.

"I'm listening," Dominick said in a hard voice.

Wallace spoke in a 'there-there-good-buddy' tone Dominick loathed.

"Someone, I'm thinking from JL Industries, contacted me two hours ago and had it sent over. Trying to deep-six you ahead of time. And send us into a scramble."

This wasn't a curveball thrown by a wily pitcher. This was someone sneaking up behind him and hitting him over the head with a bat.

"What exactly was said?"

"I was told I had a sensitive delivery going to my office for my eyes only, arriving in an hour. Normally I would have called horseshit. But they called my private number right after I got word about Arthur. Blocked ID."

"The messenger?"

Wallace shook his head. "Some guy on a bike, barely spoke English. Was paid in cash by a customer he didn't know."

Convenient. Dominick kept himself from shaking his head.

"Who have you told about this?" He looked at Wallace to gauge his response. But Wallace looked surprised at the question.

"You."

Dominick didn't bother attempting to hide his thoughts. *And if you believe that*, Dominick thought, *I have this amazing bridge to sell you.*

"Look," Wallace said as he held up his hands. "If somebody's airing your dirty laundry, they don't need my help. Personally, as long as you're increasing market share I don't care who you're giving it to. But if you're going to be our guy I need you to know someone's coming for you. And I need to know you're up for this."

"Are you kidding me?"

That's what Dominick was supposed to say, of course. That he meant it was immaterial, even as Wallace nodded. But there was something more here, wasn't there? Yes, there was. And he only had a few more seconds to uncover it.

Mr. Wellington, a master negotiator, had schooled Dominick in the psychological warfare it involved. Dominick had to get beyond what he was supposed to say and how he was supposed to feel and instead grasp what initial reactions would normally obscure. Yes, he felt blindsided, embarrassed, outraged, and even afraid—but what was on the other side?

And more importantly, how did it benefit Wallace?

His face softened when it hit him. Just in time, because Wallace opened his mouth to conclude things.

"Okay. Then what do you say we—"

"Cut the shit, Wallace. What do you want?" God, did the heat in his face feel good.

"Want?"

"Yes, want. What do you expect for coming to me in this 'You Can Trust Me, I'm on Your Side' kind of way?"

Again Wallace held up his beefy hands.

"I get it. Given what's in your lap you'd be a fool to not be paranoid right now. But this is on the level."

"On the level."

"Swear to God."

*Now, about that bridge,* Dominick thought.

Dominick closed his eyes to keep from rolling them. It was time to set his trap. He took an obvious breath.

"My apologies," Dominick said. "Shooting the messenger has a certain appeal at a time like this."

Wallace shrugged. "Like I said, I get it."

With the line baited, it was time to toss it. Dominick looked out of the tinted windshield and squinted for effect.

"Is there anything I don't know? Before he collapsed, Mr. Wellington was cryptic. Vague. Not like himself."

Dominick trailed off, his eyes still out the windshield, and waited for Wallace to bite. Wallace exhaled.

"Arthur loves you," he started. "We all know that. Hell, I used to be worried about it." Wallace rubbed the rubbery creases of skin on his forehead. "If he was trying to tell you something, it's right there for you. You just need more time with it."

Wallace shrugged as Dominick could almost hear the door of opportunity slam shut. Even as he nodded at Wallace with the appropriate level of feigned gratitude, Dominick was surprised by how much ire he felt for Wallace. What had the voice called him? A fat pig-fucker?

Adding insult to injury, Wallace thumped him on his shoulder.

"I'll let you get back to your god-brother and tend to that little item." Wallace motioned to the envelope still in Dominick's lap.

"No, you should come in and meet him. He's a good guy."

The words were out of Dominick's mouth before he'd even registered their meaning. It was as though he'd spoken from a fog. Why did he say that?

Wallace looked as surprised as Dominick felt. But then the big man shrugged.

"Why not?"

*      *      *

Dominick walked through the door with Wallace close behind. His jaw was tight from his latest defeat as his mind was hard at work on the contents of the manila envelope in his hand. Was Dai in trouble now as well? Jesus Christ.

He had no idea what would unfold after including Terrance in their conversation, but there was no harm in keeping Wallace around a little longer. Perhaps he'd make a mistake and allow Dominick opportunity to make up some ground; as it was he felt he'd been blitzkrieged.

Terrance rose to greet them as they approached the table. Later, Dominick would realize he missed Terrance's too-wide smile. Had he noticed, he would have been better prepared for what followed.

"Wallace, this is my god-brother Terrance."

Wallace pumped Terrance's arm with his usual enthusiasm.

"Thanks for taking care of our man here," Wallace thundered. "Wallace Purdie."

At the mention of his full name Terrance paused and cocked his head as if in recognition.

"Wait," Terrance said. "Facial humiliation, right?"

Dominick's heart exploded into his throat.

Wallace blinked. "Facial what?"

"Facial humiliation. Aren't you an authority on that?"

Wallace shook his head.

"Sorry, partner. Don't even know what that is."

"It's where a group of men ejaculate on a woman's face en masse," Terrance said, releasing Wallace's hand but still smiling. It was as if the room had fallen silent. "But you already knew that, didn't you? So why don't we save the bullshit for the pasture and you tell us why you're here."

Terrance's audacity hit Dominick like a prizefighter, but the reality of Wallace's reaction hit harder still. The trap had been so expertly laid that even Wallace, with all his experience in evasion, couldn't escape it. For the barest moment Wallace had been absolutely stunned; that he then feigned ignorance cemented his culpability.

Wallace's eyes flashed with menace. The veins in his neck pulsed and the muscles of his jaw pressed through the sides of his face.

"I don't like your tone, buddy," he growled.

Terrance's smile didn't fade.

"And I don't like your secrets. Buddy. But tell you what? How about you sit your fat ass down, tell us what you and the board have planned for tomorrow, and we'll keep your 'investments' between us."

Wallace vibrated with indignation. He edged towards Terrance.

"You listen to me, god-brother Terrance." His tone was low, deadly. "You listen to me like you've never listened to anyone your entire insignificant life. I could chew you up and spit you out three times before breakfast. You and your family. So how about next time you get your facts straight before you open your ignorant mouth?"

Terrance stood his ground with his smile unchanged.

"Given your future triple bypass surgery, I'd avoid using eating metaphors to make threats. And speaking of facts, there's one of which you're currently unaware. The knowing of which changes things."

Without taking his eyes off Wallace, he reached into his back pocket and pulled out a black leather square bearing his golden badge.

"Would you like to rephrase that last statement about me and my family, sir?"

Wallace blanched, then straightened up.

He blinked and turned away. And then Dominick snapped.

In an instant the scope of Wallace's betrayal exploded into Dominick's awareness

*(Wallace Purdie is a racist, a porn addict, a—)*

and yet the high-octane rage pouring into his veins slowed time itself. So he actually felt his right fist clench tight and draw back, his shoulder engage and his torso rotate to increase momentum, his left foot plant as his weight shifted forward, his throat vibrate hoarsely as fury poured over bared teeth and the punch sailed towards Wallace's head.

Thankfully, Terrance was faster.

He deflected the blow and locked Dominick in a vice-like grip that held Dominick's arms at sides. Wallace recoiled at Dominick's scream and turned with startled eyes.

Unnerved but attempting to salvage some dignity under the eyes of the remaining people in the restaurant, Wallace stiffly—but quickly—made his exit.

Once Wallace had exited the door, Terrance released Dominick. His head spun. Worse, the intruding voice was screaming inside his head again.

*Get him! Kill him! Don't let him get away!*

Terrance held up his badge to the room.

"It's all right, I'm with the police." He turned to Dominick, who again had his hand at his temple. "You okay?"

"Given that I almost assaulted a board member in the presence of law enforcement, I'm fantastic." Dominick's head throbbed.

"That was a good-looking punch. I didn't know you still had it in you." Terrance gave him a patronizing pat on the shoulder. "Shall we?"

"Let's shall."

Dominick was aghast. Of all the times for him to channel his inner Detroit Ghetto Boy, now? He grabbed the manila envelope from the floor and started towards the door.

"Oh wait," Dominick said, stopping. "The bill."

Terrance took him by the arm.

"I took care of it."

Dominick looked at him with surprise. Terrance rolled his eyes in spite of the smile dancing around his mouth.

"Yes I have money of my own, asshole. Let's go."

\*      \*      \*

# CHAPTER FOUR

## Sunday Night

*Walk and breathe, walk and breathe*, Dominick told himself as they strode towards the door of the restaurant. Ms. Pierced Eyebrow watched them with her mouth a little O of surprise. *Yes, yes*, Dominick thought, *almost a fist-fight at hipster-ass Swingers.* Grandma would be shaking her head. *You're bringing down the race*, she might say—one of her most damning admonitions.

The moment they reached the open air his phone was to his ear. Baxter answered in one ring.

"Yes, sir?"

"Eyes on Antoinette, immediately. No contact, but have her watched at all times until further instruction. Threat identified."

"Copy, eyes on Mrs. Reinhart, no contact, high-alert until further."

"Confirmed."

"Shall I come for you?" Baxter asked.

"No, I'm with Detective Faucon. Will contact when in need."

"Understood."

Dominick disconnected as they reached Terrance's smoke-black Dodge Challenger.

"Where to?" Terrance asked.

"But wait, there's more."

Dominick handed him Wallace's manila envelope. Terrance pulled out the photos and groaned. After trading a look they got into Terrance's car.

"No," Terrance said the moment the doors closed. "Absolutely not."

"You're just checking on her and letting her know."

"And you're just smoking rocks if you think I'm doing that."

"What other options are there?"

"You have a car."

Dominick rolled his eyes. "Because me going anywhere near Dai is a great idea, right?"

He knew Terrance wouldn't acquiesce without a fight, but they were out of options. To his surprise, Terrance shrugged his shoulders with a resigned sigh. Dominick took that as "okay."

A moment later Terrance was typing on his phone. "How do you spell his last name? I'm contacting vice."

"P-u-r-d-i-e. And he's covering his tracks this very moment. Guaranteed."

"These guys never stay clean. And good call on bringing him to me, by the way. Didn't think you would."

Dominick shifted, then looked out the window to hide his discomfort. His suggestion that Wallace meet Terrance had left his mouth before the idea had formed in his mind. Strictly speaking, that wasn't possible.

But somehow it happened.

"I'm glad it worked out," Dominick said. "As did your subtle, indirect questioning."

"Says Mike Tyson."

The v-8 engine growled to life and they leaped onto Beverly Blvd via an illegal U-turn. A silver sedan bleated its displeasure, but with Terrance's heavy right foot the sedan was soon a distant memory.

"We both see Dai," Terrance declared. "Right now. Just wake her ass up. If anyone tries to misrepresent it later I'll swear under oath to the contrary." He was using his Cop Voice, as Dominick called it. He only did that to Dominick when he was spooked. For him to do so now meant he wouldn't be seeing Dai alone.

Dominick glanced at the clock—almost 3 AM. It was far from ideal, but Terrance was resolved. It was Dominick's turn to shrug and sigh his assent.

"While we're on the subject of things you don't like," Terrance continued, "before Porky interrupted us you were telling me something important. Something about the kids." He looked at Dominick as they pulled to a stoplight. "No, I hadn't forgotten."

Dominick hadn't forgotten either, but nor was he in a rush to tell the strangest part of this bizarre story. Fate intervened.

As they idled at the red light a young man crossed the street before them. Thin, early twenties, and dressed in unkempt dark clothes, he looked unremarkable. But when he glanced their way his eyes showed surprise and recognition.

Excited, the young man approached Dominick's side of

the car; Dominick's heart rate spiked in irrational fear.

"Sir, sir!" the young man exclaimed. "She's coming, they're all coming, to see you! Oh my gosh!"

"Tweaker," Terrance mumbled, but he sounded miles away. Dominick was lost, as if hypnotized, as the young man scurried to his window.

"Listen to the animals!" the young man cried. "Super important, trust the animals!"

The light turned green and Terrance stomped on the gas.

"But not the voices!" the young man screamed as they tore away.

The city began to blur by them. A moment later Dominick's blood ran cold.

"Stop the car!" he yelled.

"What?"

"Stop the car, stop the car!" Dominick's hands shook in desperation as he looked for the young man. Already more than a block away, Terrance jammed on the brakes.

The voice in Dominick's head screamed.

*You fucking lunatic, what are you doing?*

Wincing from the explosion of pain at his temples, Dominick was already out of the car. Where was that kid? Terrance yelled his name as Dominick trotted back towards the stoplight, but even as he scanned all directions he saw nothing.

"Hey, kid!" Dominick cried. "Kid!"

The LA night remained silent.

Dominick trotted on, still looking, when again his head piped up.

*Now you've done it! Now Terrance knows you've lost your marbles. It's all downhill from here.*

He'd never wished for an internal mute button before, but

he now longed for one with a fervor that surprised him.

"Kid!" Nothing.

His efforts soon abandoned, he stood near the curb and replayed the encounter in his mind. Coincidence? Addict babble meets extraordinary circumstances? Possibly. He mentioned 'animals?' Yes, Dominick was hearing voices. But animals?

Then he blinked. "The deer."

Hands on his hips, Dominick cocked his head. Already he'd forgotten the other unscheduled encounter while in a car this evening; it was indeed of the creature variety. That had only been hours ago, but in this nightmare evening it felt like days prior. Coincidence?

Terrance pulled up beside him, the Challenger's ABS narrowly preventing a screech of tires.

"What the hell is wrong with you?" He was all Cop Voice now.

Dominick looked at him as he considered the impossible.

"Maybe I should think about that blowjob." He got into the car and snapped on his seat belt with Terrance's eyes all over him.

\*                    \*                    \*


Five minutes later they were in silence. Terrance, of course, had demanded answers. Dominick was prepared to give them—some of them—but he needed a few moments. He wasn't stalling; he needed silence to craft his response as well as prepare for his next improbable encounter of the evening.

It was a dangerous silence. The longer he indulged in it, the more he risked exasperating Terrance at a time when his trusted friend was worth his weight in platinum. And yet, if Dominick filled it prematurely he risked running into the brick wall named Dai when he was ill-prepared and unguarded—and that was risky indeed.

"Play this," Dominick said. He handed Terrance his phone with a song queued to play. Moments later the haunting bass lines of Miles Davis' moody "Teo" engulfed the car. Dominick closed his eyes and reviewed his current to-do list. He needed to give Terrance answers; he needed to find his way through his own confusion, doubt, and apprehension; and he needed to remember his strength before they reached Venice, before they reached Dai. Collectively, it represented a tall order. Bizarre a choice as it may be, if listening to a dark jazz-waltz would help him find his way, he would take it.

Miles Davis, his trumpet piercing and terse, offered the opening chorus as if in sorrowful prayer. He then picked his way through the first solo, placing notes in precise fashion as one might place feet while stepping through a field of thorns. Dominick opened his eyes; they would navigate the thorns together, he decided. Let the sad and angry trumpet lead the way.

"He mentioned them," he began. "The kids. Before Mr. Wellington collapsed he said to find Violet, and apologize. Said Vincent was his fault."

Terrance didn't respond. Some riddles didn't need answers.

"It made me think of a thing people don't understand about death," Dominick continued as he watched a sleeping Beverly Hills blow by them outside his window. "Everyone knows that the dead freeze in memory. Their hair, clothes, their laughter. They stop changing. But as I change, and Vincent doesn't, there's this schism. It's like a gap inside me. And it gets bigger every day—every day that I'm different but he's not. No one talks about that."

His eyes burned. But this time he didn't feel the moisture. Instead, he listened to John Coltrane launch into his offering to their musical prayer. As he plowed through notes at a blistering pace, Dominick heard his desperate supplication. Coltrane knew pain. Coltrane would understand.

"It's like my boy is on an island, alone. And I'm on a ship leaving him behind. Each day he's getting further away. But it's not like I don't know it. It's not like he's forgotten. I feel the growing distance. But I can't jump off the boat. I'm tied to the ship. I'm powerless."

He wiped a tear from his cheek. Not for the first time he noticed an aspect of the song that meant nothing and yet somehow pried his chest open just a bit more: the horns never play in unison. One was angry, the other was desperate but unrelenting, and yet both were isolated from each other. Neither offered the other comfort or support.

Fitting.

"Antoinette said Mr. Wellington told her goodbye. She thinks he knew it was coming, and she asked me if he said goodbye to me too." Dominick shook his head. "She's right. Before the end he said, 'We're out of time.' He knew. But his literal last words to me were, 'please find my granddaughter, tell her I'm sorry. Vincent was my fault.' Then he goes inside and falls over like a sack of potatoes."

The song massaged the silence between them. Miles returned to restate the main theme, but instead of concluding it, his sad-and-angry trumpet lingered on. But eventually his haunting trumpet fell silent, and the voices of the rhythm section, in turn, gave way to the dark stillness. Dominick settled into himself; the song had indeed helped him find his way to telling Terrance the truth, but it had gone too far by guiding him to feelings he usually avoided. It was a dangerous balance.

Moments passed as the city streamed by. Finally Terrance spoke.

"You didn't tell her, did you?"

Dominick's silence answered for him. Terrance grunted.

"Porky and company aren't going to give her a pass because you two aren't seeing eye to eye."

"No," Dominick sighed. "I just need to reel her back in. That's why I haven't told her yet." Maddening woman or not, she was still his maddening woman. "But if she finds out I saw Dai in the middle of the night, even with you—"

"If you want to warn Dai, we're seeing her together."

Dominick's mouth tightened but then relaxed. Terrance's hard-line stance was inconvenient, but not unexpected.

Appropriately, at that moment they passed a tanning facility. What an oddity that in Los Angeles, which saw warmth and sunshine almost every single day of the year, there still existed thriving tanning salons in affluent areas. To Dominick that somehow spoke to the fundamental difference between Antoinette and Dai. At times the vanity that pulsed within the city's veins fit Antoinette. As a younger woman she'd frequented tanning salons until her dermatologist begged her to stop.

Dai, on the other hand, was more likely to firebomb such a place as a form of protest, or performance art, or both.

With no traffic it was a short and silent run to Venice. As

they neared their destination Dominick began his concentration exercises. His imagination was again dancing along a knife's edge when Terrance spoke again.

"Are you sure she still lives there?"

"I am."

They stopped before a sizable craftsman home behind a wooden gate. Lush trees loomed overhead, he noticed. She'd re-landscaped. His heart rate accelerated in anticipation and he took a steadying breath.

"I don't mind waking her, but what if she's not alone?" Terrance was anxious; Dominick would be managing his friend's misgivings tonight as well as his own.

"She's alone."

Street parking didn't exist, so Terrance pulled into a red zone in front of her house. One of the perks of his job was parking ticket forgiveness.

"Are you doing the talking?" Terrance asked. "Or am I?"

Dominick couldn't help but smirk.

"She will."

He unbuckled his seat belt when Terrance spoke again.

"Are you seeing anybody about Vincent? Therapist, counselor, anybody?" Against his will, Dominick's eyes dropped. "You should. You're not okay."

Feeling no response was the best response, Dominick glanced his friend's way, grabbed the manila envelope, and left the car.

\*  \*  \*

Moments later they were at the mahogany gate. Jittery, Terrance reached towards the buzzer, but Dominick motioned his hand away. Without a word, Dominick pulled out his keys. Even in the diminished light Terrance's dumbfounded expression was clear as Dominick inserted a key and opened the door.

They crossed the lushly landscaped yard; a tire swing hung off the main tree, and a table with two chairs sat nearby. The ashtray on the table contained the remains of a cigar; Tio Rodolfo's if Dominick were to guess.

They mounted the porch, which featured more chairs and unlit candles. Sculptures of a mustachioed sun and a feminine moon flanked her mahogany doorway. After one last deep breath Dominick produced another key and opened the front door. The rich smell of incense greeted them. Regardless of his efforts to steel himself against nostalgia, the familiar patchouli scent spiraled his mind back to the first time he smelled it in her hair while holding her body to his own.

The voice in his head interrupted this reverie.

*You're sunk already! What the hell are you even doing here?*

Dominick stopped. He'd already forgotten about that lovely little phenomena, and being reminded of it now added fuel to his slow-burning apprehension.

He pushed ahead. As they entered the front room he was embraced by its clean lines, rich tones, and open feel. These and other details marked it as Dai's: framed family portraits, accent walls with textured finishes, and candles everywhere. He almost smiled in spite of himself. It was like seeing her before seeing her.

Music played from somewhere further in the home. They walked towards it.

"Dai?" Dominick called. The only response was the appearance of a black and white cat, which padded his way and rubbed itself against his shin. He petted the beast absently.

"Hello, Chango the cat," he mumbled, distracted. He'd recognized the music and was breathing through the resultant chill it brought. It was Joe Henderson's rendition of Miles Ahead. But it was far more than that. It was a song he played for them as they soaked in a hot bath of richly salted water by candlelight. It was what he played for her their beautiful and forbidden day and night in San Rafael.

"What is it?" Terrance asked.

Ignoring this, Dominick continued towards the music, which coincided with the greatest light source visible. Already his composure was leaking away from him, and with each step he fought to reclaim it. Of the millions of recorded songs on planet earth, what were the odds that she would be playing that one when he walked unannounced through her door at three in the morning? Even as he and Terrance strode with confidence towards the light, he wondered if moths imagined themselves similarly as they drew towards flame.

As they neared the light another smell because unmistakable: the piercing, chemical-scent of fresh paint. They rounded a corner and came into a large, bright, high-ceilinged room that was nearly devoid of furniture but whose high walls were dominated by large paintings. Drop cloths were positioned at various points on every wall. There was a large table buried under dozens of tubes of paints, jars of fluids, and several containers stuffed with brushes of every size.

And there, in the far corner perched on a six-foot folding ladder, holding a palette in one hand and brush in the other, was Dai Santana.

She turned to face them, with black-rimmed glasses halfway down her sharp nose, her massive black mane held absently in check by a folded bandana. It had been eight months of silence, but she hadn't changed in the slightest. Same Asiatic eyes from her Cantonese father, same full lips from her mixed-race mother, same gold nose ring looping from her right nostril, same perfectly arched eyebrows, same deep, soul-searching gaze.

Without a word or even a change in expression, she dismounted from her ladder, cleaned off her paintbrush in a nearby jar, walked over to the nearby wireless speaker and reduced the volume on the jazz quartet. She wore a t-shirt, tights, and those ballet flats he hated on her. And yet she was beautiful.

Again she faced them and this time removed her glasses as if to turn the power of her eyes to full blast.

"The king returns," she said. "And with him comes his jester. Or should I say fool?" Her voice was richer than expected out of her petite frame, and the slight staccato Cuban accent surprised most as well.

"It's good to see you too, Dai," Terrance quipped. Her eyes didn't leave Dominick.

"I'm glad you used your key. And yet now that you have come to me it is with a chaperon and a face hidden behind a mask." She tilted her head in the adorably curious way he'd missed. "Not like you. Is something rotten in the state of Denmark?"

Not sixty seconds in her presence and already his steely resolve was under assault. So he pretended the opposite. Stone-faced, he walked towards her with the manila envelope extended.

She smiled. Too late he realized that by pretending to be stronger than he was he may have played into her hands. She didn't take the envelope.

"Have you no words for me either? This envelope speaks for you? Or does the ring on your finger also serve as a gag?" Maybe it was another faux pas to extend the envelope with his left hand, he realized. But she could have tossed that barb either way. She took a step towards him. "I'm not interested in a messenger. Or in a boy-man in need of a babysitter. Show me the man I have loved or leave me to my peace."

His face remained stoic, but hot desire spiked in his chest. God, what a woman. Nonetheless, he edged closer to her. This tennis match, he knew how to play.

"As much as I enjoy this—and I do enjoy it—we wouldn't be here if it weren't important," he said. "Please."

Her lips pressed together in what he believed was annoyance. With a huff she started out of the room.

"Not in my studio," she said without stopping. Terrance rolled his eyes as both he and Dominick followed.

When they re-entered the front room she was already lighting candles. That done she left the room and returned with a mug of strongly-scented coffee and sat on the couch, and Dominick chose the love seat across from her. Terrance lingered in the doorway with his arms crossed.

Dominick placed the envelope on the coffee table between them. She sipped her coffee before looking at him with a shake of her head. Disappointment, maybe? Eventually she grabbed the envelope and opened it.

"I see. Our little secret is no longer." She thumbed through the pictures without interest before tossing them onto the table. "And that would be important. Except it stopped being a secret eight months and twenty-two days ago, as Antoinette would be happy to remind you."

"Good, she doesn't care," Terrance said. "Guess we can go."

"I think the philanderer is anxious to leave," Dai cooed. "Perhaps his penis has an appointment. Into a jar of vaseline maybe?"

"Will you two relax for a moment?" Dominick said with an attempt at force. "No, it isn't a secret. But that doesn't mean it's public. If I was under surveillance even then, who knows what these people are really after and what they're willing to do to get it. And since you're on their radar, you need to know about this."

"A warning, how sweet of you." She sipped her coffee. "Especially since I'm certain he resisted the idea. Speaking of, why is he here again?"

"I thought we were just waking you up," Terrance snorted. "I'd have resisted a hell of a lot more if I knew we were going to talk to you."

"I'm grateful he's here," Dominick redirected. "Because of him this meeting can't be used against either of us."

"He's not a necessity, he's a liability. In more ways than you know."

"Jesus, what is your problem?" Terrance already sounded near the end of his patience. Dai had gotten under his skin in record time.

"I know what you did, is my problem," she spat with eyes of ice. The force of her conviction surprised both men.

"What the hell does that mean?" Terrance said.

"It means it's not my place to out you as the degenerate that you are, *mentiroso*." Her eyes blazed at him. "But your time will come."

They were dangerously off-track and Dominick was about to redirect again when his head got lighter. He blinked, but the feeling continued. He then noticed that Chango the cat had climbed onto the couch and was sitting next to Dai.

His unblinking eyes were riveted onto Dominick.

Again the voice in his head intervened.

*You're freaked out by a cat now? What kind of leader are you? Tell her to shut up and listen!*

Dominick winced—the outbursts were getting louder. As the pain subsided he was aware of two things: a queasiness in his stomach, and an absence of speaking around him. He noticed both Terrance and Dai were watching him.

"Headache, I'm fine," he said. He took a deep breath to re-engage Dai, but she turned to trade a look with her cat. Since when did cats hold gazes with people?

The cat again turned to Dominick, and Dai did the same.

"Who's the red head?" Dai asked.

Dominick blinked. "What?

"You're not seeing a red head?"

"What are you talking about?" he asked.

She didn't answer, but continued to look at him.

As did the cat.

His head, meanwhile, was getting lighter by the moment. It was as if a string was attached to his awareness, and someone far above him had grabbed hold of it and began pulling him up.

"We should go," he said with as much authority as he could muster, but it was little more than a mumble. His vision was dimming and all that stood out were two green circles staring into him from across the table. Cat eyes.

He tried to stand but faltered—and that's when a firm hand was on his arm pulling him up. To his surprise, Terrance was now beside him.

"You all right?"

He looked at Terrance as if awakening from a dream.

"I'm fine."

"You should stay here," Dai said with concern in her voice. "And not for that. Something is rotten, but it's not the state of Denmark. It's you."

With his head still clearing Dominick didn't know what that meant. But he decided it didn't matter.

"I said I'm fine. And you know I can't."

"Let's get the hell out of here." Terrance tugged Dominick towards the door. Dai rose.

"Dominick." He still loved the way she said his name. "If you leave now you will return. But you won't be happy to do so."

Dominick pulled away from Terrance and met her stare. Again with certainty he didn't feel he returned to the table grabbed the manila envelope and the pictures.

"Take care of yourself, Dai."

She put a hand on his shoulder.

"I could feel you on your way over," she said. "That's why I was playing the music." Her eyes were swallowing him whole. "Something's happening, and you're at the center of it. And you need to find Violet. But we'll talk about it when you return to me."

She cupped his face with one hand, kissed his cheek, and left the room.

He stroked his head, not knowing what to think. Terrance shrugged. They started towards the door.

"Until then, please be careful."

Dominick stopped, turned. That was Dai, and she sounded very close. But she wasn't in the room. He looked around. Why did his head feel foggy again?

"What?" Terrance was at the door looking back at him.

"You didn't hear—?" But Terrance's confused expression confirmed that he did not. "Never mind." He walked out, his mind awash with uncertainty.

\*                              \*                              \*

Ten minutes later they barreled through sparse pre-dawn traffic. Terrance was asleep in the passenger's seat and Dominick couldn't help but grip the wheel too tightly.

How much madness could one day hold? Twenty-four hours ago he was sleeping soundly, about to enjoy a day of skiing with his mentor and father-in-law, and preparing himself for a board meeting where he'd be voted the company's new chief executive. Then Pandora's box opened and hell was unleashed. And hell's epicenter seemed to correspond with his exact location.

"But when you're going through hell, keep going," he muttered to himself. Predawn West LA did not disagree. "Call Lawrence Silvers," he told his phone.

Within moments the phone rang over the car's speakers, and a clear voice answered.

"Law Offices of Silvers and Richards."

"I need to get an emergency message to Lawrence Silvers. This is Dominick Reinhart."

"Of course, Mr. Reinhart. I have a note from Mr. Silvers to route you. Please hold."

Dominick bet that Linda, his assistant, had already put legal on notice about a possible request. That woman was a godsend.

"This is Lawrence Silvers," a sleepy voice said over the speakers.

"I'm sorry to wake you, Lawrence. I'm sure you've heard about Mr. Wellington."

"I have."

"I'd like to meet as soon as possible to review the bylaws. Specifically, the language as it pertains to succession under such circumstances."

"Of course. I anticipated this request when I got the news last night. I had my staff review it over the night, and I'll review it myself before we meet. Is 6 AM at my office a possibility?"

"It sounds perfect. I'll see you then."

Dominick disconnected the line. Times like this he was grateful for their well-oiled corporate machine and his ability to navigate it at 70 mph on Interstate-10. He may have stepped into a nightmare, but he was determined to wake up and return to living the life he'd created for himself.

Again he thought it over. What Mr. Wellington said about Wallace was troubling enough. That Wallace then tried to throw him off-base with the pictures made things worse. After Dominick verified his future as leader of their corporate empire was still secured, he would reevaluate all the members of the board. Earlier tonight he'd called Wallace a consistent ally! Add to that Higgins' flat refusal and Leftwich's uncharacteristic evasion—the questions were piling up.

The kids, mentioned once again. Dai couldn't have

known that Mr. Wellington had mentioned them earlier, so for her to bring up Violet was astounding. But as much as Dominick would love to question Dai further, seeing her again was out of the question—despite her strange prediction to the contrary. The damage that would do to his marriage would be incredible, and seeing her created more questions inside of him than answers.

Now was a time for answers.

Nonetheless, Dai was accurate in one regard: with conspirators out there, he'd best get a handle on Violet, and right now.

The sky had gone from black to gray, and traffic had intensified. He'd get to Lawrence's office in mid-Wilshire about an hour before their scheduled meeting. That was enough time for him and Terrance to grab breakfast and some more caffeine beforehand. He considered leaving Terrance asleep in the car while he met with Lawrence. But after last night's weirdness he'd take as much support as he could get.

He drove with the sounds of the road and Terrance's snoring beside him. What a soundtrack for a man hours away from assuming the reigns of a worldwide conglomerate with offices on four continents and investments in everything from cloud computing to coffee beans. But the road to glory was often less-than-glorious, and he was fine with that as well.

\*　　　　　　\*　　　　　　\*

# Monday Morning

The office of Lawrence Silvers was on the 36th floor and offered an expansive view of the smoggy Los Angeles skyline. Cars scrambled below them on Wilshire boulevard like lines of insects.

With manicured nails, circular black glasses, and a tailored dark suit, Lawrence looked the part of the soft-spoken high-powered attorney. He rose.

"Good morning, Mr. Reinhart."

"Lawrence, please. It's Dominick. And this is detective Faucon. A long-time friend. Please speak freely in his presence."

"Detective." Lawrence nodded as they shook. "May I offer you a drink?" He indicated the wet bar in the corner.

"Thanks." Terrance motioned to their seats. "I'll pour, you sit. Dominick?"

"I'm fine."

Terrance went to the elegant collection of bottles and glasses as Dominick and Lawrence sat. The moment he settled into his seat Dominick again felt his head lighten. His heart beat faster than appropriate. As at Dai's, it was as though someone above him pulled on the string of his awareness.

Dominick swallowed his exasperation. He would grit his teeth and focus through it. *Sometimes, child, you just have to be a man*, Grandma would say.

Terrance poured alcohol and Lawrence adjusted his glasses before indicating the thick packet of papers before him. Dominick's head was light but bearable. So far, so good.

"The bylaws are clear in this respect," Lawrence began. "In the event that the Chief Executive becomes incapacitated without a replacement named, the board of directors selects an interim replacement from within the company via a simple majority."

It was during that word *majority* when Dominick first spotted it; as Lawrence finished the word something thin darted out of his mouth then retreated just as quickly. Dominick's brow furrowed.

Terrance didn't stir. Lawrence scanned his notes and continued.

"Said replacement then serves until the board of directors conducts a search and locates a well-qualified candidate who is to be appointed to the position of Chief Executive by an absolute two-thirds majority vote."

"And there are no ambiguities?" Dominick asked.

"Correct."

Lawrence took a deep breath. And as he did, Dominick again saw something thin shoot from the dark cavern of Lawrence's mouth, and then draw back in. It shot out once more, but this time it wagged up and down before retracting. Dominick glanced at Terrance, but again he didn't react. Dominick's jaw tightened.

*Now I'm hallucinating*, Dominick told himself. *Awesome.*

"The language is precise and specific," Lawrence continued, "and there are no reasonable grounds for alternate interpretations. The criterion for the interim replacement is also clear. The individual must be from within the company's executive team, intimately involved with the company's day-to-day affairs, in direct and continual contact with the presiding Chief Executive, and someone who has demonstrated a quantifiable history of successful executive leadership."

Lawrence leaned forward and pointed his nose at the stack of papers before him. That's when the snake, black-emerald and shimmering in the new day's light, slid from his mouth and onto the desk.

It poured forth as though living excrement; it arched its head from Lawrence's desk as if gaining its bearings. Its eyes, crimson orbs bisected by black vertical pupils, seemed to point right at Dominick. Its forked tongue flicked towards him obscenely.

A whimper escaped him. He felt Terrance turn towards him, but he couldn't take his eyes off the great black serpent now staring at him from his attorney's desk.

A line from a half-remembered dream floated into Dominick's awareness: *I fear madness will take him in short order.* He nearly gagged.

The snake continued to pour from Lawrence's parted lips; it also seemed to grow fatter once it encountered the air. Indeed, the beast now amassing on Lawrence's desk was far too large to have emanated from a human mouth.

Nonetheless—

When the tail exited Lawrence's mouth he looked at Dominick and resumed.

"Of course there is no guarantee that the interim Chief Executive will be selected to serve as the permanent replacement."

The serpent opened its mouth wide, barring two gleaming curved fangs, and Dominick heard a voice. It was breathy, deep, distorted—and yet Dominick understood it.

"Lawrence Silvers hates his father," it said. "He visualizes himself urinating on his father's grave. He hired a Spanish-speaking attending medical staff for his father's medical care because he knows he hates Mexicans."

"You okay?" This was from Terrance, who was staring at

Dominick.

Dominick gulped as his face throbbed with fear. Still, he couldn't take his eyes from the snake. It closed its mouth and stared at him.

After a second gulp Dominick found his voice.

"I'm fine."

He motioned to Lawrence to continue, even as the snake edged closer to Dominick. Pain shot up his arms as he gripped his chair. His heart raced.

"From the clear language of this document," Lawrence continued, "there is little to no way that the Board of Directors can legally bar your candidacy as the forerunner for interim Chief Executive. From the documents here and from what you've shared, Mr. Wellington had openly spent time in an obvious, even scheduled, professional development capacity in relationship to you."

Lawrence again settled into his chair, heedless of the giant viper inches away from him. It opened its great mouth again.

"Know this about Lawrence Silvers," it said. "Anger is his food. Spite, his air. Upon it he feeds. Gains succor. And yet it will also kill him. Soon, in fact. Because who he hates most of all is himself. In this man you trust your empire."

"While it isn't impossible to rule out other potential candidates for the interim executive position," Lawrence droned on, "it is difficult to argue for another candidate's legitimacy over yours on the basis of the criterion stated here."

"Good," Dominick said, his voice thin. Now at his eye level, the snake flitted its tongue and stared at him. "I'd like a hard copy of the bylaws as well. Right now."

"Of course," Lawrence said. "Is everything all right, sir?"

The snake, though expressionless, seemed to smile at

Dominick. He thought he might faint.

"Yes," he said, but it came out as a squeak.

Lawrence typed, with rapid precision, on a nearby keyboard.

"My staff will provide you that hard copy within moments. Would you like to discuss this further? Or is there anything additional that I may provide for you?"

"Or maybe that drink?" Terrance prompted.

The serpent, however, opened its mouth once again.

*Since I'm hallucinating,* Dominick thought, *how come I can only hear it when it opens its mouth?* Involuntary tears of despair came to his eyes.

"Welcome to 'what is,' Dominick," the snake said.

Dominick stood.

"No, that'll be all. I'm not feeling well. Thank you, Lawrence."

The attorney stood and outstretched his hand inches away from the serpent's head. The snake tilted its head Dominick's way. Did he dare?

Dominick's throat worked as his stomach began to pitch.

"I can't. Probably shouldn't have earlier. Make sure you wash that hand."

"Oh, of course," Lawrence replied. "Shall I call you a physician? You look—"

"No, no," Dominick said. "Thank you for your time, as always." Terrance stood and shook Lawrence's hand as Dominick made for the door. He opened it, but turned once more towards Lawrence.

Lawrence stood there, still watching. And there, inches before him, remained the giant black snake—and it still seemed to be smiling at him.

Dominick grabbed the nearby wastebasket and retched as he staggered from the room.

\*            \*            \*

# CHAPTER FIVE

## Monday Morning

"What the hell was that?" Terrance demanded.

Dominick, his stomach contorting, glanced at his watch as they climbed back into Terrance's car. It was nearly seven; the board would meet in four hours. He had time to nap, shower, change…and wake up from this nightmare.

"That wasn't rhetorical." Terrance was back to using his Cop Voice.

"What do you think it was? Bad food."

"And I'm supposed to believe that? Got a nice bridge for me too?"

*That's my line*, Dominick almost said. But that would be nonsense to Terrance, and would only exasperate him further.

"Head downtown," Dominick said, feigning his normal authority. "I'm fine. Sue me for the night's festivities getting to me."

Terrance fired up the car and started out the parking deck.

"Which is why I thought getting some good news would make you feel better. Not have you puking your guts out." He shot a glance Dominick's way. "You should've seen yourself. I thought you were going to faint."

If he wasn't so shaken, Dominick might have smiled. He fainted twice yesterday. That was a walk in the park compared to what he'd just experienced.

He shuddered. The snake had looked shockingly real; he was haunted by details like the black slits in its red eyes and the shimmer of its scales in the morning light. How could he hallucinate with that level of clarity when he'd never taken time to look at a snake?

He was pondering the relationship between sleep deprivation and hallucinating when they passed a young man stepping onto an orange city bus. The memory came in a flash: *listen to the animals! Super important, trust the animals!*

"Oh, fuck me," Dominick blurted out.

"What?"

Dominick stared ahead as two pieces of this nightmarish puzzle tried to fit together. He desperately wanted to ask Terrance if he'd heard what the young man had said last night; it was as if he felt himself edging ever-so-closely to the realm where reality itself was becoming more difficult to trust. Having an outside party verify that *that had actually happened* would be of supreme comfort.

Except he couldn't ask; Terrance was already too concerned.

"What is it?" Terrance repeated. Dominick could feel his friend's concern radiating from him. Dominick sighed. If he was going to continue temporarily losing his mind he'd have to get better at hiding it.

"It's just—" Dominick started, but stopped. He'd have to

tease this out in his head while talking about something else. He closed his eyes. "I had a thought," he said.

Terrance had seen the young man last night and called him a tweaker—a speed addict—which meant he wasn't a hallucination. And since Dominick hadn't experienced real people saying imagined things, the young man may have indeed encouraged him to listen to animals. A snake definitely counts as an animal.

Yet could Dominick honestly entertain the notion that a babbling speed addict had commented on his future hallucination?

*He also mentioned the voices*, Dominick thought bitterly. *And note he said animals, plural.* Dominick put his head in his right hand and squeezed.

"Lawrence," Dominick said. His head throbbed. Could this nightmare get worse? "What if the board got to him?"

"You think?"

"After last night I don't know what to think. But I had heard some potentially embarrassing information about Lawrence personally. Never looked into it because it didn't matter. But if the board got wind as well they could've used it for leverage. Now would be a great time to verify or disprove it. And it wouldn't hurt to get a second set of eyes on the bylaws."

"Sounds paranoid. Misleading a client would cost him everything." Terrance mused for a moment. "But after the photos I can't blame you for some paranoia."

Maybe this could be a good thing, Dominick realized. With the snake telling him something he could not have known, something that he can now disprove, he could write the whole thing off as a waking dream and feel better about his grasp of reality. All it would take is a little detective work.

That, and giving credence to something he heard from a giant viper that slid out of his attorney's mouth and started talking.

"I need someone to look into Lawrence's family life," Dominick said. "His father specifically."

"What are they looking for?"

*Now the leap*, Dominick thought.

"I heard his dad is racist, and that Lawrence, to spite him, hired a Hispanic medical staff for his care."

Terrance chuckled. "Poetic justice, huh? Not much to pin on a guy, though."

"But worth checking out."

"Yeah," Terrance said. Dominick felt a little more relaxed already. "Who told you? One of Baxter's guys?"

*No*, Dominick thought, *a snake came out of his mouth and told me. Didn't you see it? It spoke plain English. Didn't even hiss like they do in the movies. Apparently real talking snakes don't do that.*

"It doesn't matter."

Terrance shrugged as they crawled through commuter traffic headed towards downtown. "I'll get somebody on it."

Dominick nodded, but then wondered what to make of the rest of the young man's words:

*She's coming, they're all coming, to see you! Oh my gosh!*

Dominick shook it away. Five hours from now he'd be one of the most influential executives in America, and here he was trying to decode the babbling of a street junkie and passing along info he got from a talking snake.

"And you're sure you don't want to head home first?" Terrance asked. Dominick shook his head.

"No time. You get the side investigation started. I'm

going to get outside counsel to look at the bylaws. I've stayed downtown before. I'll have someone get me a room and some fresh clothes, then be ready for the board meeting."

"And you're sure you don't want me to come with?"

Dominick was sure of no such thing, but this wasn't the time to say so.

"I can handle this myself."

\*                         \*                         \*

Three hours later he awoke in a room at the JW Marriott downtown. While the company had an account with the more opulent Ritz-Carlton next door, he felt that excessive for what amounted to a four-hour stay. This would more than do.

Before his nap he had addressed several items. A copy of the by-laws had been sent to the nearby offices of the Ryu Law Group for their "corporate and transactional expertise." Rachel was en route with fresh clothes for the meeting, and she'd make sure the town car left at the hospital would get returned. He'd checked the hospital for Mr. Wellington's condition; no change.

Antoinette didn't answer her phone. But Baxter confirmed she was still at the Kelleys' and had not been approached by anyone.

Blinking away the cobwebs, he sat up on the bed. His head felt like dead weight upon his shoulders. He had an hour before the meeting, which was five minutes away. A shower would do him wonders.

He relieved himself in the bright and geometrically-decorated bathroom, and then he took a long, hot shower. He inhaled the steam with deep heavy breaths, and he imagined the hot water relaxing his muscles from without even as the warmth of the water vapor relaxed his body from within. He imagined blood running freely throughout his entire circulatory system. He saw his brain, the magnificent switchboard that was biology's great masterpiece, working as a portrait of health and efficiency. He saw himself relaxed and in harmony with all that was transpiring within his entire being.

He would be ready for the events transpiring around him. Nothing before him was worse than that which was already behind him. He'd risen from nothing; he'd been the son of a drunkard who eventually abandoned his family, and yet Dominick had put himself through both college and business school. Along the way he'd won the favor of one of the single most successful self-made men in business. All this, he told himself, was proof he was a man of destiny.

No, it hadn't been easy. But he saw it through. Violet was conceived unexpectedly when he was barely out of his teens, and rather than abort or give her up for adoption he bet on himself, went well above his pay grade, and married the most beautiful girl he'd ever seen. He promised her that he would take their brave little family far beyond the life the statistics had predicted for him. And he succeeded—because he saw it through.

Their nineteen-year union had been besieged with hardship, and none greater than the loss suffered that fateful September day. But like the Redwoods, those timeless, majestic giants they'd visited that tragic day, they withstood the test of time. They'd all been battered; Violet rebelled, he had erred with Dai, yet they remained intact. Imperfect as they were, they were still a family. He had seen it through.

Today's meeting would be no different.

By the time he finished his shower the last sixteen hours had indeed felt like a fantasy from which he was finally awakening. He looked into the mirror and watched the steam retreat from its surface. As the haze dissipated he watched his reflection take shape. It was like watching himself emerge from the depths— like a sunken treasure, once lost, now being hoisted from the black sea and into the brilliance of the daylight.

He was still a leader. He was still a winner. He was still himself.

He let these feelings of gratitude and confidence fill his being. Whatever challenges lay before him, they too would fall.

"'I see only my objectives—the obstacles must give way,'" he quoted to his reflection.

He put on the complimentary robe, which itself was a delight to his skin. Upon leaving the bathroom he saw a blinking light on the room phone. *Rachel,* he thought with satisfaction. Life was returning to the way it was supposed to be.

He picked up his phone and enjoyed the feeling of a smile on his face.

"This is the front desk, how may I assist you?" a smiling voice said to him after he'd depressed a single button.

"This is Dominick Reinhart in 1162. I believe there's a message for me?"

"Yes, sir. Miss Rachel Myers dropped off some items for you. Would you like me to send them up?"

"Yes, please."

"My pleasure. They will arrive momentarily. May I assist you with something else?"

"A butter croissant, a carafe of orange juice, and a bowl of mixed fruit, please."

"Right away, sir."

"Thank you."

He disconnected with a smile. He spent several moments at the window taking in the sunlight of the new day. Damn, did it feel good to be himself again.

He noticed his cell phone blinking with a notification alert. He picked it up and to his surprise there were ten missed calls from Linda. How had he missed this when he first woke up? Before he pushed the call-back button there was a knock on the door.

Delaying his phone call, he opened the door to two smiling young men. One had his food, and the second was holding a full garment bag, a shoe-box—and an envelope.

Dominick regarded this last with interest. On it read his first name, written in Antoinette's handwriting.

His call momentarily forgotten, he tipped them, hung the garment bag upon the door hook, and looked at the envelope. His smile, so confident moments ago, faded slightly. Noticing this, he took a deep breath, re-discovered his gratitude, and then looked at the envelope again. Now was no time to forget fundamentals.

He took a letter opener from the desk and cut open the envelope. Inside he found a note, a photograph, and a small pouch. The photo was a recent candid shot of Antoinette, smiling radiantly, sandwiched between Bill and Elizabeth Kelley. A surprising sadness stabbed through his grateful defenses; she hadn't smiled at him like that in years.

His eyes found the note—and froze.

*I wanted you to see that I'm happy now. I'm sorry for my*

*mistakes and I forgive you for Dai. You deserve to find your happiness as well. Goodbye.*

Numbness infiltrated him. He fought the tightening of his stomach, even as he looked at the small linen pouch that had accompanied the note. He had an idea of what was inside even as he loosened the pouch into his palm.

Her wedding rings fell into his hand.

They were Tiffany-designed rings. The primary diamond was a full carat weight with VVS1 clarity, and it was set in a platinum band amidst a ring of smaller accent diamonds. The ring set constituted a $15,000 purchase he proudly made as part of their tenth-anniversary celebration. They renewed their vows and the white beaches of Martinique, and he remembered her eyes sparkling when he slipped this ring onto her finger. It was stunning, even from his uninformed Midwest American male perspective.

And now they were discarded items in a pouch sent to him like forgotten trinkets of yesteryear.

He sat heavily onto the bed. He stared at the rings in his hand and felt their delicate weight. He remembered snapping a secret picture of Antoinette's left hand—no small feat in the era before cell phone cameras. She'd recently gotten a French-manicure, as was her habit, and he used the picture to help mock-up a design he thought would look beautiful on her finger. Even the jeweler was touched by his level of consideration.

Their first set of wedding rings was a modest affair from the leaner days; so for their tenth he not only raised the bar, but put it into a different atmosphere. He'd considered these rings an astonishing achievement of that endeavor.

Now here they were, rejected old knick-knacks that had

outlived their purpose.

*Maybe you should have remembered all this before you cheated on her,* the voice in his head offered.

Dominick shook his head and stood. Enough was enough. Enough with the shitty voice in his head, enough with the sob story of victimhood, enough with the current Antoinette melodrama; it was time to get his life back in order *right now.*

He was reaching for the phone to call Linda and then Antoinette, but then he froze again mid-reach.

*I wanted you to see that I am happy now.*

The sentence screamed in his mind, but this time with it came a thought that stole the breath from his lungs. He grabbed the picture and the note again.

"You deserve to find your happiness as well," he reread aloud. It couldn't be. "But why else would she say it like that? And then mention Dai?"

Tears of a unique sort began to well in his eyes now—not from grief, but from the sheer magnitude of emotion.

*I am happy now. You deserve to find your happiness as well.*

Like she'd found happiness—with them.

WITH them.

"No." He shook his head. That's ridiculous. It was the stuff of porn films and hippie communes. It was crazy talk. He was reading too much into it, being too cerebral like she'd often accused him in the past (more so in recent times). She *couldn't* mean—

He studied the picture again; he noted how the three of them beamed at one another. He noted the closeness of their bodies to one another, and how they weren't grinning for the camera, but laughing together. And although the table was large and circular, the three of them were bunched together—

like it was important they remained close. Antoinette was in the middle, laughing and leaning into Elizabeth Kelley, with her hand placed on Bill Kelley's shoulder. Together.

"Impossible."

He remembered last night. When she was at the hospital over Mr. Wellington's bed—they'd been arm in arm, all three of them, again with her in the middle.

"No."

He remembered Antoinette's look of defiance. Her green eyes aflame, her lips pressed tightly together. She'd assumed her battle stance after he announced that this was a family matter.

"'They are family.' That's what she said."

That's when Bill Kelley told her "not now." Because Antoinette was going to tell him right then.

"She was going to tell me exactly who they are to her. She wanted to."

But as things would have it, she chose to wait—almost twelve whole hours.

*Goodbye.*

His breathing had accelerated, and yet he felt he was barely breathing at all. The more he panted the less air he received; his lips tingled and his head spun. He put his hand to his chest but realized he was still holding the picture, *their picture,* and he tried to throw it far, far away from him. But his hands also felt numb and his limbs were going rubbery.

*Hyperventilating,* he thought. He hadn't done this since childhood, when his dad, drunk, would make to beat him.

"Breathe, breathe, breathe," he whispered asthmatically, recalling his mother's calming chant of the same words so many years ago. Even as his heart raced with both panic and irregular amounts of carbon dioxide, he fought to breathe smoothly. He remembered the times when he'd fainted dead away as a child, and he couldn't risk doing so now.

*Stop her!* Again his head exploded in pain. *Kill them if you have to! Don't let her humiliate you like this! That's your wife, YOUR wife!*

"Stop it, stop it," he whispered as asthmatically as he had "breathe" moments ago. The room started to rotate and the lights dimmed before his eyes, but still he fought to focus. He focused all his attention on breathing.

Ages passed. The panting became more manageable, and the swimming of his head receded. An atomic bomb of emotion remained within him undetonated—for now.

The room phone rang. After panting a few moments longer, he answered in a daze.

"Yes?"

"Good afternoon, is this Mr. Reinhart?"

"Yes."

"Your car is here, sir."

Dominick blinked, his chest still heaving. He looked dumbly around the room. The discarded rings and pouch lay on his bed like tiny corpses. The picture and note on the floor, the murder weapons. But a glance at the clock told him all that mattered right now; it was time.

He was still in the complimentary bathrobe, but now each fiber of it seemed to stab at his skin.

"Yes," he said finally. He'd almost forgotten that he was still holding the phone. "I'll be down shortly."

*      *      *

The 1.5-mile ride in the chauffeured black Mercedes happened, but only because Dominick found himself outside the skyscraping US Bank Tower that held their corporate headquarters. He had no recollection of the ride itself. They'd passed countless people in the short ride through downtown LA; the mentally ill, strung out and homeless had crossed his field of vision; he'd seen dozens of business people hastily scurrying to their various engagements. Upscale bars and hotels with valet staff at the ready, law enforcement patrolling around on both their bicycles and in their vehicles, children and tourists and people with no particular place to go, had all passed him. Some of them had likely seen him as well.

But he retained none of it. Time had opened up, absorbed him whole, then spat him out just as he arrived.

The moment he stepped from the car Linda and his younger second assistant, Derrick, were all over him.

"Sir, here is the brief that was disseminated to the board moments ago."

"Sir, can I get you something on your way up? The food has already been served."

"Sir, I want to tell you how sorry I am to hear about Mr. Wellington. My prayers are with you and Mrs. Reinhart right now."

That somehow pierced the fog. Mrs. Reinhart. She was HIS wife. And she was *sleeping with Bill and Elizabeth Kelley? HIS wife?*

"Thank you." His voice was cold and tight as he strode towards the expansive white lobby. "Anything else I need to know before the meeting starts?"

Derrick shot Linda a look.

"What?" Dominick asked.

Linda, with some exasperation, pulled him along by the arm like a mother would a child even as she lowered her voice.

"Sir, I've been calling you all morning. The time was moved up. The meeting started almost an hour ago."

He stopped.

"Moved up by whom? And when?"

Fifty and tough as nails, still she fretted fractionally before answering.

"Mr. Higgins' office contacted us after midnight and left a message about the time change. I don't know how the rest of the members heard about it in time."

His heart double-timed and his face blazed like a Texas July. *Higgins!*

He stormed into the lobby with fury mounting with each step. Linda and Derrick pattered behind him, and he was dimly aware of sympathetic glances his way and the occasional "good morning, sir" from others in the lobby. But all this was lost in the rage-born haze.

He'd spoken to Higgins not twelve hours ago, and he'd said nothing of changing the time. He'd spoken to Leftwich afterward and had even seen Wallace later still. Yet no one told him. This was five steps too far.

He turned back to Linda. "Get the Ryu Law Group on the phone and let them know I want that analysis ASAP. And get Lawrence Silvers down here right now."

"Yes, sir."

"Derrick, call Terrance Faucon and let him know of these developments. Tell him to come as soon as he can. And both of you, don't say a word of this to anyone else."

"Yes, sir."

He stepped into the executive elevator and punched in the 54th floor. He stood there, boiling in place, waiting for the elevator doors to close and contemplating the spew of righteous indignation he would soon unleash upon Higgins— when a woman screamed the words *Dominick Reinhart*.

It was the leader in him, he'd later realize, and not conscious thought that spurred him to step out to face the commotion. For good or ill, he'd learned it often was the small choices that had the greatest impact.

Already security was converging around the disheveled-looking woman with wild red hair and rumpled clothing as she attempted to pull her worn linen bag away from a security officer.

"His name is Dominick Reinhart!" she shouted. "Dominick Reinhart! Gold BMX bike with red wheels! Red wheels, you hear me?"

He froze, and at that moment she looked over and their eyes met. Her face lit up like a child's on Christmas morning.

"Dominick Reinhart!" she squealed in delight.

Again time ground to a halt. His jaw loosened as realizations, each one more unbelievable than the last, tumbled like an avalanche within him.

In a flash, the pertinent recent memories
*("She's coming, they're all coming, to see you! Oh my gosh!")*
*("Who's the red head?")*
blended with the inexplicable truth:

The woman before him had just described a bike of his youth that had also been a recent dream;

The woman before him had been in that same dream, in which he re-lived an awful memory from when they were both children over thirty years ago;

110

The woman before him was his elementary school classmate Sherrill McKinnen.

He was almost accustomed to a degree of insanity temporarily residing inside his head. But this insanity was outside his head. It was standing twenty feet away.

*Walk away,* the voice in his head screamed. *Walk away,* WALK AWAY!

This time, he barely noticed the voice.

"Let her be!" he yelled.

"Sir, you know this woman?"

Ninety-five percent of him wanted to close his mind to this fantasy world and get back onto the elevator as though nothing had happened. But five percent of him *needed* to know what was going on.

"Yes. Release her." He waved them away as he stepped forward.

"Sir, are you—"

"I said release her."

They were still reluctant, but they nonetheless parted before him. Her smile widened the closer he came to her.

She clapped her gloved hands together in glee. She was dressed for colder weather, he noticed.

"Dominick Reinhart!" she laughed.

Even standing in front of her, he could barely believe his eyes. "What are you doing here?"

"Oh no." Her smile was bright and brilliant. "Not myself yet, need more time. But you!"

She reached out and sweetly touched his face with her hands. Security edged forward but again he waved them back.

"You, you need to meet!" Her muddy blue eyes were lit with enthusiasm, but then she lowered her voice. "We'll have time. When I'm myself we'll have time." She clapped again. "Dominick Reinhart!"

He could feel his training, experience, and reasoning faculty working furiously. In a split-second he had a viable theory: like the photos of him and Dai from the night before, she was an imaginative distraction intended to throw him off-balance at this key juncture. That's why she knew about his meeting. This was an extraordinary implementation, but a classic distraction maneuver.

Except

(*"Who's the red head?"*)

(*"She's coming!"*)

she'd also been in his dream. Further, she had described his bike from that dream with details he hadn't mentioned to anyone. All he had was another mystery.

"Derrick?" He called out without taking his eyes off Sherrill McKinnen.

"Yes, sir?"

Dominick pulled out a couple twenties.

"Take her nearby and get her something to eat. Stay there with her and I'll have you notified when I get out of the meeting."

Derrick remained hesitant but a look from Dominick convinced him.

"Yes, sir."

Dominick turned back to Sherrill McKinnen.

"Sherrill, this man works with me. He's going to get you something to eat, and then we're going to talk. Okay?"

She spared one concerned look at Derrick, but then brightened up again when she faced Dominick. She nodded with another smile.

"Great," Dominick said, and smiled with a warmth he didn't feel.

Again she placed a hand on Dominick's cheek. Did her fingertips feel softer on his face now than moments ago? Was that his imagination? She took her hand away and then looked at Derrick with excitement.

"Lunch?"

She then hooked arms with the uneasy young man and turned away.

The unlikely pair headed for the door and Dominick turned to the building's head of security.

"Have someone follow them, not closely, and stay nearby. Make sure they get there safely and that nothing happens to either of them. Either of them, understand me?"

"Yes, sir."

Dominick addressed Linda.

"Silvers here, right now, with his copy of the bylaws. And I need that other analysis."

He strode back towards the elevators.

\*                         \*                         \*

Moments later the eerily-fast elevator opened its doors and welcomed him to the 54th floor. Whatever had happened in the lobby and whatever it meant, it would get handled later. This moment was his.

The company had several floors of this particular building, but here is where their most important conferences were held. When they worked around-the-clock with a previous competitor for a potential merger that would increase their market share in the financial sector by an astounding 30%, it was here. When Mr. Wellington informed the board of a hostile takeover attempt that they then spent weeks fending off with all their corporate might, it was here. Virtually every decision of vast importance throughout their far-flung corporate empire took place here.

Today there would be, perhaps, one more.

He strode through the wall-paneled doors into the lobby. He'd always thought it looked a bit like a posh hotel that was somehow a little unforgiving even in its luxury. Mr. Wellington had told him that was intentional.

*Those who serve here don't need to be truly comfortable,* he'd said. *Great power should never be.*

Dominick entered the vast waiting area with purpose. Several assistants, drivers, and bodyguards—themselves employees of others on the board—milled about. Those who had been seated in the overstuffed chairs all sprang to their feet when he entered.

He glanced at them but said nothing. But he noted, for the first time, that Wallace's driver was much prettier than any driver he'd seen. White gloves, hat, and blindingly white starched shirt, she could have been a model playing dress-up sans the make-up. Where would one find a woman who looked like that to simply drive his car? And how had he not noticed before now?

She stared back at him with piercing blue eyes. He smiled to himself with amusement; even the hired help knew that new battle lines had been drawn. News travels fast indeed in this new era.

He strode past them and towards the doors. Once he

crossed the lengthy floor, the well-dressed security officer posing as the boardroom's receptionist unlocked the door for him without a word.

    \*           \*           \*

# CHAPTER SIX

## Monday Morning

The room fell silent. Upon entering Dominick imagined an announcer gesturing grandly towards a stage as crimson curtains parted. *"And now the would-be CEO recently usurped by this very board! Ladies and gentlemen, I give you—Dominick! Reinhart!"*

The security man closed the massive doors behind him.

The rectangular room was dominated by an obsidian-hued table lined on both sides with board members. Higgins, dressed in a gray suit with a smart bow tie, hovered near the head of the table—Mr. Wellington's customary seat.

Still as granite, Dominick studied each of their faces. Wallace stared back at him dully; Leftwich looked ill-at-ease and pallid. The other four spanned a spectrum of reactions to his entrance: bored, impatient, amused, avoidant. Higgins, his deep olive-complected face impassive, stared at Dominick with a blank expression.

"Dominick," he said, elongating his name. "How good of you to join us. We can now conclude the day's business."

Dominick ignored him and directed his words to the board with an even gaze.

"I sincerely apologize for the delay in my attendance. I was not adequately informed of the time change. Strangely so."

He directed this last at Wallace and then to Leftwich. The larger man didn't bat an eye; Leftwich coughed.

Higgins, however, chimed in.

"We indeed noted your absence, and there is still business—"

"Yes, there is," Dominick answered. "Principally, the business of the void left by Mr. Wellington's untimely illness. As you know—"

"That's been handled," Higgins announced with the annoyance of a schoolteacher restating previous material. Dominick's head nearly exploded from his shoulders.

"What do you mean, 'handled'? The bylaws—"

Higgins tossed a packet of paper in his direction. Without sitting, Dominick grabbed it. It was already bookmarked and highlighted.

"The bylaws clearly state," Higgins droned, "that in the event of an emergency vacancy at the position of Chief Executive, the presiding chairman of the board of trustees is appointed interim CEO until as such a time that a suitable permanent replacement can be located."

Dominick looked at the other board members, but no one uttered anything to the contrary. Seized by equal parts outrage and mounting panic, he tore through the copy of the bylaws before him.

The sections highlighted were different from what he'd seen with Lawrence that morning. The language here was clear; in the absence of the CEO (Mr. Wellington), the acting Chairman of the Board (Higgins) would assume the interim role until the replacement was appointed.

A different set of bylaws? That was absurdity made manifest. Did they think they could change the bylaws that morning without notification to suit their own purposes?

Dominick looked at Higgins. He could feel his eyes burning with the heat of a star gone nova.

"This, I find interesting," Dominick said as calmly as he could manage. "I studied the bylaws just this morning. It was clear that the interim CEO is chosen from within the executive leadership team already in place. This leader would be someone who had demonstrated a history of success and familiarity with the company. Someone who was intimately aware of the day-to-day functioning of the business." He looked from Higgins to each face of the board. "Someone who sounds a lot like me. Since I was the one being groomed by the existing CEO to do his job. So I find it curious that this situation has been 'handled' without my knowledge or participation."

"Fantastic!" Wallace said as he threw up his meaty, paw-like hands. "Are we here for story hour about the bylaws or are we going to handle business?"

"I understand your frustrations and I too value our collected time," Higgins said without the slightest indication of disturbance. "And it is vital he understands the language of the newest version of the bylaws."

Dominick's eyes narrowed. Newest version of the bylaws?

"Mr. Wellington himself moved that we amend bylaws a month ago," Higgins said with a small smile. "The meeting was recorded, of course. You were furnished a copy of the new bylaws as well as the video recording of the meeting. As was legal. Did you not receive it?"

Dominick felt like a trap door had opened beneath him and he'd fallen not only out of sight, but into another world. This couldn't be true. They changed the bylaws without him? Upon Mr. Wellington's request? Higgins was now leading the company, on a day that was supposed to belong to Dominick? Without him knowing anything about it?

"This is an outrage." Dominick's words were quiet, dark. "I helped build this company. Shape it into what it is. I have recruited and trained the people who are, to this day, continuing to make this company the powerhouse that it is. I am the one—"

"Yes, and I'm sure you have an excellent golf swing too," Wallace groused. "Now can we get along with the meeting?"

"I agree," said another board member, this one named Rebecca Tisdale. "I don't want to reschedule the charter."

"What they mean," Higgins said placidly, "is that the remaining agenda item can't be covered without you."

Dominick ground his teeth. They had the gall to make a request of him this morning? He would hear it, if only to use it against them.

"I'm listening."

Higgins settled himself into Mr. Wellington's seat and motioned to an empty seat.

"I'll stand," Dominick said.

*Grab him by his pencil neck and put him through that window,* the voice in Dominick's head recommended. Dominick kept his game face unmoved.

"This may come as some surprise to you," Higgins began,

"but I'm not actually interested in running this company. In fact, I have neither the time nor the inclination to do so."

He was wrong: it didn't surprise Dominick because he didn't believe a word of it. It was an old tactic played by con artists of all ages and stripes. Disarm the mark by showing that you mean him no ill will, and that you want to give him what he wants. Then explain that there's just *one little thing* that he should do...

"This company needs a proper Chief Executive," Higgins continued. "Arthur Wellington made it clear that he saw you as this company's future. But his eyes aren't ours." Higgins leaned forward and folded his hands. "It is the opinion of this board that it's best to hire a capable insider. We will do our due diligence, but we'd like to offer you a chance to shine. In case you are, in fact, ready for the next big step.

"We've created a new position for you: Worldwide Chief Operating officer. You will report directly to me as interim CEO. The duties, however, fall on your shoulders. Your compensation will be adjusted accordingly, and your primary responsibility will be executing the directives laid out in the organization's founding corporate objectives. You will be tasked with achieving these goals by whatever means you ultimately deem fit. What matters to those assembled here are the results."

His smile was pleasant. Dominick, silent, waited for the con.

"Please understand," Higgins continued, "no one is disputing your track record. You are obviously a strong candidate. But this isn't make-believe, role-play, business school, or theoretical practice. If we hand you this company, we expect you to make us even more wealthy than we already are. So now is when you prove yourself as capable as Arthur hoped you'd be. Do that and you'll make our job of picking a permanent CEO a simple affair."

Dominick waited for the rest. They'd sweetened the deal, flattered his ego, and now they'd address their need.

"That's all," Higgins said with another telepathic smile.

Bullshit, Dominick thought. They were offering him a raise and a chance to run the company as he saw fit as an audition for the CEO position. That sounded fantastic—except they held a secret meeting a month ago, changed the by-laws, and then met for a full hour this morning without him.

*Tinkle on my head and tell me it's raining, why don't you?* Grandma would say.

"We'll have the offer sent to your office immediately," Higgins concluded. "Take the next two or three days off. Look it over, think it over. Then let us know."

Higgins stood, as did everyone else. Dominick hadn't moved.

"With that," Higgins said, "this meeting is adjourned."

\*                           \*                           \*

Board members gathered their belongings and made for the exit, and Dominick immediately went to Christian Leftwich. Slow-moving and growing more pallid by the moment, he was easy to corner.

"Christian," Dominick said in a low voice. "Talk to me." The older man shook his head and avoided his eyes. Dominick pressed. "Why didn't you tell me?"

Something shifted in the old man. He coughed over

his opposing shoulder, but then stood a little straighter. His cloudy gray eyes drilled into Dominick's own.

"You know what I wondered? Too late, when it didn't matter? How many times have they done this? How many other companies, organizations, kingdoms, clans? How many pawns have they had, just like us? Genius. Evil genius." He laid a hand on Dominick's shoulder. "Last night I couldn't speak freely. But now that she's here, my part's finished. It'll make sense later. Unless we failed. Good luck."

He squeezed Dominick's shoulder and moved away.

Surprise, fear, and confusion all jockeyed for position inside of Dominick's stomach.

*Respond, don't react*, he told himself. He was about to re-corner Leftwich when he saw Rebecca Tisdale outside the boardroom motioning for him to join her.

Leftwich was already in the lobby area being assisted by his driver.

In a split-second choice, Dominick let Leftwich go and instead headed towards Tisdale. She was the yin to Wallace's yang. Colleagues and sometimes competitors, it was no secret that they had professional respect for each other. Dominick bet that interacting with her would ultimately gain him more leverage.

She dug into her purse as her entourage surrounded her. One of her assistants was in mid-instruction when Dominick reached them.

"You need to be in the air by—"

"Give us a minute," Tisdale said she said in her husky smoker's voice. She retrieved a stick of gum and some folded papers from her purse. Her assistant seemed taken aback.

"Of course, but just to be clear you only have—"

"I'm clear. And I need a minute."

The assistant nodded and they all shuffled away. Tisdale lowered her voice, even as she chewed her gum vigorously.

"It's not my business but I wanted to tell you,"

"Tell me what?"

"Two things. The first is about Antoinette."

The mention of her name thrust into him like a blade of ice. Still, he kept a straight face.

"What about her?"

"She called me last night," Tisdale said. "Asked me about property in the Hamptons. And not for vacation."

"She said that?"

"How else would I know if she hadn't told me? She said she wants a house for her and her new partners. Wants to be my neighbor." Anger and surprise surged forward in their battle for prominent positioning inside of him. "I don't know if she's trying to embarrass you or herself," Tisdale continued, "and either way it's not my business. But I thought you should know. And the second thing, someone sent this to my hotel room last night."

She extended the folded papers his way, and he had an idea of what it was even before he opened it. Anger pulled into the lead inside of him.

"I don't care what you do in your personal life as long as you protect my interests," she said matter-of-factly. With effort, he maintained a neutral expression as he again looked at pictures of himself with Dai.

Rebecca Tisdale looked over at her entourage and motioned with her head.

"Good luck with—"

"Did you know about Wallace's investments in

pornography?" Dominick asked.

He'd let the question fly from his mouth without bothering to consider the tactic; there came a time when you just had to start swinging.

When he searched her face, however, he saw not a trace of shock or surprise, only dull contempt. She leaned in towards his ear.

"Do I care is the better question."

She turned away and her entourage trailed after her.

Dominick then noticed that the other board members had already made their way to the elevators; he was alone in bare moments.

Video cameras monitored this room. So keeping the appearance of outward calm was a necessity despite the swirl of explosive emotion in his chest.

What came to his mind was a speech Arthur Wellington gave many years ago; at the time Dominick was a young man fresh from business school, and Arthur was speaking at a conference for young business leaders.

"The successful leader is a student of himself," he said from the lectern. "He is knowledgeable of his strengths, far more versed in his limitations, and crystal clear of his own breaking point and the warning signs that precede it. The best leader recognizes that her most precious resource is her own ability to lead—and that it, too, is finite."

Dominick grasped the wisdom of this, but he didn't find his redline limit until he overshot it that awful September day. The heart-wrenching weeks that followed then ripped his family to shreds, and he, the highly-trained executive and powerful leader, could do nothing to save it.

That wretched time had taught him the warning signs of

his limit. Standing in the boardroom lobby, stewing in fury and fear, he recognized one of them.

Godzilla Mode, he called it.

It would be comedic if not for its consequences. During his childhood, he'd been endlessly amused by the 1950s black-and-white version of Godzilla where the giant reptile laid waste to every tall building in Tokyo in a spectacular fit of rage. Upon reaching adulthood, that memory became a marker for his own personal boiling point—and a warning of the damage that lay beyond it.

Even as he stood there, forcing his hands to remain still while his mind sprinted

*("newest set of by-laws")*

*("good luck")*

*("don't know if she's trying to embarrass you or herself")*

a warning was whispered from deep inside him. It was a warning that the Godzilla urge was forming at the center of his stress; it was an urge to lash out at everything around him for the sole purpose of watching it burn. Let the anger, the frustration, the confusion, the white-hot fury spew forth in an uninterrupted stream of destruction. He was already imagining how good it would feel.

Dominick nodded. This was another game he knew how to win. Just like before, he would stand here, he would breathe, and he would remember who he was.

It was already working. He could feel his jaw relaxing and his heart rate decreasing. He started breathing more deeply, when his mind, traitorous, let slip a forbidden memory:

Vincent, his gapped teeth in a huge smile and his light brown eyes alive with joy, excitedly held a baseball that he'd just caught on his own for the first time.

*I got it, Dad! I got it, I got it!*

A shock of grief rippled through Dominick. His eyes moistened and his hand wiped the tear away just as fast; he was already moving towards the elevator and whipping out his phone with his free hand. Before he'd gotten to the elevator, his call to Linda was already initiated.

Breathing time was over; it was time to move.

*　　　*　　　*

Questions flew through his mind as the elevator whisked past dozens of floors.

How could *no one* in his office hear anything of a board meeting or of updated bylaws that came from it? How could Mr. Wellington preside over a meeting where succession was restructured and then fail to mention it to Dominick? Was this all a ploy to keep Dominick off-balance until their actual objective was revealed? What could he do to stop them?

The talk about making them even wealthier was smoke and mirrors. What were they planning? He thought of Leftwich. Why in God's name did both he and Mr. Wellington choose now to speak exclusively in riddles? Shaking his head, Dominick pulled out a pad and pen and scribbled Leftwich's words.

*It'll make sense later. Unless we failed.*

He also considered Rebecca Tisdale and her evasion. He jotted down those notes as well, and they immediately brought thoughts of Antoinette. Those he shoved away.

The elevator chimed to let him know he'd reached the

ground floor. Per his call before entering the elevator, Linda was there to meet him.

"Where is Lawrence?" he asked. "And where is Terrance?"

"Detective Faucon is about an hour away with traffic," she said, uncomfortable. "Lawrence Silvers' office says he hasn't been seen today."

Dominick shook his head, exasperated, but she could only fidget.

He looked around the lobby as if it might offer further explanation. The people had changed, but the pace remained. It was like an ant's nest, alive with activity, and yet the end goal of all that activity was a well-obscured mystery. People merely went along their way, flitting to and fro, like impulsive children on a lazy summer day. It was staggering to know this was merely another day for most of the working world; for him it was a bizarre day with a now-record level of unexpected chaos.

*You're creating more chaos for yourself,* the voice inside his head told him. *Why don't you stop? Get away from it all!*

Ignoring it, Dominick headed for the front doors and motioned for her to follow him.

"What exactly is Lawrence's office saying?"

"They said it's highly unusual for him to be out of communication but they haven't been able to reach him. Other attorneys are assisting his clients. I can get one of them—"

"No, keep trying." Lawrence Silvers hadn't been late for a single appointment with Dominick in a decade. Something was wrong.

Maybe Lawrence has his own family problems, Dominick reflected. According to the snake he certainly did. But the idea was to discredit the imagined snake's insight, not give it credence. He turned to Linda, about to speak, when he remembered something else the snake said about Lawrence.

*Anger is his food. Spite, his air. Upon it he feeds. Gains succor. And yet it will also kill him. Soon, in fact.*

Dominick froze.

"Sir?"

"I saw Lawrence Silvers, alive and well, six hours ago," Dominick said with adamance. "He's out there. And I need to talk to him."

"Yes, sir."

"I also need you to find a recording of a board meeting from a month ago. And a copy of the updated bylaws produced in that meeting. They claim it was already sent over. Also, an offer from the board is coming as well. I need it evaluated the moment it arrives."

She tapped notes on a tablet as they reached the building's door and exited into the LA afternoon. There was one more mysterious subplot introduced by this baffling day, and although he was loathe to give it his time, it could prove to be important.

*But now that she's here, I've finished my part.*

It was a hell of a coincidence that Leftwich would say this immediately after a mysterious "she" showed up in Dominick's lobby. Compounded by the coincidence of the tweaker referencing the arrival of a "she" the night before.

*She's coming, they're all coming, to see you! Oh my gosh!*

Disgusted, he looked around for Derrick and Sherrill McKinnen among the passers-by on Fifth street.

"Have you heard from Derrick?"

Linda shook her head.

"I need to talk to that woman." He looked around. "Call

him and—"

"There." Linda pointed.

Sure enough, he spied Derrick and a woman walking towards them. The woman was different though, not Sherrill McKinnen. Her hair, though red, was combed into a neat ponytail, and her clothes, smart and casual, looked brand new. This woman might be a tourist visiting downtown LA, or perhaps a comfortably-dressed local enjoying a day off.

Nonetheless, the woman smiled at Dominick, as might an old friend. They drew closer, and Dominick's eyesight confirmed she was indeed Sherrill McKinnen. He stiffened.

"Dominick," she said with a casual smile as they walked. He stared at her, too suspicious to care that he hadn't responded, and then looked at Derrick for an explanation. The young man shifted at the unasked question.

"I took her to a café like you said. She went to the bathroom and came out someone else," he stammered. "She asked to go to the Gap and then—"

"Let's have a do-over," Sherrill McKinnen said in a clear, even voice. "I was someone else earlier." She extended her hand to Dominick. He shook it, not moving his eyes from her face. "Good to see you again," she said. She then motioned to the street. "Shall we?"

Dominick looked at her a moment longer, then spoke to Linda.

"I need Terrance, I need Lawrence. Yesterday. And call Baxter and tell him to update me."

"Yes, sir."

He stepped towards Sherrill McKinnen, and she took his arm and fell in stride beside him. They walked before the building on the massive concrete walkway. The relative lack of people passing by afforded them some open-air privacy as they strolled down Fifth street.

"This had better be good," he said.

"My explanation? I'm afraid you'll likely be disappointed."

"Try me."

"Let's hear your theories first."

"Why?" He could feel his irritation rising. She smiled easily but didn't look his way.

"Because you'll feel better having said what's on your mind."

He stopped walking and turned towards her.

"Trust me when I tell you I'm in no mood to dance."

"When a band plays and one is standing on a dance floor, I think it's a pretty good idea to do so anyway," she said, her voice calm and steady. "But we can do it this way." She smoothed out her hair. "It'll just be harder," she added.

He opened his mouth to speak, but opted to stare into her brilliant blue eyes instead. Had her eyes been this bright before? He didn't think so.

"Theory one," she said. "Corporate conspiracy. Our last meeting was a performance by me. You're in the midst of a grand show orchestrated by your enemies, and I am a paid agent on their behalf. I was hired by them because 1) I am from an obscure corner of your past, and 2) I am far removed from the workings of your normal world. My abrupt appearance, today of all days, is intended to distract you from whatever nefarious plan is underfoot until it's too late for you to do anything about it."

She said it simply, without edge, and yet he could feel his blood rising with each syllable.

"You say it like it isn't true." He studied her face. In truth she said it neutrally, but he wanted to see her response to the accusation. She only smiled and continued.

"Theory two. Con. Our last meeting was still a performance on my part, but one aimed to disorient you and draw your attention to me. Thus my ultimate goal is to ensnare you into a web of deceit that will end in an attempt to capitalize on your money or influence. Or both."

"A common tactic of a con is to state the possibility of the con and then refute it," he rebutted. His heart pounded; already he disliked the simple way she articulated his thoughts. Again, she didn't react to his accusation.

"Theory three. Insanity. You are in the midst of a dream, a drug-induced delusion, or perhaps a psychotic break from reality, and none of this is happening. It feels real, it looks real, and certain people within the dream behave normally. Then someone like me appears and proves that this cannot, in truth, be actually happening."

A splash of fear bloomed within his gut, but he ignored it. He was obviously engaged with a skilled adversary, and he didn't have time to field his own fear.

"I told you it would be harder this way," she concluded. "How did I do?"

Her playfulness angered him further.

"I have yet to hear a reason why I shouldn't walk away from you, get back to my life, and tell security to keep you out of my sight."

"Yet you have done none of those things," she said with her perturbing calm. "I'm sure you've noticed that I've said things that a corporate spy or a con artist wouldn't know. Perhaps you suspect that my appearance, like several things for you recently, is not what it seems."

That quickly, she'd maneuvered him to another crossroads. Should he call her bluff and walk away? Was he willing to leave this mystery unresolved? What was the alternative? Could he entertain a fourth possibility; this was somehow all on the level? Could he risk that when the first two theories (which were still the most credible) painted her as an enemy?

Mr. Wellington would call her bluff, he thought.

Yes, he would. It was time to step away from this madness.

The corners of his mouth started to stretch into a sarcastic smile. He was about to say "good day, madam" as a parting shot before he turned away. It was going to be so perfect that he was already proud of himself for doing it—but when he opened his mouth to speak the voice in his head screamed at him.

*Don't walk away from your enemies! HURT her! Make her regret ever seeing you!*

The words surged through him like a hungry wildfire. Maybe it was the lack of sleep; maybe it was the tumult of the last twelve hours; maybe it was the timing, because he'd felt so good about himself before this blast of anger shot through him. Whatever the reason, he was so shaken by the voice that he couldn't help but wince.

He looked at her, about to make an excuse about a headache, when she motioned to his head and spoke.

"And there's that," she said.

He stopped. Alarms blared in his head. It was as if there was a safety engineer somewhere inside him screaming and waving his arms in a desperate attempt to avoid catastrophe. She couldn't, simply *could not,* have known what happened in his mind and made a comment about it.

Without conscious thought he grabbed her by both arms

132

and pulled her close as if to shake the truth from her.

"What do you mean? *Tell me what you mean!*"

Then he realized he actually WAS shaking her. With this realization came a wave of horror. He released her and backed away. His mind, now a white-hot daze, went blank.

"It's okay. Dominick, it's okay," she said from far away. He barely heard her. His mind was lost in a memory from two years prior. It all came back to him: her face, so petulant, and the fire within him bursting through; she was wearing a pouty, defiant little girl's expression, mocking him, and he wanted to slap it right off her face.

*Antoinette*, he thought, *I grabbed Antoinette, I was one of those guys, I could be—*

Revulsion shot through him.

For the first time Sherrill McKinnen looked concerned.

"No, you need to stay. The portal is open, people and events will be drawn to you that you won't understand. Dominick! Listen to me!"

She reached out as if to steady him, but he backed away. He saw her lips moving and he heard sounds emanating from them, but it was unintelligible. He turned and walked away.

"Dominick!"

He walked away as fast as he could. The alarms in his head blared on, as if the whole thing could blow at any moment.

He made a right turn and trotted towards the upscale bar towards the end of the block. She yelled something one final time, but her words were lost to the city.

*      *      *

# Monday Afternoon

Minutes later Dominick was at the bar with an empty Grey Goose Martini before him and another on the way. The muted chatter of other customers surrounded him, but it was all white noise. The only noise he truly wanted to drown out was within his own head.

His new drink arrived and he took a long sip. He'd requested his drink in a lowball glass—Martini glasses felt inherently feminine to him. Today his ego needed as many reminders of his masculine power as it could get.

He was so focused on forgetting the past few hours it wasn't until the man slid beside him that he remembered one of the realities of bar culture. He'd forgotten that sitting alone at the bar was often regarded as an invitation for random conversation.

"What's her name?" the early fifties man said with a wicked smile. He was wearing a well-tailored suit and a loosened tie. His face, while flushed with alcohol, looked like it had been a recent victim of sleepless nights.

Dominick was about to decline conversation when the man put up his palms disarmingly.

"No, wait," the man interjected. "How impolite of me. I should go first. Another Maker's 46, please?" he motioned to the bartender then turned towards Dominick. "Like I said, I should go first. My name's Roger. And her name was Victoria. She never went by Vicky. Said Victoria brought out her inner queen. Hell, I guess her real name could have been Gertrude.

134

Never saw her ID."

"Is this a boy meets girl story, boy loves girl, boy loses girl story?" Dominick asked in spite of himself. The alcohol was working.

"With a twist. This one definitely has a twist."

The bartender placed the bourbon before him; he took a generous gulp before continuing. "Boy did meet girl, and you might even say boy loved girl. If 'loved' could include seeing many waking moments as an opportunity to think of girl, remember girl, and imagine what girl might like that boy could give her."

"I don't think the twelve-step groups call that love. That one usually goes by obsessing, I understand." Two horns had grown out of Dominick's head, he realized. Yet neither of them seemed to mind.

"Who's the feisty listener today?" Roger said with a smile. "Perhaps they do call it that. And maybe that obsession was inspired by love. Somewhere deep within the recesses of boy's tender heart." He placed his hand on his chest with another smile. "Call it what you will, but it was real. And maybe it was indeed three parts love, one part obsession."

"Or vice versa."

"Or perhaps even vice versa. Nonetheless, boy had feelings about girl, and those feelings inspired quite a bit of internal activity within boy about girl."

"Girls have that tendency, don't they?"

"Funny, isn't it? And these internal activities can get us boys to do wacky external things too. It's like some strange closed system that feeds itself. Or maybe it only feeds on boys."

The sadness absent in his voice but present in his words nonetheless spoke to Dominick's own. He felt something unhappy shift within himself as Roger stopped for a moment to have another gulp. Again Roger smiled before resuming.

"One recent night—let's just say last night for the sake of the story—internal activity and love-obsession gives boy a brilliant idea: let's surprise queen Victoria girl with her favorite ice cream. Not Ben & Jerry's but the high quality, slickly-packaged, pure ingredients, expensive, organic gourmet ice cream."

"What girl doesn't like her favorite ice cream?"

"Great idea, right? And boy doesn't get all passive-aggressive with it. Boy decides to not suggest a movie in case girl would be open to watching it while she ate the ice cream he so generously brought her. Boy considers it, sure. But boy recognizes it would be a shitty way to try to make girl spend time with him."

"It's admirable of boy to recognize that."

"Thank you. Boy thought so too. So boy goes out and gets the over-priced gourmet mint chocolate chip ice cream—disgusting stuff to boy, but girl is into it, and that's who matters here—and boy takes that over to girl's condo in West Holly."

"Here's where I remind you that West Hollywood is the very gay part of town. Not that there's anything wrong with that." He laughed. "And clearly not everyone in West Holly is gay because girl lives there. And girl is sleeping with boy, and that strongly suggests that she isn't gay."

Dominick could feel his own stomach tightening. *Oh Antoinette,* something in him tried to whisper.

"Yeah, you see where this is going," Roger said with a humorless smile. "But that's not the twist. Yes, it is true that I pulled up to her door, cold storage bag of over-priced ice-cream in freakin' hand. And yes, it is true that exactly when

I'm about to buzz her place I turn and see her come around the corner. And yes it is also true that there she is, holding hands with another girl while they walk her little yappy dog. Yes, my heart goes into my throat. But like I said, that's not the twist.

"Twist starts when she sees me. She lights right up! No 'oh shit I'm busted' look. She gets an excited grin on her face, turns to the other girl with a smile, and points at me. Like, look there he is! I smile back, because at this point I don't know what the fuck else to do. And she actually does a little skip up to me, hugs me, presses her hot little early-thirties yoga body into me and I can smell her hair. She kisses me, then turns to the girl and says, 'hey this is Roger.'

"The other girl comes over. She's a little older than girl but still younger than you and me. No make-up. But pretty, and still a girl, you know—wearing heels and a fitted top with some cleavage. Nice rack, if I'm being honest. And she shakes my hand. Tracy, she says. Shakes my hand and smiles at me."

Roger gulped down the rest of the bourbon.

"So my guts are tap dancing. Tap dancing, I tell you. But I'm thinking, okay, maybe I'm jumping to conclusions. These days I guess girlfriends walk down the street holding hands even if they're not doing it, you know? I mean, she's not acting like she's been busted.

"So I play it cool, and I pay no attention to the fact that I want to puke because I'm so uptight. I hand her the ice cream and she gets all super excited, kisses me again, talks about how good the night is going to be. Tracy is smiling, I'm smiling, we're all smiling. She says, 'let's go inside and have some.' Yes, we, like all three.

"I want to say something, but what the fuck am I going to say? She's *happy*. She *wants* to spend time with me, and who cares if Tracy-with-the-nice-rack is coming in with us? Sure, they were holding hands looking like a lesbian couple. But it's not about that, right? We're going to be three people eating ice cream in her cute little place in West Holly.

"So we go inside, and the first thing she does is pull out spoons, bowls, and shot glasses. For shots and ice cream, she says. Like that's a thing that people do. But my guts are still tap dancing, so I could probably use a drink. Calm the hell down, you know? So we do three rounds of shots. She's touchy and flirty and kissy and friendly with me, and I'm like, okay. This is good. And yeah she's touchy with Tracy too, and I don't know what I'm seeing and that's a little weird. And then we're all lounging over each other on the couch while we're eating ice cream, which is also a little weird.

"And then Tracy starts massaging her shoulders and yeah I'm starting to get a stiff one even though I'm also a little sick to my stomach watching this. Then girl comes over and kisses me, then leans over and kisses Tracy. Like it's no big deal. 'I'm so happy,' she says. 'This is amazing,' she says.

"I'm sick and turned on at the same time, and I'm trying to be cool, so I have another shot. Then they make out, right there in front of me. And she rubs my arm and smiles at me and kisses me too, and I smile back. Cause I can be cool, right? Why I'm being cool, I can't tell you. Just seems like a good idea to be cool.

"I keep drinking. We make out. They make out. We make out. They make out. They go at it. Really go at it. Right there on the couch, right there in front of me. I watch. It's hot. I want to whack off. But I can't do that. What am I, twelve? What am I still doing here? What is even happening right now?"

Roger shrugged as if still mystified.

"So boy watches girl get it on with other girl. Once they're done girl wants to get it on with boy so other girl can watch. Boy thinks this is crazy, but boy is strangely turned on. But boy is also drunk and hurt and angry so boy is a little rough with her. Girl seems to enjoy it. Even encourages boy. Other girl enjoys too. Gets herself off while watching. This confuses boy further. Boy is ashamed of himself. When it's over he cries in the bathroom. Actually does puke. And then boy passes out cuddling with girl who is sandwiched between boy and other girl. He wakes up with no earthly clue what the fuck just happened. Boy leaves, but only after kissing girl as requested."

Roger took a deep breath. Dominick smoldered. What were the odds that he'd hear a story like this, right after his discovery about Antoinette? Right after what Rebecca Tisdale told him?

*Roger's a plant,* he thought. *Someone, probably Rebecca Tisdale, paid this guy to jerk my chain. Goddamn her.*

"So now boy goes to a bar, gets drunk again, and finds someone to share his story with?" Dominick allowed his irritation to infuse the words. Roger again didn't seem to mind and only nodded in response.

"Boy does indeed. But that's skipping ahead in the story."

"There's more?" Dominick had long stopped believing a word; he was busy considering how he was going to make Rebecca Tisdale pay for this. Roger's smile was cold and distant.

"There's absolutely more."

Roger looked at his watch. Omega, Dominick noted. An actor of some means, Roger was.

"I apologize, Attentive Listener. We're not going to have time to get to your story."

"Pressing appointment?"

"In a sense. But to conclude. Boy goes home, boy sobers up. Boy then has a disturbing thought: what if girl thought he was just a play-thing all along? What if everything that happened last night was okay in girl's mind because she thought boy and girl didn't have anything special? But how could they not be special? Boy loves girl, remember? And boy acts like it. Could she possibly not understand this?

"This thought drives boy a bit crazy. One might say over the edge. So boy does something he shouldn't have. Boy returns to girl's cute little West Holly home. After other girl has left. Boy brings a certain item with him."

To Dominick's shock Roger reached into his suit jacket and produced a small revolver. Holding it low, he considered it as a stage actor might an important prop.

"What the hell is this?" Dominick demanded.

Roger shook his head.

"Boy loses it. But he doesn't hurt girl. He'd never hurt girl. He loves girl. But he does tie girl up though. So she doesn't try to run. So that they can talk. Too late boy realizes he's gone too far. It's over with girl. And he's ruined himself. He's committed a felony. Several, as the District Attorney will point out. The DA that boy helped get elected, in fact. You see, even though boy has been acting like an errant, tender child, he's actually a man of some influence. A man with a career. A staff. Shareholders. Now all of that is going down the toilet because boy couldn't keep it together one stupid night. His competitors will feast upon his ruin. He's humiliated himself."

Dominick, dry-mouthed, tried to interrupt.

"Roger—"

"So boy leaves, boy gets drunk, boy finds another sad-looking boy with a nice suit and expensive watch, and boy spills his guts. The end."

His bloodshot eyes wet with tears, he rose from the stool.

"I'm sorry we don't have time to hear your story. My office has people looking for me, and they're probably close. But you can tell me her name. The girl in your story. What's her name, Attentive Listener?"

"Roger, listen to me—"

"Please." His voice was steady even as tears streamed down his face. "It can't be just me."

With Roger's anguish evident, Dominick's own heart split.

"Antoinette," he breathed.

"Is she beautiful?"

"Most beautiful girl I'd ever seen. She was my angel."

Roger nodded. They locked eyes. Roger smiled through the tears.

"My angel is at 7925 Romaine Street, Unit 2," he said. "Make sure you tell them that. I'm sure she has to pee by now."

"Think of your family, your friends—"

"It's too late."

Dominick slid off his stool and moved slowly towards Roger. Roger retreated, gun in hand, and shook his head.

"Roger. Look at me. There's always a way through," Dominick said. "Always. Just give me the—"

"You should close your eyes now."

"Don't—!"

Roger put the gun under his chin and fired.

*       *       *

# CHAPTER SEVEN

## Monday Afternoon

Three hours later Dominick exited a chauffeured Town Car and stepped onto his driveway. He stared up at his home, his castle. The setting sun painted a wash of golden light across its Italian lines, but instead of producing an ad-worthy image it cast angular shadows that made his home look menacing. It reminded him of the storybook gingerbread house that beckoned two starving children named Hansel and Gretel. The exterior was inviting, but what lurked inside?

A voice from the recent past:

*If you experience sleeplessness or vivid recurring nightmares of the event, please consult your physician immediately.*

Having completed its task, the Town Car retreated beyond the property gates and into the street. Within moments it faded into the distance. He was alone.

*These could be strong indicators of post-traumatic stress disorder. Irritability, lack of focus, depression, and trouble relating to others are also common symptoms.*

Did he dare go inside?

He grunted. Years ago, before he was even a junior executive, his daily practice was to imagine himself living in a magnificent dream home. And now his once-unbodied dream stood before him; he now lived in six thousand (over-priced) square-feet of gated Brentwood awesomeness. Closing on it was one of his proudest days. Within it he'd find refuge from the horror-show of the last twenty-four hours.

Right?

*Counseling and medication have proven to be effective treatments for PTSD. Receiving treatment immediately can lessen the effects. Do you already have a therapist?*

He remembered Roger's eyes; in them was a portrait of pain that poets sought to immortalize. Roger's anguish had been as plain to Dominick as the status symbol before him.

Then with a squeeze of a trigger—*bang*—Roger was gone.

"Why'd you do it?" Dominick asked aloud.

Standing in his driveway and looking at his house like an awestruck simpleton, he felt forbidden thoughts bubbling around in his mind. Yesterday Mr. Wellington fell into a coma. Today Roger died. Coma, then death—didn't that sequence sound familiar?

Dominick put his head in his hands, but he also forced the tear away. Roger had a family who would mourn him, and Dominick was not among them. Roger's death, albeit tragic, was his choice. It was completely unrelated to what happened to Vincent.

And yet...

*Here's my card. Please call if I can be of any assistance.*

The counselor, who'd come to the scene at the behest

of the police, had been a pale man with perfect teeth and a disturbingly neutral demeanor. Dominick was sure he'd experienced more empathy from toast.

Yet in this strange time, that man—a stranger—was more available to Dominick than his wife.

He looked to the sky. The blue expanse matched the distance he felt from Antoinette. She knew nothing of his current hell. His last two hours—the screams at the bar, the hastily placed tarp, the flashing lights, the bitter coffee, the traumatizing retelling of the incident—were all stories of which she had yet to hear. A partner at Lawrence's firm had helped him craft his statement to the police; Terrance checked in before leaving to assist his colleagues with freeing "girl" (whose real name was Victoria Watson).

Antoinette's phone had gone straight to voicemail. And why wouldn't it? She was likely in the company of the only two people from which she cared to hear.

He longed to tell her about the sadness in Roger's eyes, about gagging while stepping over bloody pieces of the man's head on the polished floor, about how he shuddered every time the *bang* played again in his mind. He wished for the comfort of her thin frame in his arms, the softness of her lips, the radiant love in her eyes. At one time he'd had all that and more.

Now he'd have better luck embracing a ghost.

How had they come to this? He looked again at his empty palace with no queen. How could the woman ignoring him be the same person who played his favorite version of "All Blues" when he arrived home to a surprise 30th birthday dinner? How was she the woman who remembered what he liked to see her wearing so she could dress for him on special occasions? What happened to the Antoinette who had called him 'my king' when she wanted to seduce him—or be seduced by him?

What a goofball she'd once been. Years ago, when Violet was seven and Vincent was still a baby, a box of Halloween costumes arrived at their home. The devilish look in Antoinette's eyes told him trouble lie ahead. S'mores, she laughed. Her grand idea was to dress them all up as ingredients for s'mores—a joke about them being an interracial family.

Being an Important Man at the time, dressing up as a giant graham cracker was out of the question. But Antoinette's glee would not be denied; she donned her own graham cracker costume, Violet dressed as a walking chocolate bar and they got tiny Vincent into a marshmallow puff costume without difficulty. They all couldn't stop laughing, and Dominick couldn't refuse. That turned out to be one of the best Halloweens they ever had as a family.

Distant memories, those times. In a post-Vincent, post-Dai, post-Kelleys era, shared laughter and moments of seduction did not exist. The most affection he got was being allowed to kiss her on the cheek. Lately, even that had vanished.

"She hit me," he remembered. She slapped him the night of the heart attack. Last night, he reminded himself. In the unending parade of extraordinary experiences, he'd somehow already forgotten the most damning indicator of their crumbling union.

She wouldn't understand why he stood outside their home. They'd never seen eye to eye in that way; as far as she was concerned a car was a car and a dress was a dress. The objects themselves held no significance for her. Yet for him, the house contained a thousand little memories. He could find the black dress she wore to dinner the night they flew to San Francisco to catch the symphony perform her favorite Ravel.

God, what a night that was. With her hair pulled into a perfect ponytail, her neck sparkling with diamonds he'd given her the year before, her skin contrasted by the black shimmer of her dress, her smile brilliant and free—she was breathtaking. They barely made it into the doorway of the hotel room that night before peeling off their clothes like horny high schoolers.

How far-fetched that seemed now.

Her clothing was but one reminder of their collapsing marriage. How many more would he find inside? On a day where he might be approaching a nervous breakdown, could he risk further agitation?

"So should I stand outside my house like an idiot?" he asked no one.

He wondered if the voice inside his head would answer. They hadn't been together long, but now that the two of them were alone and he could perhaps even use the company, it kept silent.

He pulled out his phone. When stalling, it's always better to do so productively.

"Yes, sir," Baxter answered in one ring.

"Status?"

"Mrs. Reinhart is still at the home of the Kelleys. Detective Faucon arrived six minutes ago and is currently in the home as well."

Dominick frowned.

"Go again?"

"Mrs. Reinhart is at the Kelley residence and was joined by Detective Faucon six minutes ago. Now seven."

"You're certain it was Terrance?"

"I saw him enter with my own eyes and I'm looking at his car. Is that a problem?"

"No," Dominick said. "But keep me updated via text as to when he leaves. And notify me if anyone else arrives."

"Yes, sir."

Dominick disconnected. What the hell was Terrance doing there? Baxter had clearly assumed that Dominick had sent him. That would have been a fool's errand of the highest order; Antoinette was about as hostile towards Terrance as Dai; as different as the two women were, disdain for him was among their commonalities.

He prayed Terrance wasn't trying to appease Antoinette on his behalf. That would only infuriate her further.

Dominick started up the walkway—and then stopped as he remembered Dai's words with a chill.

*He's not a necessity, he's a liability. In more ways than you know.*

Dai had always openly disliked Terrance, but last night was different. She referenced a specific crime she was convinced Terrance had committed. Coincidence that today he's at the Kelleys'?

Paranoia, he thought. Terrance was his oldest and best friend. But more of Dai's words wafted into his awareness.

*Who's the red head? You're not seeing a red head?*

A feeling of disquiet snaked through him. When Dai said that at 3 AM it was nonsense. But upon seeing Sherrill McKinnen hours later, Dai's words were among the first to come to mind. What were the odds? Speaking of Sherrill McKinnen...

Again, he pulled out his phone and dialed.

"Yes, sir?"

"I need you to run a background on a name."

He went through the description of Sherrill McKinnen.

"Of course," Baxter replied. "Sir? In light of recent events, I strongly suggest you allow me or one of my men to be at your side at all times."

Dominick again looked at his house. It was his castle, his lion's den, his secretly-favorite status symbol; doubtless within it he could make himself comfortable. Yet something else would comfort him even more: answers. He knew where he could get a few more of those, and the sooner the better.

"In time," Dominick replied. "I need to do something first. I'll be in touch."

"Yes, sir."

Dominick hung up and headed for the garage.

\*                              \*                              \*

Traffic out to Venice was heavier than it had been at 3 AM, but Dominick barely noticed.

With much less fanfare than before, he again used his keys to let himself into her home. Rather than music from their past, this time he was greeted by the sight of Dai herself—sleeping peacefully on her couch. She was curled under a large Mexican blanket with her hands clasped under her face.

Without thinking, he took a seat opposite her. He absently wondered how long he'd watch her sleep, but her almond eyes soon opened.

She pressed her lips pressed together into the beginnings of a smile. Blinking, she sat up as Chango the cat leaped onto the couch beside her.

She stretched and began to pet him, but as she looked at

Dominick her hand stilled. Even as Chango continued to vie for her attention she only squinted her eyes at Dominick with a growing look of concern.

She moved the cat from her lap and stood.

"Come." She moved from the room.

*You're in charge here!* the voice inside his head screamed. *Who is she to tell you what to do?*

Dominick actually found her decisiveness reassuring. He rose and followed her into the kitchen without protest.

Like most spaces in her home, the kitchen was a visual experience. The walls, with their rich complementary colors and coarse irregular texture, looked artful and intentional. Iron pans of various sizes, cutlery, bowls, strainers, were all hung up or precisely-placed on open shelving; it was a working kitchen, but it was also an art installation.

She lit the small white candle at the center of a nearby table and whispered something in Spanish into the dancing flame. She then went to the sink and washed her hands.

"Don't you want to know why I'm here?" he asked as she pulled food from the refrigerator.

"I have my *abuela's* eyes. I can see why you're here."

"The priestess?"

"*Santera,*" she corrected.

"What do you see?"

She shook her head. "First a meal. And while it cooks you can unburden yourself. Atlas."

He smiled. With all that had transpired in the last day, her simple kindness touched his soul. But he was here on business.

"I need to know why you asked me about a red head," he evaded.

There was a chance that Dai was in on it, of course. The

people who had hired Sherrill McKinnen, probably the board, could have enlisted Dai to help plant her in his mind. They had pictures of him with Dai; why wouldn't they try to use her against him? In that way Dai's red head comment earlier could have been part of the script.

That theory was problematic, however. One, Dai's response to a blackmail attempt would be a war declaration, not capitulation. Two, there was the dream. Dreams originated in the mind of the dreamer, period. So Sherrill McKinnen's appearance in his dream one night and then in his lobby the next morning made her a singularly alarming presence. Adding Leftwich's insinuation about the arrival of a "she" only compounded that reality.

"I don't have much time so I need to be direct," Dominick added.

"Time isn't what you think it is." She deftly sliced onions. "Or is it that you don't trust me?"

He stood. She laid down the knife, her onions momentarily on hold. She faced him as the silent moments crept by.

"I didn't wait for you," she almost whispered. She maintained eye contact, but he could see it was a struggle. "I changed the locks six months ago. You had her, why should I be alone? But he wasn't you. So I kept the old locks. And after I asked him to leave, I had them changed back."

He lingered in her stare. He wanted to bolt away; he wanted to embrace her. So he stood in place and let his heart pound. After a moment, he dropped his gaze and the truth fell out of him.

"I'm sorry. My life's gone crazy." He opened his arms and met her eyes. "I need answers."

"As do I, *Dominito.*" She gave him a small smile and

returned to her onions. "Ask away. But be prepared to answer as well."

He noticed the stiffness of her posture as she chopped. She was on edge. Why had he thought this would be simple and easy?

*Dames*, the voice in his head lamented.

"I need to know why you asked about a red head," he said. "Because one turned up in my lobby a few hours later."

"Who is she?" She added meat to a saucepan and the kitchen came alive with the scent of garlic and lime.

*She's in on it,* the voice in his head proclaimed. *Don't tell her a goddamn thing!*

Dominick rubbed his temple; he could scarcely believe that an hour ago he'd almost encouraged it to say something.

"What is it?" she asked. He cursed his own distraction; she'd turned his way and he hadn't noticed.

He took a breath and again settled himself in her eyes. In the mosaic of emotion between them, he could still see simple, genuine concern on her face—concern for him. The truth poured out of him.

"Last night Mr. Wellington made bizarre statements about the board, pricked my finger with something, went into the cabin, and had a heart attack. Now he's in a coma. Since then I've had this voice in my head that periodically yells at me. And my life has gone bat-shit crazy." It felt strangely good to say it all out loud. "And the red head, she knew about it. The voice. She referenced it, casually. But I hadn't told anyone."

Dai nodded. She returned to her stove, and again her movements looked more focused than necessary.

"She's not just any red head, is she?"

"How did you know that?"

151

"I can see her on you. She's a part of you, but in a way I don't understand. What's your history with her?"

Dominick wiped his head; the rabbit hole was deepening beneath him.

"She was a classmate in elementary school. We didn't get along. But she had something of mine, another kid had given it to her, and we went to her house to get it. But then her stepfather comes home, drunk. Thinks we're there to mess around. Goes ballistic. She begs me to deny it, but I can't. I'm too afraid. So he hits her, pulls out a gun. Threatens me. I run away. I hear her screaming as I run.

"We never talked about it. I wanted to apologize. Always thought if I had said something he wouldn't have beat her. But I didn't. Then she moved away." He took a deep breath. "So no, not just any red head. And she's in my lobby today, of all days. First she's a deranged homeless person. An hour later she's calm, collected, well-spoken. And she knows something I haven't told anybody."

*You confide in your lover but not your wife?* the voice screamed. *What the hell is your problem?*

Dominick trailed off and rubbed his temples. "Your turn."

She added some spices, then poured some broth into her pot and set it to simmer. She turned to him with apprehension dancing about her face.

"She's not what she seems. I don't know what she is, but she isn't your grade school classmate. And she's not the only thing that's on you. There's something else from the other side."

"Other side?"

"*Abuela* often said what we experience is only one level of life. But life occurs on different levels. Some people call that life aliens, others call them ancestors. Ghosts, angels, demons.

It's all life beyond our five senses."

*Horseshit,* the voice asserted.

Dominick wiped his face and tried not to grimace. He recalled something Mr. Wellington said about his "greatest weakness."

*You are my champion, my dream made flesh in every regard but one.*

*You lack faith in things unseen.*

Dominick shook his head.

"You don't believe it," she said. "Even with it staring you in your face."

"I didn't get where I am by believing in fairies or energy."

"And this is where you want to be?" Her tone had sharpened.

Dominick motioned around them. "You have all this because of your intelligence, your drive, and your talent. You made this with hard work. Not fairy dust."

He watched her watch him. With a cut of her eyes she returned to cooking.

"You make me crazy. Your confidence in yourself is charming. And stupid."

They'd gotten off track. Rather than reply he enjoyed the increasingly enticing aromas wafting about the kitchen.

She didn't speak again until she put a plate before him; *arroz con pollo,* he saw. A simply-made but vibrant dish with saffron, garlic, and cumin creating a savory celebration.

She sat opposite him with a plate of her own.

"Thank you."

"Please eat." She was still rattled, he noticed. But he'd have to let her share in her own time. They began eating, and it was even more delicious than he'd hoped.

Moments passed before she spoke again. "I didn't see anyone spying on us in San Rafael. But last week I noticed a van on my street. It felt familiar." Dominick's heart-rate accelerated. "What I felt on the van is similar to what I see on you now. Yes, there's the woman with the red hair on you, but I don't mean her. Something dark is upon you. It was on the van. It was on the pictures you showed me last night." She trailed off and seemed to consider her words with a twirl of her fork against the plate. "It was on your father-in-law."

Dominick stopped eating.

"Meaning?"

"Meaning there's more to him than you probably know." She returned to her food, but Dominick didn't feel as hungry. More riddles. "You said he pricked your finger?"

"Yes, with like a tiny stake, but made of stone, not wood."

"Black?"

"Yes," he said cautiously, but she kept utmost attention on her food. "How did you know that?"

"Keep going."

"I'm having the little stake tested for psycho-active substances, because that's when the voice in my head started and the world went crazy. But back to the van. You think someone's watching you?"

She took another careful bite.

"Forget the van. Did he take blood from you?"

"Yes. And why should I forget the van?"

"Because I can take care of myself." Her volume surprised him, and her eyes were suddenly riveted on his own. But then she softened. "Except where you're concerned."

She continued eating. Dominick picked at his plate, distracted. Who was watching Dai? The board? Someone else? Why?

"Any painter worth anything is a student of symbols," she began again. "And if a painter had a *santera* for an *abuela*, even more so. Blood represents life, everybody knows that. But in ritual, blood of the living is special."

She continued to eat, even as she returned to avoiding his eyes. He resumed eating. He was willing to pretend that this conversation was normal if it would support her. Eventually she went on.

"You hear stories about teenage girls using a lock of a boy's hair to grab his attention. High school games." Her voice remained measured. "Blood ritual is different. Blood is sacred, central to life. It comes from pain, from sacrifice, not a comb. So if you want to create a powerful connection to something on the other side, to life beyond the five senses, you use a person's blood. And you get it with sharpened obsidian, volcanic glass, which has long been known to unblock energy. Speaking of fairy dust."

She eyed him with a moment's contempt. His jaw clenched as disbelief gnawed at him; he was supposed to believe that his mentor had cast a spell on him?

He took a breath and considered. That Mr. Wellington had taken his blood was above denial. He forcibly held Dominick's hand until he got blood into the bowl. In turn, the bowl reacted to it immediately. But that seemed like a chemical reaction and not much of a "spell."

The cat padded his way into the kitchen, shook his tail, then sat near the table. Again his eyes went straight to Dominick.

Dominick's head lightened. The world seemed to shift beneath his feet.

"Why does your cat stare at me?"

He looked at Dai dreamily, but she said nothing. Had he asked the question out loud? Suddenly he wasn't sure.

"Animals aren't always what they seem either."

Dominick tried to blink the fog away. That wasn't Dai; who said that?

Dominick's fingers were again at his temples applying pressure. The world cleared a bit, but he felt woozy.

"Freaking animals," he mumbled. Then he noticed her staring at him again.

"What do you mean?" Her voice was concerned.

He looked away, embarrassed. He imagined trying to describe it: *nothing, your cat just freaked me out there for a moment...*

Then he remembered another inexplicable line from the recent past, this one from the drug-addled young man near the hospital.

*Listen to the animals! Super important, trust the animals! But not the voices!*

Dominick couldn't help but groan. "Animals," he asked. "What do animals symbolize?"

"Depends on the animal."

"Stag, snake. Cat."

"A stag is the horned god. Protector of the forest, the gatekeeper. A snake can mean many things, but commonly the knowledge of good and evil. A cat can be patience, curiosity. Immortality."

At the word Dominick felt a spark within his chest without knowing why.

"Immortality," he said. "Tell me more."

"All three suggest immortality. The cat has nine lives. The

snake sheds its skin and is born anew. The horns of the stag regrow. Life flows on."

Dominick stood and paced. It almost made a strange, sick sense: life, death, immortality. Unfortunately, it was also crazy. Without a word she cleared the table.

He wrestled with his thoughts as she rinsed dishes. Symbolism and talking snakes and prophetic dreams and traumatizing childhood memories—what did it all mean?

He snorted to himself as he stared out of her kitchen window.

"I hadn't thought about Sherrill McKinnen in twenty years," he said. "But in one way she's been with me every day since fourth grade. Because of her, I'm decisive. After being too afraid to speak that day, I got to hear her scream. I said never again." He shook his head. "And now it's come full circle. This morning I was going to take decisive action and walk away—from her and all the madness. But it drew me back in."

He wanted to finish; two words remained, and they were the ones that he most wanted her to hear. He turned to her to say them, but something in her expression kept him silent. So the words *I'm scared* remained in the confines of his mind.

An eternity passed in her entrancing brown eyes, and then, strangely, she smiled. She went to him and drew him into a stiff hug that felt distant.

"My star-crossed lover," she whispered into his ear. She was still smiling, he heard. "You're stronger than you think. Open up. And believe."

She released him and lay a hand on his cheek. Her eyes were wistful, even as they shimmered with tears. Understanding struck him.

"You can't," he protested. "Not now. Please."

"I want nothing more than to stand by your side and face every dog of war hell sends your way. I love you. I can feel you in my sleep." Her ferocity gave him chills. Yet she took a step away from him. "But you are not mine to love."

Her voice cracked. Something inside him splintered at the sound.

Still, he took a step towards her but was halted by a raised hand.

"I kept the new locks too." Her voice was tearful but firm. "If you come again, please knock."

She moved to the doorway, her steps stiff, and then turned to face him. Even as he was caught in her wet eyes, his world clouded over; it was like seeing her through misty glass.

"Find your baby girl." Her voice was clear but he didn't see her mouth moving. "Find Violet."

She left the room. Chango the cat flicked his tail, blinked at Dominick, and followed her out.

*             *             *

He was in the car, almost home again and still in a daze, when vibration in his pocket brought him back to reality. Baxter.

"Yes?"

"I have an update on the name you requested. Did you get my earlier text about Detective Faucon's departure from the Kelleys'?"

Dominick had forgotten he'd even asked for that.

"No, but thank you. What do you have?"

"Sherrill McKinnen has several arrests related to alcohol and vagrancy. Under-aged drinking, two DUIs, public intoxication. Trespassing. Destruction of property. Did a stint in the psychiatric ward of Henry Ford Hospital. I'm forwarding it to you via email."

"Good." Dominick pulled into his driveway. "I'm home, so send someone here. You stay with Antoinette. And put someone on Dai's block as well. Counter-surveillance stance. She's been watched."

"Copy that. Man on you, counter-surveil Dai Santana."

"Confirmed."

He disconnected, turned off the car, and typed a text message to Terrance. *I'm home. How soon can you get here?* it said. He should have contacted Terrance as soon as he left Dai, but nausea kept him from thinking clearly. Whatever his previous record for stress in a 24-hour period, he'd surpassed it.

He had pointedly not thought about Dai en route. He would get home, get into comfortable clothing, get into his study, and he would write out everything in play on his gigantic whiteboard. It was a puzzle, and once he got it out of his head and onto a visual medium he could make sense of it.

But before that, he would have a stiff cocktail. Or three.

The moment he entered his home and disarmed the security system his phone buzzed again. The number was LA area, but unfamiliar.

Weary but attempting to sound otherwise, he answered.

"This is Dominick."

"And this is Sherrill McKinnen." Her voice was eerily vibrant. "I'm very sorry about earlier today. But we need to talk."

He closed his eyes and stroked his head. It never stopped.

*Mind your manners when someone's trying to help you, child* Grandma said in his mind.

"Great, now Grandma too?" Dominick said aloud. He knew he was being nonsensical but he didn't care.

Sherrill McKinnen sounded unfazed.

"It's only going to get worse. We need to talk."

*Talk, talk, talk,* the other voice in his head screamed. *Everyone wants to talk! Tell them all to go suck it instead!*

He didn't trust what would actually exit his mouth, so he kept it shut. She filled the silence.

"Realistically, do you not stand to gain more than you can lose at this point?"

He instantly remembered how much he hated her second, no-longer-homeless incarnation.

"What do you want from me?"

"We need to talk," she said for the third time as if it were the first.

He grimaced. His comfortable clothes, his whiteboard, his several drinks—but now someone else wanted him to leave?

"I can meet you at your place," she offered.

"Stop reading my mind!" he spat. Regretting it, he calmed himself. "How would you get here, even if you knew where here was? This morning you were homeless. How do you even have a cell phone?"

While he'd expected, even hoped, that this would provoke an exasperated response, her vocal quality didn't change.

"I'll tell you as much as I can, but unfortunately that isn't nearly as much as you'd like. But if we do not speak I fear madness will take you."

Another shock went through him and he grabbed a nearby

wall to steady himself.

*I fear madness will take him in short order.*

That was a memory from somewhere in the hazy recent past. Wasn't that in a dream? Wasn't that from the same dream where he'd seen Sherrill McKinnen yesterday? Didn't she herself say that in the dream?

His head throbbed. This wasn't happening, he was still in a dream, he was stuck in a—

"Dominick, please. We have to meet."

Like a drowning man, he cast frantic eyes skyward. Maybe he could find air, even if he was flailing. Maybe he could save himself.

"Fine," he managed. "My address is—"

"I'm already here. Open the outer gate."

His heart skipped. He started to ask the obvious, but instead he hastened to the security panel and pushed the entry button. He was excited, euphoric even, at this strange development. Something was happening, surreal as it was.

Within moments he opened the door and received his next surprise.

The homeless woman from this morning with the rumpled clothing, matted hair, and ruddy complexion was now a fiercely-styled femme fatale who strutted towards him in stiletto heels, slinky designer jeans, and a fashion model's attitude. Her eyes, a piercing blue, sparkled in contrast to her buoyant, freshly-styled red mane.

He stared. In hours she'd gone from pitiable to dazzling.

"How—"

She put a finger to his lips, and her cool touch silenced him even as it sent a tremble through his body.

"You shouldn't look at me for the next few minutes. Please

trust me."

She walked past him, through the grand entry-way, with her heels clicking sharply against the hardwood. She moved past the baby Steinway and to the overstuffed couch in the living room.

Within moments she'd slipped off her heels and curled her legs underneath her in the way he'd found utterly adorable since his youth. He recalled a fight with Antoinette after he'd let his eyes linger too long on a vivacious Japanese model, the date of an oil man he was entertaining, as she executed that same gesture in that very chair. Even as he'd apologized to Antoinette he'd secretly wished she sat like that more often.

Sherrill McKinnen glanced at him, looking like a splendid vision of effortless femininity. Something in the timing of her look made him feel caught, just as he had with Antoinette years ago.

"You must try to look away," she said.

Indignant, he rolled his eyes. Instead of sitting opposite her, he opted to sit on the piano bench and face the keys— which put her out of his field of vision. Immediately he had a two-fold experience. He felt a palpable discomfort with having this strange woman in his home without the ability to watch her.

Yet he also felt less dazzled; it was as if looking at her encouraged his dreamlike daze. He sighed. Enough with the craziness.

"Why don't you tell me who you are, who you're working for, and what this is all about." He was using his authoritative voice.

She paused. Without the benefit of visual cues, her pauses felt absurdly long.

"We can't start that way, because I can't tell you everything. But I promise I will tell you everything I can." He heard her shift in her seat. Doubtless it was some effortless, elegant way.

"Before we begin, there are two rules that you must follow, and one of them is critical."

"What's that?"

"After we start *you must not look at me until we are done.* At some point facing me will seem the most sensible thing to do. But you must not. If you do, you risk madness right here and now. Do you understand?"

"No. What does looking at you have to do with anything?"

"You think it a coincidence that as your wife slips through your grasp and your lover distances herself from you that I become more beautiful?"

Dominick was stunned into silence. How in the name of God—

"I will explain it as best I can." Her velvet voice was insistent. "For now please trust me. Do not look at me until we are complete; if you do you will pay dearly."

Madness, he thought to himself.

"Fine. What's the second rule?"

"You must keep a calm and open mind. The more open, patient, and calm you remain, the more I will be able to reveal. Skepticism can be revisited later. But if you aren't open, you further limit what I can share. And if you let your upset run you, you risk ruining this entire dialogue."

"What are you talking about?"

"The tightness in your throat is what I'm talking about."

He indeed noticed that the feeling of tightness around his throat had increased. Exasperation was replaced by apprehension.

"Your time is limited, we must begin," she said. "Are you as ready as you can be?"

"What do you mean, my time is limited?"

"Dominick. Please."

He closed his eyes and took several deep breaths. After forcing his mind to nothingness, he opened his eyes. Game on.

"I'm ready."

"A doorway has been opened from my reality into your consciousness," she began. "But it is a doorway that accommodates your enemies as easily as it does your allies. This is why I cannot tell you everything; the more I tell you, the wider the doorway becomes. The wider the doorway, the more access the darkness has to you.

So I cannot tell you directly who I am, nor can I share all that is occurring. But I can tell you who I am not. I am not Sherrill McKinnen. She is the vessel. She is the means through which I am able to come to you. Can you accept this?"

Dominick's jaw had tightened, but he desperately clung to Dai's words. *Life beyond the senses. I don't know what she is, but I can tell you she isn't your classmate from grade school.*

The voice in his head took another view.

*Time in the psychiatric ward,* it reminded him. *Bat-shit. Looney-tunes. Koo-koo for cocoa-puffs.*

"I'm trying," he said. "But that sounds insane, and you could be a crazy person."

A long pause ensued, and upon not hearing a response he nearly forgot his promise to not turn to her.

"You're failing already." Her voice was deeper now, and gone was her maddening neutrality. An edge had replaced it. He was already re-thinking the wisdom of allowing a possible schizophrenic into his home with the promise that he wouldn't look at her.

"You're asking me to believe that you're not the woman my eyes and ears tell me that you are." He tried to sound reasonable. "And that you're from an alternate reality that you can't talk about. This is after you appeared in my lobby clearly addled and speaking near-nonsense. Do you realize how that sounds?"

"Then our conversation will be over before it starts." Her voice had dropped further; she sounded almost sinister. "And gone with it will be your chance to see. The madness will take you. So choose now, and choose well. Otherwise, have a look at me and let us be done."

He breathed, relieved. He was being baited, and he would resist that on pride alone. He had no reason to look at her other than the ridiculousness of the circumstances. He didn't have to lose this bizarre game so quickly.

"No," he sighed. "I will play a little while longer. Give me a moment to find a way to accept this."

"Much better." Her voice had brightened. It wasn't as lush as before, but closer. "Elaborate aloud. It will support us both."

What a strange game, he thought. But he was fully engaged now.

"I hadn't seen you since elementary school. And you materialize in my lobby, right before the biggest meeting of my career. You were in my dreams last night. And you knew about my meeting, which wasn't public information." He kept his voice rational, as if he were discussing an intriguing merger possibility. "And when I see you again, barely an hour later, you've cleaned up and become a different person. You reference something only I know about, and when I leave you

I then step into a storybook hell.

"And now a few hours later you're different again. So I can definitely say there is something strange about you. How you got here from Detroit I don't know. How you've repeatedly changed I don't know. How you got to my home, knew where my home was, or even got my personal cell phone number, are all things I don't know. So, yes, whoever you are and however you came to be here is indeed unusual and perhaps even extraordinary."

Although he'd detailed some of the reasons why he didn't trust her—shouldn't trust her—he'd also satisfied the basic assertion that she wasn't what she appeared to be. Even if she was mad, she was a well-resourced version of mad that merited interest.

"Much, much better." The lush lyricism was back in her voice. "You can evaluate my words when our time here is complete. You'll likely have the rest of your life to do so, as we may never meet again."

He heard the breathy smile in her voice. It stimulated something within him, even as his head felt lighter. Even with his back to her, she felt intoxicating; it was almost as if he'd had that cocktail after all.

*She lies, the crazy bitch,* the voice in his head said bitterly. *It's always the hot ones.*

Without warning, he thought of Roger. The board. Mr. Wellington. Antoinette. Dai. A fresh pang hit his stomach.

"Focus and listen," she invited. "Listen with an open heart and mind. You'll have time for all the rest later."

She was in his mind again, but instead of dwelling on that he turned his attention to the sheet music in front of him. It was a collection of Chopin's nocturnes. In these sad, poignant pieces he'd recently found some solace that had otherwise eluded him.

"Why don't you play?" she asked. Her voice floated into him like a song. For some reason he didn't mind that she was reading his mind now. The dreamlike quality of the moment made it matter less.

With a smile that surprised him, he thumbed through the sheets and pulled out his favorite. It was the piece that drew him to nocturnes. Antoinette sometimes listened, but she never understood it. The beauty was in the "stormy chromatic center;" it was where the music rose and fell, went this way, then surged that way, then circled back around again with fury, only to land with sweetness and innocence like a petal falling from a rose. It was delightful. How could the critics have panned it?

"Haters," he mumbled as he poised his hands above the keyboard.

The opening bars of the Chopin Nocturne Opus 32, No. 2 in A-flat major laid out before him like a luxurious blanket. The piano came alive beneath his fingers. He'd expected to stumble his way through; he'd not played in at least three days and he hadn't warmed up. Yet he felt strong and fluid anyway.

As a boy he fantasized about a ballerina dancing to his music. Over time the fantasy became more elaborate and he saw himself playing in the expansive living room of the palatial estate home he'd bought once he was wealthy and powerful.

Antoinette had in fact been a ballerina, but after an injury she'd vowed to never dance en pointe again. So he kept his fantasy to himself even after he'd become (fairly) wealthy and (somewhat) powerful and then bought an (almost) palatial estate home.

He blinked, even as he kept playing. Why was he thinking

about all that now? Why weren't they talking?

As if on cue, she spoke.

"Dominick Reinhart, you are being shown 'what is' at an extraordinary level. You have the unenviable task of retaining your sanity nonetheless."

"Apparently 'what is' is the grandest lie of all creation," he breathed airily. His awareness drifted towards the ceiling again; he was watching himself play, watching himself listen, watching himself speak. "Mr. Wellington told me so last night. It was one of the last things he said to me."

He wasn't supposed to be giving *her* information. But he was losing track of agendas. These chords demanded so much attention; the progression from F-sharp minor to A-flat major was always so gratifying if he let it breathe. Chopin was a genius, critics be damned.

She laughed. The sound of her smile was an added gust for his elevation beyond their vaulted ceiling.

"Your mentor bet his life that you were a better man than he. He underestimated his enemies, who had in fact been his true customers and collaborators. He colluded with them, knowingly, to create the 'what is' he referred to. That's why it was always a lie, and he a liar. His empire was his prison."

Dominick played the "agitated atmosphere" that was the nocturne's center. He was playing more quickly than he liked to. The storm wasn't supposed to be *this* choppy.

"He's been the kindest, most decent and moral man I've known," he felt himself saying. "But he hid things from me. They had a secret meeting. They robbed me."

"By alluding to the truth to you, the uninitiated, he signed his own death warrant. But you are his champion. He bet his life that you could end the madness and destruction."

"End the madness? I'm the one going crazy!"

"You are not yet mad."

"Yet!" He laughed. He found his way through a few more gratifying measures, which made him feel a little better. How could he forget how good this was?

"There are unseen forces interested in the activities of your company." Her voice was strong, beautiful. "I am one of them. The evil that speaks inside your head is as well. But the balance is a deadly one, Dominick. The more I assist you, the more the darkness will attempt to destroy you.

"Already it has doused you with its essence to empower your grief; to draw others who grieve into your path; to repel those sensitive to it who would otherwise support you; to reveal wounds in those around you that have been hidden from your sight. It will tempt, it will distract, it will consume. The hell through which you have journeyed is one deliberately crafted. It is the endgame of the darkness."

He shook his head as he remembered Roger's defeated, agonized eyes. "You mentioned limited time before. Why do I have limited time?"

"The portal will close in what you call two days. Almost half of that window is already gone."

"What happens when it closes?" For the first time, she paused. He called out louder. "What happens?"

"It is unclear."

He fumbled over the keys. "You don't know?"

Again she paused. "No champion has ever made it that far."

"There's been others? What happened to them? And what the hell do mean by—"

"Dominick, please focus." He was heading back into what

169

was supposed to be a gentle reprise, but he careened into it instead. As he took a deep breath she continued. "The last champion was corrupted by the darkness. If corruption fails, they will attempt to kill you. If you survive but the portal closes before you succeed, you will likely be driven mad."

"If I don't win I'll either turn evil, go crazy, or be killed? Those are my only options?"

"Yes."

"What the fuck? I didn't ask for any of this! I just want my dream job!"

"This is your destiny. Your mentor groomed you to be the man he couldn't be. So now you and the portal are one. You are the bearer of light and the beacon for darkness. You are the champion."

"Why didn't Arthur. Just. Tell. Me?" Dominick demanded as he picked his way through a re-harmonization.

"He could not speak on it directly; alluding to it landed him into a coma." Her voice was darkening again. "His accomplice Leftwich is not far behind. They abdicated the responsibility of guiding the thrust of the story to you. Now only you can destroy the prison they built. But to do so is to draw the wrath of those who profit from its misery.

"Or you can do as your mentor did; you can profit from the blood and assuage your guilt by seeking a champion and hope he or she is stronger than you."

"But how—"

"But know this, Dominick Osiris Reinhart, son of an addict and true friend to few. Your fate will go as you go. This conversation goes as you go. As you dispute it, your enemies and their designs grow stronger. Not even I am immune. You will know regret, and they will delight in their newest devotee."

Her voice had become seductively rich; it was like syrup he wanted to dab onto the neck of a lover. He replayed the tune as if possessed, and he distantly heard…movement. Footfalls. His heart sang.

Was she dancing? Was Sherrill McKinnen his ballerina?

He fought to retain some degree of focus. "What do you want? How are you not my enemy?"

Her voice was moving, *gliding*, from one location to another. Oh, if only he could see.

"I stand against that which seeks to destroy you. Others like me have done so for generations. Our fight is your fight. But the endgame is upon us, for good or for ill. Your triumph will be our triumph. Your failure will be our destruction, with yours soon to follow."

"No pressure!" He fumbled over a run of triplets.

"Yes, the challenge is great. But I see why your mentor bet everything he held dear—his life, his career, even his only child—on you. You are remarkable. Yet you must ever be vigilant and discerning on your journey. Me, light, darkness, you, your allies, your enemies—on this side of the veil we are not altogether separate. Your chance for victory may be delivered to you by your most loathsome enemy."

Riddles, he thought. But from the heights upon which he currently soared, he didn't mind the double-talk. He had music to contend with. Such fine music!

It would not release him. He played furiously, even as he heard her lithesome figure delighting around him. Maybe he could slow the storm. Maybe he could restore to the chaos its earlier tranquility.

*You imbecile, she's dancing!* his head screamed at him. *Don't slow the storm, give her something to dance to! And bloody watch her! Why are you wasting this?*

He smiled. The venom, when coupled with the chaos of the musical storm, made a strange sense.

"You're all betting on a madman," he sang in time with the music.

"The rage and the cowardice that scream inside your head is not you," she breathed. "It is the darkness within you empowered from without. The madness that awaits you should you fail holds much worse than anything that voice can deliver. You have not yet tasted fracturing of your consciousness."

"I haven't yet tasted fracturing? Beg to differ, ma'am, beg to differ."

"True fracturing respects neither time, nor space, nor even identity. As much as you've withstood thus far, Dominick, tempt it not. It can break you."

The ivories before him continued to sing. The waters were choppy here indeed, right where the meter changed from sweet 4/4 to breakneck 12/8; this was a grown man's piece of music.

He yearned to see the lines of her body given shape by the stormy, powerful music. What a sight it would be!

"Fly, fly, fly," he sang. The music, the confounded music, was trying to get ahead of him. He would tame it.

Then another image danced into his mind—one from years ago that was somehow this morning. He again saw the snake grinning at him.

His fingers fumbled. Crazy talk. He was losing his mind. A snake slid out of his attorney's mouth and spoke to him. Chango the freaking cat almost made him faint!

"What's with the animals?" he screamed as the music blew back into 4/4 time. "This all started with a deer with a death wish!"

"They are messengers. The darkness is frightfully strong. Sometimes messages of light may only enter through the smallest of cracks and be heard through the most unlikely voices."

The snake suggested he not trust Lawrence. Then Lawrence disappeared when his information was proven unreliable. Coincidence? How far gone was Dominick to be thinking all this? For someone not who was yet mad, he sure did feel like it.

Then there was Vincent to consider—his poor, sweet Vincent. Despair flooded into him.

"You're losing, Dominick." Her voice was husky. "Focus!"

"No, no, you don't understand," he moaned. "It's all crazy now. And I miss him. I miss him so much."

"They will take advantage of your pain." Her voice darkened with each syllable, but it was somehow even more alluring. "If you fall prey to their tactics, we are all lost."

"Riddles, double-talk, light, dark, gray, snakes, divorce, suicide," he sang bitterly. His eyes were leaking. Tears on the ivory? There was a fitting song title.

She responded with a deep, lilting moan. It rose like a tidal wave, gathered power, and then pitched forward. The storm was building again. He blazed into the chromatic re-phrasings again and again. He would find its true pace. If only he could stay on top of it!

"And Antoinette, how could she?" Dominick screamed. "The Kellyes? We were a family!"

"Evil knows no restraint. The darkness will twist any knife available to push you over the edge."

"It's working!"

"You have a choice!" she screamed. It thrilled him.

His hands flew faster than he thought they could move;

his fingers, now lit with pain, danced over the keys like a line of madmen. He couldn't stop the storm.

"I just wanted to love her." Tears blurred his vision as his fingers danced. "I wanted to be a good man who loved his wife and children. How did I lose the only things that mattered?"

She shrieked again, this time with animalistic fury. He'd never heard the mating calls of the great cats but wondered if the Serengeti was witness to shrieks like that.

He again thought of Roger. He was a charming, successful man who could have dated any number of women. Yet his love for the one he chose drove him over the edge. And in choosing suicide he left behind far more wreckage than he probably realized. Dominick, who had just met Roger, was shaken to his core. What of Victoria Watson? What of Roger's family, his friends, his staff?

"It was a waste," he mused to the storm.

*A waste like your time with Antoinette,* the voice inside him said grimly. *Roger wasted his life loving a woman he didn't understand. You wasted your life loving a woman that's leaving you to have threesomes with hippies!*

There was another shriek, loud and heartbroken, and Dominick realized it was coming from his own throat. The storm had reached a fevered pitch.

He was on his feet now, not knowing when he'd stood and not caring. Pain shot up the length of his fingertips through his wrists, up his forearms, past his elbows and shoulders and into his back. Yet he hardly felt a thing. He was laughing and salivating and crying—and there was power, such power.

This is what the Almighty must have felt on that blessed seventh day, he thought. The power here was delicious. The strange words of Henry Ward Beecher leaped to mind, and he screamed it with all his might.

*"We are but a point, a single comma, and God is the literature of ETERNITY!"*

He felt incredible forces surging through him; he felt like a mighty tsunami preparing to reshape continents. The destruction would be spectacular; he, as its author, would be God.

Again at the end of the song, instead of relaunching it he slammed his hands on the keys with a final cry. Before he turned a warning surged through his body

*—Dominick don't—*

but with his mouth frothing, he whirled around.

His living room had tripled in size; it was now filled by a swirling golden cloud of energy spiraling fantastically from the center. The air was alive with golden sparkles dancing like living firelight around him; speckles of green and red hues nipped at his skin.

At the center, suspended mid-air, was a seductive witch-goddess ablaze in a rich yellow flame; her eyes glowed blue like an infinite sky, and her graceful arms were outstretched as if to embrace.

Or to consume.

Robbed of his will he strode towards her. Her lips, shapely and beautiful, increased the power of their invitation with each step.

In a breath he was upon her. His arms swept around her and his mouth prepared to inhale her, but then his awareness went to black.

\*          \*          \*

# CHAPTER EIGHT

Disorientation struck first; like a tidal wave it pounded Dominick senseless. Where was he? The light was different. New smells filled his nose. Unfamiliar clothing clung to his skin. What was this?

In moments his senses revealed the setting: he was inside an unfamiliar café, seated alone. Before him was an iced coffee, an untouched omelet, and an open copy of *Time* magazine.

But Dominick couldn't move. He was conscious of his body but unable to command it.

Without warning his left hand came into view, as if self-directed, and his right hand, equally autonomous, pushed aside his sleeve cuff to reveal a Rolex watch on his wrist. His chest sighed and his hands picked up the magazine. Dominick's fear exploded. Not only had his body moved on its own, but the hands he'd just seen were not his own. They were smaller, more wrinkled, and Caucasian.

He was someone else.

Incredulity howled in protest, even as Dominick watched the right hand that could not possibly belong to him nonetheless grab the iced coffee and bring it to his lips. As he swallowed the bitter liquid another sensation came to him; a burning itch on his right hip sang in angry tones. Dominick's hands, indifferent to it, returned to the magazine article.

He was experiencing the most intimate form of theater. He was aware of sensations throughout his (his?) body, and yet he could control none of it.

Bells chimed as the front door opened, and his eyes darted towards the entrance. A spike of excitement surfaced, but then subsided when he saw an older woman with curly hair make her way inside. He felt himself begin to look at his watch again, but instead he returned to his article. The door chimed again, and again his eyes darted up at the sound. Again there was a spike of excitement in his stomach, but this time the excitement continued as the well-groomed, broad-shouldered young man entered the café and briefly met his gaze.

Dominick's eyes lingered on the young man momentarily, then again looked at his Rolex. He continued looking at the article, but his eyes only stared at the page as if pretending to read. His nostrils flared, his heart beat more quickly, his breathing shallowed.

Within moments the handsome young man, mid-twenties, sat across from Dominick.

"Thanks for coming," the young man said as he adjusted his chair. Dominick's small hands put his magazine down leisurely, even as his heart galloped like a thoroughbred.

"Good timing," said the voice from Dominick's throat. "I just finished with a client and I have a break before the next."

His throat was dry, and the manner of speech was familiar to Dominick. He felt his face stretch into a falsely-patient smile. "What's on your mind?"

The young man shifted.

"I'm just going to say it." Uncomfortable, he managed a sheepish smile anyway. "I got called to the minors."

Dominick's stomach turned dramatically, but his outward demeanor remained unchanged.

"You're taking it, obviously," Dominick heard himself say in the oddly familiar voice. "When do you leave?"

Again the young man hesitated.

"I go in for my physical tomorrow and head to the bus right after. But we're still good for tonight."

"No, of course not." Dominick's heart raced, even as his familiar voice remained calm. "You have to pack and prepare. Good luck and congratulations."

The young man looked surprised.

"Seriously?" He shook his head. "It doesn't have to be like that."

"Like what? I'm not angry with you. But I'm also not interested in wasting my time." Dominick's hands retrieved the copy of *Time* magazine. "Or yours. We knew this wasn't going to go very far."

"Larry."

"You don't have to let me down easy. This isn't my first rodeo. And seriously, don't be afraid to have a good time." His slight hands leisurely thumbed through his magazine, even as his heart split.

The young man sat back in his seat.

"So that's it?"

The pain in the young man's eyes brought a new blast

of emotion to Dominick's chest. Still, his face felt blank and expressionless.

"What else is there?" his voice asked the young man.

"Tonight!"

Dominick's wild heart-rate increased further.

"With you leaving I should get ahead on some work," his mouth said. "It's only proper."

"So I'm dismissed?"

His voice was louder now. Dominick felt his eyes almost look to the other customers, but they stayed on the young man. There was a new warmth in his cheeks.

"I find that a curious perspective when you're the one leaving."

"You're acting like I planned this." The young man's voice cracked.

"And you're acting like I'm supposed to take this differently. Did you imagine I'd receive this as good news?

"No, I imagined you might even be happy for me, and that we could go out and celebrate."

Dominick's hands sat the magazine down and stared at the young man. There was something more to say; he could feel it lurking within his gut and begging to spill out.

Instead what he heard himself say was: "Then you were mistaken."

Empty silence passed between them. The young man's eyes moistened.

"Fine." He rose from his chair.

Dominick's mouth tightened as he started to say something more, but then his eyes stayed on the magazine as the chimes of the door clanged again. His stomach burned.

Dominick looked into a nearby satchel and pulled out a

small vial of pills. He opened them quickly, furtively, and took two. He gulped some of the iced coffee and felt it mix with the fire in his stomach; instead of extinguishing the flames it increased his nausea.

With his heart racing and his cheeks hot, Dominick reached into his bag and grabbed a cell phone. St. Augustine Manor, missed calls x 6 and voicemails, his phone said. His elevated heart rate shot up further as he grabbed his satchel and headed for the door.

He pushed out the doors, phone to his ear, already checking the voicemail.

"Mr. Silvers this is Dr. Hernandez at the St. Augustine Manor. There's an emergency with your father, please call us right away at—"

He strode to a large Lexus sedan and threw open the door. He pushed the icon to return the call, and as his car hummed to life the sound of the ringing phone came over the car's internal speakers. He put it into gear and jerked the car into the street. A loud horn responded, but Dominick's head didn't turn to look.

A new voice answered the other end of the phone line.

"St. Augustine Manor, this is Jenny how may I assist you?"

"Lawrence Silvers for Dr. Hernandez, right now."

"Please hold."

Dominick suddenly understood. He was dreaming that he was his attorney. That's why he wasn't controlling himself; he was having a hyper-realistic dream about being Lawrence.

Lawrence maneuvered the big Lexus through the streets of Mid-Wilshire with generous pressure on the gas pedal. Dominick noted that their speed was unsafe, even by LA standards.

A man's voice came over the car's speakers.

"Mr. Silvers this is Dr. Hernandez. I regret to inform you that your father suffered two strokes this morning and his organs have begun to fail. He's—"

"Wait—what?"

"Your father suffered two strokes this morning and is now in critical condition. He's in intensive care but as his organs fail there's—"

"He's dying?" Lawerence exclaimed. Dominick felt his face stretch into a mad grin. "He's dying, right now, as of this moment, he's dying?"

The moment was overwhelming, and Dominick could feel it all: the twisting knots in Lawrence's stomach; the angry fire at his hip; the delirious heat of his cheeks, the unmoored, unfocused quality of his thoughts.

And Dominick felt his foot depress the gas pedal even further.

"It appears that way, yes," the doctor replied.

"I'm on the way," Lawrence declared with a smile on his face and nausea in his stomach. "Don't let him die until I get there! "

"The attending medical staff will of course do their best, but we cannot—"

Lawrence cut the call, his grin stretching further. The world flew past in a near blur as the Lexus careened around traffic. The interstate 10 was ahead by perhaps a half-mile. Cars could be seen on the overpass as they darted in a westward direction. Dominick felt his own fear in conjunction with everything inside of Lawrence. If this is how he drove on the street Dominick feared what would happen when they reached the highway.

"He's dying," Lawrence said. "The bastard is finally dying!"

He was moments from the highway entrance now, with two more traffic lights to go. But as the light before him turned yellow and then red, Lawrence pushed the gas pedal to the floor—and a black Yukon already in the intersection attempted to make the left-hand turn.

Time slowed for Dominick, but it was as if Lawrence didn't register what was happening. Dominick, horrified, realized that Lawrence had disconnected. All he saw was himself at his father's bedside; all he saw was the opportunity to spit in the old man's face as he finally left his stubborn, selfish, worthless life. Lawrence wanted to laugh and cry, celebrate and curse, raise his arms in triumph and simultaneously shake his father into oblivion. All he saw was imminent victory. The Yukon had disappeared behind the

(madness)

complex veil of his own emotions.

His foot never left the gas.

Two-and-half tons of Japanese luxury slammed into the perpendicularly-oriented Yukon at over ninety miles per hour. There was no blaring of his horn, no attempted emergency deceleration, no screech of tires. There was only an explosion of metal and glass and the concussive white blast of airbags. Dominick could only scream before the world went black.

\*　　　　　　　\*　　　　　　　\*

Dizzy, Dominick opened his eyes. Even through the fog of his most recent horror, he realized that once again his eyes were not his own. They remained half-closed, and he felt himself taking deep, controlled breaths.

Whoever he was, he was sitting in a small dimly-lit room. A fountain babbled nearby, and Buddha in quiet repose faced him from the nearest opposing wall. A line of candles flickered before him. He felt a small smile on his face. Nothing was familiar, but he noticed a calm feeling within him. His smile got wider, and beneath it, like a child playfully peeking beneath as sleeping parent's bed sheet, was a sense of excitement.

He rose from the chair and walked—glided really—towards the doorway. It had been covered with a beaded curtain that had been neatly pinned aside. He stepped into the doorway, carrying this sense of serenity and excitement with him, and entered a short hallway. The hardwood floor felt cool beneath his bare feet, and he was struck by the upright gliding manner in which he moved across the floor. It was familiar.

He strode through a short hallway and into an adjoining room. It was a small living room, richly carpeted, and it featured a lit fireplace, several more candles, and plush jeweled-toned cushions and pillows.

Dominick felt his smile widen when he looked across this modest-but-loved living room to the people near the small kitchen.

Sitting on a stool at the counter was Elizabeth Kelley; across from her in the kitchen was Bill Kelley. They both looked over to Dominick and smiled.

"I'm ready," Dominick heard himself say with Antoinette's voice.

*No, no, NO, NO!* he screamed inside of himself. As the Kelleys made their way towards him he screamed again. He wanted to sprint away, but as they closed in on him, their eyes soft with adoration, he had no escape.

Elizabeth Kelley reached Antoinette first and planted a kiss on her mouth that revolted Dominick, even as Antoinette lingered in it. The women held each other and Dominick began to weep even as he smelled Elizabeth Kelley's hair through his wife's nose. Antoinette then turned towards Bill Kelley, who'd been standing by with a look of appreciation. Antoinette uplifted her face towards him in an invitation.

Unheard was Dominick's cry of horror as Bill Kelley came towards her leading with his smile. His face joined hers, even as Dominick howled, and the three of them held each other in the doorway.

Trapped in their triangle, Dominick could feel himself disappearing into the horror, the dismay, the revulsion, the anguish now plowing through him. When he felt Bill Kelley's hand caress the small of her back—*her back, my wife's back* he screamed—he could also feel himself shattering. When Elizabeth Kelley kissed her again and he could not vomit in response, he prayed his destruction would come quickly.

Because the alternative was to stand idly by while Elizabeth and Bill Kelley had sex with his wife. Dominick, a prisoner, would be forced to not only watch it but to experience every moment of it. It was as though he'd stepped into Roger's nightmare and then elevated it into his own first-person hell.

*Roger,* he thought. *Oh, Roger.*

Yes, anguished Roger, who Dominick misjudged, opted to put a bullet through his head rather than face humiliation.

Dominick remembered Roger's eyes. He never blinked. Riddled with sadness, they were on Dominick's own when he pulled the trigger.

Was it not a waste? Roger was a successful man with a

career, staff, shareholders, and a future. All of it was lost to a single bullet in reaction to a bizarre, heart-wrenching night.

What had he said to Roger that final moment?

He remembered: *There's always a way through.*

Dominick's descent into the darkness slowed, even as the pain continued its assault upon him. He was, in his own way, just like Roger, standing with a gun to his head with the option to end the torment. What would he choose?

He felt the darkness in his heart receding. It did nothing to ease the stinging pain. But it helped him see that the situation around him had changed.

Antoinette was no longer making out with Bill Kelley. He had returned to their modest kitchen and was now coming back with a serving tray. Antoinette turned and re-entered the hallway, and all three of them went into the room where she'd first been.

She then faced them with a lightness in her chest. The three of them sat upon a set of pillows with Antoinette, as ever, in the middle.

"You'll want to take this first," Elizabeth Kelley was saying. She'd picked up a pill off of the tray and was offering it to Antoinette. "It's a magnesium supplement."

Dominick felt the cool pill go into her hand, and then she reached for the glass of green fluid on the tray. She swallowed the pill with the thick green liquid; it smelled like a garden and yet tasted of fruit juices. The Kelleys did the same.

"It helps with the serotonin depletion," Bill Kelley said. "People sometimes have stiffness in their jaw, or bite their lips afterward."

"Don't want that." Elizabeth Kelley brushed a flirtatious finger across Antoinette's lip.

Dominick cringed, even as Antoinette beamed.

"We'll have a meal afterward, and another multivitamin," Bill Kelley continued. "The vegetables in the drink have tryptophan, which will also help. Doing what we can to keep those lips beautiful."

"Oh I see what you're into now," Antoinette said with a smile. "The rest of me can go to shit, but as long as my mouth stays nice, you're good."

They all laughed, and Bill Kelley choked on his drink. Elizabeth Kelley clapped her hands.

Dominick experienced the odd contrast between his feelings and what he felt from Antoinette. They were enjoying their time together. This was a quiet, intimate moment in their inexplicable love affair, and he was lingering inside of her like a common peeping-tom. Even with the sadness and revulsion at the scene playing out before him, he also felt a sense of shame. This was their life. She was their lover. And he was an unwelcome intruder, and that upon which he was spying was killing him.

He began entertaining inviting the darkness to consume him anyway, but then a shot of apprehension from Antoinette got his attention. Even with circumstances as bizarre as this, when he became aware of his wife's distress he reflexively made its cause his business.

The cause of her uneasiness surprised him; she was looking at a small piece of chocolate wrapped in tinfoil. Bill and Elizabeth Kelley each had one in front of them, and both had identical supportive smiles on their faces. Granted, Antoinette's apprehension was microscopic compared to what he'd experienced with Lawrence

*(Lawrence! What happened to Lawrence?)*

but nonetheless it stood in stark contrast to her calm of earlier.

"There's no pressure." Bill Kelley sounded reassuring, warm-and-fuzzy. Dominick ached to punch him.

"I'm ready." Antoinette reached down and unwrapped the tinfoil. Bracing himself for a surprise, Dominick saw only innocuous-looking chocolate. *What the hell?* he thought. "This is for us." Antoinette popped it into her mouth.

It was chocolate, to be sure—but within moments her taste buds informed him that it was also something else. There was something dry and disgustingly bitter in the chocolate; he felt Antoinette gag at the taste. Nonetheless, she persevered and swallowed it. The Kelleys chewed chocolates of their own, and Bill Kelley started a timer on his phone.

"Forty-five minutes?" Antoinette asked.

Bill Kelley nodded. "By then the psilocybin will have fully activated within your consciousness. You'll know it. And then we'll take the other."

"The MDNA will further open your heart." Elizabeth Kelley smiled sweetly. "It's a beautiful journey of discovery and communion."

Antoinette's eyes went to a small pill on the tray. Again, there was one for each of them. She then smiled and reached out to her lovers.

"Thank you." Dominick felt tears in her eyes. "I feel loved."

Again, as though by pre-arrangement, both of the Kelleys held her hands. They all closed their eyes, still holding hands, and breathed deeply.

Shock didn't describe the depth of Dominick's surprise. He should have realized it before, with all the talk of serotonin depletion and jaw clenching. She wasn't preparing to have sex with them. She was taking drugs with them, apparently for the first time. They were doing it as some kind of shared experience of "discovery and communion." She'd been meditating before; that's what she'd been doing to prepare for this "journey."

In forty-five minutes, after they were high, perhaps then they could have deep, heartfelt, shared-journey, drugged-out sex. And Dominick would experience every chemically-altered moment of it.

Fury devoured him. His wife, who played the role of an ice-queen to him, had transformed into a lecherous party-girl for a hippie couple, as if to repay him for Dai with penalties and interest. And now he would bear witness to it, as he waited for whatever was in the chocolate to work its way through her metabolic system (to be followed by MDNA, lest he forget, to further open her heart).

He didn't know what he was doing inside of Antoinette's awareness like a psychic stow-away; he didn't know what landmine he'd stepped on that had obliterated his normal and (mostly) successful life; he didn't even recall much of what had happened just before his last traumatic dream with Lawrence.

He was, however, crystal clear about one thing: someone had done this to him. Whoever they were, wherever they were, they would pay dearly. He would not suffer this way in vain.

When this hateful thought settled into his being, he felt a smile from something far away, something dark. Without warning, the world once more went black.

\*             \*             \*

The orange glow from a cigarette pierced the darkness between them. They were in a Chevette; it was an easy car to fail to notice, even in a near-empty parking lot like this one. Dominick was in the driver's seat with another man beside him. Rusk was his name, Dominick somehow knew. It was cold—cold enough to see his breath upon exhalation.

Things were different this time. Even though the environment was not at all familiar, at the same time it also made an easy sense. He wasn't a passenger inside someone else; some version of *himself* was participating. He knew this scenario. He wasn't himself, but he knew what to do. He was in his element.

"I'm thinking that you and I should stop meeting like this," Rusk mentioned after another puff of his cigarette.

"Maybe you should look into a new line of work," Dominick said in a Brooklyn accent. This, too, felt normal.

"Don't think I haven't thought about that. But I've also thought of giving up cigarettes. And retiring young and wealthy. And dating Farrah Fawcett. And helping her prepare for an audition for Deep Throat II."

"How considerate of you." Dominick scanned the area.

"I'm not all bad."

Dominick reached his gloved hand into the pocket of his heavy coat and retrieved the revolver he knew was there. He opened the cylinder, checked the six bullets, then replaced it with a sigh. Rusk glanced over.

"Somebody's antsy tonight. Got a hot date?"

"Every Friday," Dominick said.

"What's her name? Jack Daniels or Jim Beam?"

"Darts."

As they talked they kept their eyes on the Volkswagen Rabbit twenty feet away. It couldn't be much longer now.

Rusk continued. "Seriously, there's gotta be something a little more productive that we could be doing."

"That's going to get a living wage for night's work? I guess I could see how much you'd get me in the queer clubs."

Rusk guffawed and stubbed out his cigarette.

They saw them—a couple making their way towards the VW. The woman, as expected, was a petite brunette in white gogo boots. Surprisingly, the man whose arm she held was Black. He wore a heavy tan wool coat and a matching tan hat cocked to the side atop his afro.

"Well, well," Rusk said as he checked his revolver. "I didn't know she supported integration."

"The good man did say he had a dream," Dominick replied. "Watch the soul brother. I'll stay on her."

They stepped into the frigid Friday night air. Dominick placed his hand on the gun in his pocket as they moved to intercept the couple.

"Theresa. Theresa Richards," Dominick called to her. "A moment of your time please."

The woman looked up in alarm. Her bouncy curls moved a half-beat after her head. The man, drunk, looked at them curiously but without concern.

"Sorry, cats, no change for you. Gave at the office," he said with a casual smile.

Dominick stopped cold. He gaped at the man.

The man looked at him quizzically, his bloodshot eyes partially closed.

"What, like the hat?" His charming smile got wider. He then turned to the woman. "Sorry, baby. I get this all the time."

Rusk looked to Dominick suggestively. Dominick, silent, only stared.

"What my colleague here means to say, Ms. Richards," Rusk jumped in. "Is that our employer would appreciate your cooperation regarding a financial matter. A matter to the sum of—"

"What are you doing here?" Dominick yelled at the man with a hostility that seemed to surprise everyone else.

"What am I doing here?" the man repeated. "I'm sorry, jack, was I supposed to be somewhere else? What was her name?"

Hot rage gripped Dominick and he pulled his gun and smashed it against the man's cheek. He fell to the concrete and the woman screamed. Rusk, alarmed, pulled his pistol and grabbed the woman's arm.

But Dominick only saw the man.

*"Why aren't you with your family? Why aren't you with your wife and child?"* Dominick aimed the gun at the man's face.

The man shook his head and touched his quickly-puffing cheek. When he met Dominick's eyes his expression of confusion shifted to grim understanding.

Rusk, still with the woman held at gunpoint, called out in an attempted hushed tone.

"Ted! Ted! We're working, remember?" Rusk said. "We don't get paid for personal stuff. Let's just do our job."

Dominick cocked his pistol.

"Do you have any idea, *any idea,* how much your boy misses you? And you're out with some depressed junkie hooker?"

"Ted!"

"Hot dog," the man said with a shake of his head. Still he didn't look afraid, even as he gingerly touched his broken cheek. "What are the odds of running into somebody out here that knows Cathy and Dominick?"

"You mean your family!" Dominick pointed at the arm the man was using to support himself and fired. The *crack* of the pistol caused the woman to scream once again, even as the man grabbed his wounded arm and fell in agony.

"Ted! Have you lost your mind?"

"Take her. Cut her throat. Marry her. I don't care," Dominick said from the dream that was his rage. "This is between me and him."

Rusk fretted for a moment.

"C'mon, sugar. Going for a ride. Don't scream again."

"What are you doing? Where are you taking me?" she protested and struggled anyway.

As Rusk muscled her in the direction of the Chevette, he addressed Dominick one last time.

"Charles Bronson? If you're going to do him, be quick about it."

Rusk pulled the woman away. Moments later the car started and the headlights trailed away. Only Dominick and the moaning man remained.

"You want to try answering that question again?" Dominick barked.

"What do you want?" The man rocked back and forth as he clutched his bleeding arm. "You want an explanation? You want an apology?"

"YES!" Dominick bellowed, and fired again. He'd aimed just left of the man's head, and as the bullet whizzed by he jerked over and fell to the concrete.

The man re-gathered himself and tried to sit up. A different confusion clouded his face.

"You ever loved a woman, Mr. Hitman? I don't mean a whore. I mean a woman." He let the question hang, but Dominick only burned. "It's complicated. You want to give her the world. But you hate her too. Because she can hurt you like no one else, and part of her knows it. But you try anyway. Because you love her. But you're not perfect. You drink too much. And then a kid comes into the picture."

He shook his head and even managed another smile.

"And then everything changes, dig? She's all about the kid. But it makes sense because the kid needs her, you know?"

"Your son. That kid is your flesh and blood!"

"You think I don't know that?" the man screamed. "You think I don't realize there's a little guy out there that looks up to me? That thinks that I'm something to be like? I tried to be that guy, and I couldn't. I was Cathy's biggest disappointment, jack. She *hated* me. She tell you that?" He paused, as if still wounded by that. "Who's going to raise a kid in a situation like that? I can drink myself into the grave anywhere. Dom doesn't need to see that."

"That boy would give anything to have you!" Dominick fumed. "Any version of you! He hurts every night because his dad doesn't want him."

"He's got you," the man mumbled. "You can be there for him. Better guys than both of us can be there for him."

"You're the only one that can be his father!"

"You know what? You right. And I can't be his father, 'cause I'm not going to damage my kid like that. So go ahead. This is better than I thought I would get. Done by some turkey in Jersey that happened to know Cathy and Dom. That's a hell of a lot better than my liver going out. Better story too."

"I hate it when you grandstand!" Dominick fired again. The bullet shattered his kneecap and the man screamed in agony.

"God that hurts! God that hurts! Okay! One more!" the man panted. "One more, a little higher next time, about here should do." He tried to indicate his chest but could barely move his arm. "Let's just end this party now, no need for after-party cocktails."

Bloodlust was upon Dominick; the more his father joked and ran from his fear the more Dominick wanted to see him bleed.

*Kill him slowly* a deep, massive voice inside Dominick encouraged. *Three more bullets.*

He fired again, this time into the calf of his other leg. The man howled, to Dominick's delight. Something inside of him salivated.

The man continued to scream and pant, but also kept trying to smile.

"Not going into shock, boys and girls, not going into shock! Rumors ain't true, every one of them hurts!"

Dominick shot him in the shoulder, and in response he screamed and fell onto the concrete. He lay there, prostrate, moaning, panting, and trying to laugh through the agony. Dominick felt tears freezing on his face.

*One more, one more, one more,* the voice chanted with excitement. *Just one more.*

The dark voice was smiling. It was ancient, buried, hidden from Dominick's view. With no view of its face, Dominick could nonetheless feel its joy.

And beneath its joy was magnificent power.

Barely breathing, Dominick raised the gun towards his father's face. His father looked up at him, too weak now to squirm about. Still he smiled.

Dominick's finger tightened—

*(madness may take him)*

—and froze.

*Do it, do it, DO IT!* the voice screamed. The titanic darkness within him continued to move; as if by the sheer force of its will Dominick felt his finger continuing to squeeze anyway.

"No." Dominick dropped the gun. It clacked onto the ground.

*WHAT ARE YOU DOING?* The voice screamed with a force that made his cells vibrate.

The words, thick and odd in his mouth, somehow made their way out.

"I'm my own man," Dominick said.

Something burst within him, as though an unholy pregnancy had erupted, and Dominick felt thick energies flood through him. He stumbled. His body was suddenly weak, his head throbbed, and his stomach somersaulted. The world spun around him.

Flashing lights and sirens approached, even though the volume modulated and the lights alternated between being everywhere and nowhere.

He felt something else; a different smile now blossomed inside him.

"Charles Bonaparte Reinhart," Dominick said as the world spun faster and the lights grew larger. "Your son will become a successful man of power and integrity. He will marry a beautiful woman and make two incredible children. But he will also be a bit mad."

"Chip off the old block," the man said. Dominick still heard him smiling. "Tell him I love him. I'm not perfect but I love him. Dig?"

*Sure,* Dominick tried to say, but his lips had gone numb. The night sky retreated from him and reality went black once more.

\*         \*         \*

# CHAPTER NINE

## (no time)

*From the darkness came a single point of light. Without warning it expanded; in moments it spanned eternity. Disoriented, Dominick felt awash in the sea of luminescence.*

*A chorus of voices speaking as one called from the white.*

*"Come home, sister." The chorus was as rich as it was authoritative.*

*"Who's there?" Dominick tried to shout. His voice, suffocated by the light, made no sound.*

*A single voice, airy but strong, answered.*

*"I must stay," was its reply. Its voice, like all the others, seemed to swirl around Dominick.*

*"Your dance with destiny has ended," the chorus boomed.*

*"He can still succeed."*

*"Your faith is inspiring, but we fear your cause is now lost." They sounded grave. "He may soon die. And you with him if you linger."*

"Die?" Dominick again tried to cry out, but his voice was lost in the light.

"The worst is behind him," the smaller voice protested.

"Hardly. Some fracturing will continue. Madness will await him at every turn."

"I'm right here," Dominick tried to say.

"Perhaps," the smaller voice responded. "But if deserted, he will fail. I will see this through."

Although it was alone in the face of a hundred others, the single voice was also steady. The chorus responded with a breathy sigh.

"As you wish," it said.

A steady hum swelled, and the light gave way to shapes, forms, and colors. Inexorably, a new world emerged from the depths of white. From it, a new voice spoke.

"Dad?" Vincent said.

In an instant, the scene changed.

Dominick blinked against the bright sun. The mighty Pacific—six hundred and fifty feet below them according to the park sign—boomed against the coastline. Violet and Antoinette were further down the walkway eyeing a picnic table. Dominick and Vincent stood by the illustrated signs; they were still arrested by the overlook's breathtaking view.

Dominick looked down and smiled at his young prince.

"Yes, buddy?"

Vincent, sunglasses off, stared at the infinite blue majesty before them. He put one of his size-six sneakers on the wooden fence. His shoelace, untied, dangled in the wind.

"When people die, I don't think they go to Heaven," Vincent proclaimed.

"No?"

*Vincent, his face solemn, shook his head.*

*"I think they go everywhere."*

*Dominick blinked again, but not because of the brightness.*

*"What makes you say that, bud?"*

*The boy shrugged his thin shoulders and motioned around them.*

*"I think Big Mama's here. I think Snake Eyes is here." Vincent looked up at Dominick with a hand raised to shield his hazel eyes against the California sun. "I like that better anyway. They're closer."*

*Dominick was mute. Before he could respond, Vincent hugged his waist. Dominick had enough time to put his hand on his son's head and stroke his sandy-colored curls before the boy released him and skipped away. He jaunted towards his mother and sister, and Dominick smiled and began to say something more. But then the view, the wind, the sunlight, and his family all melted away.*

*"No, no, bring him back, bring him back!" Dominick tried to say. The words never came.*

\*        \*        \*

One eye opened, and then the other.

Again there was white, but this white was not blinding or all-pervading. It was dull and some distance away. After a moment his brain recognized it—it was his ceiling.

"Vincent," Dominick mumbled. "Vincent."

He tried to look around, and he could feel the muscles in his face and neck attempting to follow. He was back in his body, he realized. It felt ungainly and awkward, but it was

HIS. He was himself again.

Disoriented, he twitched. Something cold was pushing against him, and then he realized it was his living room floor. With effort, he sat up. A mighty head rush came upon him and the world momentarily disappeared from view even as his eyes remained open.

He sat there, waiting for the earth to reappear, enveloped in gratitude mixed with sadness. He could still feel his boy's arms around his waist; he could still feel Vincent's curls between his fingers.

"Vincent," he mumbled again. An ache stirred in his chest.

The world once again in sight, he pushed his hand against the cool hardwood floor. He commanded his leg to help him stand; it responded with a shot of pain and a reluctant response. How long had he been out? What exactly had happened to him (this time)? Having to pick himself up off of floors was becoming a very bad running joke.

He got to his feet and his stomach began an immediate protest. Saliva filled his mouth and he felt the need to find the nearest basin RIGHT NOW.

A guest bathroom, he remembered, was the next room over. He staggered in that direction as his stomach tossed about.

He was almost there when his legs lost their strength and his stomach contracted. He stumbled, grabbed the edge of the toilet, pulled his head towards it, and vomited painfully.

When he completed this most humbling form of worship he allowed himself to slide to the floor. Dazed, he wondered what he'd thrown up.

Omelet?

"No, that was Lawrence," he croaked. "And he didn't eat

the omelet."

He remembered the sad eyes of the young man—Lawrence's lover? He then recalled his own powerless horror when the Yukon turned into their path and Lawrence never slowed down. Had that been real?

No, of course not. Yet the experience had been incredibly specific: the weight of Lawrence's watch on his wrist; the acidic taste of the coffee; the hot and itchy rash on his hip. It all felt impossibly real.

*No, it was chocolate*, Dominick thought. *I ate a nasty piece of chocolate.*

"No, that was Antoinette."

A new wave of nausea crested over him. Again he yanked himself towards the toilet as more memories smashed home. He remembered the appalling touch of Elizabeth Kelley's hands and the revolting sensation of Bill Kelley's kiss.

He vomited once again. Little exited his stomach this time, but still the muscles of his abdomen contracted repeatedly as he dry-heaved. An eternity later, he flopped onto the floor.

"Antoinette, drugging it up with Bill and Elizabeth Kelley," he croaked. "And somehow I think I was there. She says I haven't yet gone mad. Not that I know who she actually is."

A new thought seized his attention. What day was it? Like dominoes, one after another, more memories fell into his awareness. Sherrill McKinnen had been here. That was why he was napping on the living room floor. He made a mistake

*(you must not look at me)*

and then the world went bananas. How long had he been out? From the stiffness of his body he figured days. Days! Why hadn't anyone checked the house? He could have been dead.

He pulled himself up again. The board—*the board!* What was going on with the company?

"Phone. Where's my phone?"

Sherrill McKinnen had called him just after he'd entered his home. He remembered using his phone to talk to her near the doorway. His phone would tell him what day it was.

After another lurching effort to get to his feet, he bumbled his way back into the living room. He couldn't help but observe how innocent it all looked. There was no obvious indication that his dignified living room had recently doubled as the site for some trans-dimensional, mind-splitting ritual. The sheet music for Chopin's Nocturne Opus 32, No. 2 in A-Flat Major was still at the piano; it stared at him, looking as unoffending as ever.

"Never playing you ever again," he told the silent page.

He stumbled on. There, in the foyer, near the door— there was his phone. His stagger hastened, and en-route he calculated. The board meeting was Monday the 8th. What day was it now? The 10th? The 12th? Even later?

He grabbed his phone.

Monday 8, it read. That couldn't be.

"Time."

The board meeting had been scheduled for 11 am. But Higgins had moved it to 10. After that he met with Sherrill McKinnen and then Roger—oh poor Roger! Then he'd seen Dai, gotten home by around 5 pm, and Sherrill McKinnen had called him right after. That was when the party got started. How much time had passed since then?

The phone clock read 5:19 pm.

He checked the last incoming call; it was from an unrecognized number with a 310 area code. The call came in at 5:12 pm—seven minutes ago.

Impossible. He played the Nocturne for at least a half-hour. Probably more. And then he passed out on the floor and had dreamed/hallucinated for hours, if not days.

But according to his phone, virtually no time had passed at all.

"Crazy talk," he said.

Disbelief had helped steady his legs; he crossed the length of the house and went into the entertainment room. He grabbed the universal remote and clicked on the 55-inch television and hit the "Guide" button.

Sure enough, 5:20 read as the current time. He turned it off.

"I'm going crazy."

The voice in his head weighed in.

*Forget all this. A meal, a stiff drink, and a good night's sleep are all you need.*

He sighed. It was a special irony when proof of his madness attempted to dispute the existence of his madness. He wondered if the therapist from earlier would find that interesting.

Or if he'd fit Dominick for a straight jacket soon thereafter.

He shook his head and became aware of the awful taste of digestive fluids still in his mouth. Had he even flushed the toilet?

He waved that away. Now that he was back in his own body, biology indeed had its own requirements. Chief among it was getting himself running again.

"And," he said to the empty room, "the voice is probably right to mention food."

*　　　　　　　*　　　　　　　*

# Monday Evening

He was halfway through his second bowl of oatmeal and rocking out to Led Zeppelin when Terrance called.

"I'm having the best bowl of oatmeal ever," Dominick said cheerily into the phone upon answering. Robert Plant continued screaming about his love in the background.

"Uh." Terrance sounded surprised. "Everything okay?"

"Well, right now is okay, and apparently that's a lot." Even as Dominick said it he was aware that the sentence didn't make much sense. Too late now.

"Yeah, good." Terrance sounded unconvinced. "Got your message earlier. You're still at the house?"

"Yeah. Me and Zeppelin. Tribe is in this mix too."

"I'm almost there. Got a couple updates for you."

"Great. I could probably use the company. The therapist earlier said that if I had problems relating to people I should seek professional help. So it'll be good to see if I can relate to you."

Dominick scooped up another spoonful of oatmeal.

"Just sit tight," Terrance replied after another pause. "I know it's been a hell of a day. I'll be there in a couple."

After disconnecting, Dominick wondered about Terrance's take on everything. In one sense he had a severely limited view of what Dominick had experienced since Mr. Wellington collapsed and the world (and Dominick) went mad.

Alternatively, Terrance probably didn't have voices in his head; or recent experiences of moonlighting in other people's minds; or childhood classmates reappearing as homeless people then transforming into runway models and then becoming magical spirits in the span of an afternoon.

So perhaps he was able to see things with more clarity than Dominick.

"Just the facts," he told Robert Plant. Dominick gulped down more oatmeal.

Terrance and Baxter's security man arrived within minutes of each other. Dominick stood at his front door as they conferred briefly; the bodyguard, Parker, returned to his car parked beyond the property gates.

Terrance's eyes were touched with red. His day had also been less-than-ideal, Dominick reminded himself.

"How you feeling?" Terrance asked.

"That's a complicated question." Dominick plopped onto the living room couch. It was time this room again became the site of normal, sane, non-magical human activity, he thought. He looked at the piano, daring it to misbehave, before looking again at Terrance. "You first. What's new?"

Terrance hesitated, but then pulled out a small notepad.

"Several things. Turns out Roger Anderson was the CEO of a Fortune 500 company named Sylvan-Knight Industries. A high-tech manufacturing company. His recent passing has created quite a stir. The, uh, girl in question, Victoria..."

He trailed off as he considered his notes.

"Victoria Watson. Shaken, as you might imagine."

"I might indeed imagine."

"Since you were the last person to see him before his, uh,

before he did it, she's also expressed a desire to speak with you. Get it from the horse's mouth. You don't have to, of course."

Dominick shrugged.

"Roger would like that." That they were speaking casually about a dead man was disturbing on levels he couldn't deal with at the moment. "But we have more pressing matters on the agenda, yes?"

"Yes." Terrance huffed. He took a longer-than-needed pause and then flipped a page on his notepad. He was stalling, Dominick realized. Unsure of what more Dominick could take? Dominick repressed a smile of amusement. Terrance had no idea how far gone Dominick already was. "Two pressing matters, the first being Lawrence Silvers."

Dominick took a breath. His old friend was about to give him an excellent idea of the depth of his madness; what made it ironic is that Terrance didn't even know it.

"So?"

"He's dead. Killed in a high-speed car crash this morning, soon after we left him. I'm sorry."

Christ.

Dominick's hands went to his head as he stood. Terrance eyed him warily, but Dominick suspected that it was for an entirely different set of reasons.

Maybe it was a sick coincidence, Dominick thought. Maybe Lawrence died in another wreck.

"Tell me about the accident." Dominick paced.

"Silvers blew through a red light at highway speed and t-boned an SUV making a left. The driver of the SUV was critically injured as well. If Silvers survived he'd be facing charges."

Dominick closed his eyes. It was true. Lawrence was gone

and Dominick had been right there with him. How? That was impossible!

*Some fracturing will continue.*

"Goddammit!" Dominick spat. "What time was the accident?"

"Approximately 11 AM."

"Fuck my life!" Dominick gripped his head. Terrance raised his hands as if to calm him, but Dominick barely noticed.

Eleven AM? Dominick's hands shook. Sherrill McKinnen called him after 5 PM, and the earliest he'd fainted away was soon thereafter. That was *six full hours* after Lawrence wrecked. He was on a coroner's table by then! How was Dominick there *after* the accident had already happened?

A line from the booming chorus of white light floated into his awareness: *madness will await him at every turn.*

Dominick's hands pushed harder against his temples. Madness wasn't waiting for him. It was here, now, and word of it was being delivered by his best friend.

If that was true—if his experience of the accident was truth and not fantasy—was *everything else* true as well? He'd been inside Antoinette's mind? When had that happened? Last week? Two months ago? And the episode with his father, in New Jersey in the seventies—that was real? Had he almost murdered his father—as someone else—decades ago?

Or was this all the psychotic break Sherrill McKinnen mentioned? Was he, in reality, strapped to a hospital bed with a needle in his arm as his imagination spun this fantastic tale?

"Madness," he whispered.

"I know." Terrance's compassion sounded genuine. It was misplaced in this particular instance, but genuine. "Just keep breathing."

Dominick let his hands drop to his sides. There was no way out now—he was either a raving lunatic, or this fun-house tale of the last two days was factual.

*Including people made of light that talk about me as if I'm not there and dress in the skin of childhood classmates.* His hands returned to his temple of their own will. Hadn't he just told Dai he didn't believe in fairies and energy? He needed to amend that by telling her that psychic projection, time travel, and possession by beings from other dimensions was all kosher; it was the just concept of fairies that was too far.

"Fuck my life." It was a mutter this time.

"Crazy day, I know. But you gotta just breathe and stay with it."

No, he didn't, Dominick realized. He could run out of the house right now and scream until nothing else in the world mattered. The idea held a certain appeal, in fact.

*The group said madness was waiting for me,* he thought. *They never said I'd run to it willingly.*

He sat. Yes, it was now beyond all doubt: he was either absolutely bat-shit crazy, or his life had become an episode of Black Mirror meets The Twilight Zone. Either way, the present lunacy was all he had to work with; if he was actually in a hospital bed drooling on his shoulder there was nothing he could do about it now.

"Fine," he thought out loud. "It is what it is." In the background he heard Q-Tip compare himself to Mario Andretti. The beat goes on, as they say.

"You need me to get you some water or something?" Terrance asked. "Maybe call that therapist?"

"Ain't nobody got time for that."

Terrance blinked for a moment and then laughed.

"I love that you can still make jokes." Terrance seemed reassured and looked again at his notes. "Okay. One more point on that. Small point."

"A good day for points."

"Lawrence Silver's father also bowed out this morning. He'd been fighting cancer but it was a double-stroke that killed him. The attending physician at Saint Augustine Manor provided the details. A doctor Luis Hernandez." He pronounced the name with a strong Mexican accent and gave Dominick the knowing Groucho Marx eyebrows. "I don't know if it matters anymore, but it couldn't hurt knowing that your sources had at least some accuracy."

*The snake was right,* Dominick thought. *Awesome. Next time I meet an English-speaking reptile, I'll be sure to listen to what it has to say.*

A mix of resignation and defeat swirled around in his stomach. Simultaneously, the "psychotic break" theory gained credibility.

*You need professional help,* the voice in his head told him. *Unplug and get away. Get a heavy Xanax prescription. Damn the company and take care of yourself.*

Dominick scratched his eyebrow. At least it didn't hurt anymore. Now the voice sounded afraid. Sherrill McKinnen, he remembered, had mentioned that the voice had only two settings: anger and fear. Now that he was getting accustomed to it he could hear the difference.

He also noticed that he'd unconsciously begun treating it like he did the mentally ill people who jabbered to themselves on the streets downtown LA—by ignoring it. Admittedly, it was a trifle more challenging to do when said jabbering occurred within his head.

*It's a lot harder to ignore a snake that spills out of your attorney's mouth and starts talking,* he thought. Ironically, however, the snake had offered useful, accurate information.

*Believe the animals but not the voices,* Dominick thought bitterly with a shake of his head.

"Dom?"

He looked at Terrance, somewhat startled. Dominick had forgotten about him. He sighed. He'd have to work on pretending to be sane in the company of others.

"Sorry. You said two pressing matters, the first being Lawrence. What's the second?"

Terrance looked away. "You know, I don't think now is a good time."

"You can't be serious."

"I mean, you're already dealing with a lot and this other thing is uh..." Terrance trailed off, in clear discomfort, and still avoided Dominick's eyes.

"Tell me."

Still, Terrance fretted a moment longer.

"The bowl and little stake you gave me. They were stolen from lock-up."

"Stolen?"

Terrance's words tumbled out of him in a frustrated blurt. "That shouldn't even be possible. Lock-up is more secure than most bank vaults. There's only one entrance, it's guarded around the clock, and every inch of it is under surveillance."

"Then what happened?"

"There was a power fluctuation, and emergency power kicked in immediately. Then someone came out of nowhere, I mean nowhere, not the door. Out of a shadow created by the emergency lights. Went to the bin, opened it like it wasn't locked, took the items, and walked away. Walked into a shadow and disappeared. When the power kicked on he was gone. No sign of forced entry or exit, the door never opened, it's like he vanished into thin air. No fingerprints, not even a change in ambient air temperature. It's like he wasn't there at all. But I saw the footage myself. The stuff is gone."

"What did he look like?"

"Face was in shadow the entire time."

Dominick nodded, his face blank. Terrance's frustration continued to pour.

"That room contains evidence of all types. Weapons, cash in the millions, pounds of every street drug out there. But that's all he took. I'm sorry."

Dominick said nothing as another pillar of doubt crumbled away. Terrance had described an impossible theft enacted solely for the items that began Dominick's impossible journey. That was some coincidence.

"Well, I guess that's that," he said.

Terrance looked at him with some surprise.

"You're taking this pretty well."

Dominick kept his game face intact. Even in this strange fantasy world, some things still needed to be handled with care.

"Given what you told me, I suspect everyone who is anyone in law enforcement is paying considerable attention to this. So I'm putting my attention on what I have in front of me, on what I can control, and I'm letting them do their jobs."

Terrance looked concerned, but nodded nonetheless.

"You're taking it easy today, right?" Terrance asked. "When I called you earlier you sounded a little fruitcake."

Dominick wiped his face.

"When I go fruitcake, you'll know. It won't be a little."

He wasn't sure about the rest of the evening, but knew it wouldn't include taking it easy. There were too many balls still in the air. That "newly created" position was one of them—what was the status of that? What about the rest of the madness on this side of reality, like Antoinette?

"Oh, speaking of her," Dominick said, and then realized too late that Terrance hadn't been party to his initial thought. "What were you doing at the Kelleys'? Baxter told me—"

He was interrupted by a flash of muddy yellow light; it was as if the sun itself had been dragged through the earth before shooting light into his eyes. Dominick's vision shuddered, then *altered*. Gone was Terrance, gone was the living room; instead he saw a throng of people, moving about like shadows,

—*unmask, unmask*—

with their faces half-hidden by feather masks, sequin masks, lace masks. He was surrounded by half-exposed bodies, bosoms pushed-up by corsets, and Victorian-age styled dress all around. Yet modern electronic music throbbed in the air overhead.

—*unmask, unmask*—

"Dominick?" Terrance sounded a world away.

Dominick dazed, opened his mouth to respond—but then he saw her.

A woman stood near a statue of two lovers; one of the frozen lovers was a winged god bent low to kiss a near-nude woman as she cradled his head in sweet surrender. Their rapture was complete, eternal.

The cool white surface of the statue complimented the angelic woman lingering beside it. She was clothed in sheer white with a delicate crown of lavender flowers atop her head. Familiar diamonds encircled her bare neck, and others sparkled from her ears.

Her face, although half-masked, also felt eerily familiar. Ensnared, he navigated the sea of moving bodies and wove his way towards her. In moments he reached her. Even amidst this sea of anonymous revelers

*—unmask, unmask—*

there was an air of isolation that hung about her like an empty December night. She looked at him from behind her mask, her eyes unreadable, but even as her thin lips parted to speak he suddenly knew what she was about to say.

"I'm a unicorn," both he and the woman said in unison. "But not really. Because the whole point of unicorns is that they don't exist."

The world shuddered again, more violently than before, and this time the accompanying blast of soiled yellow light disrupted Dominick's balance.

The flash faded away and Dominick's hands stopped pawing at the air around him. He was again in his living room—albeit a section of it he hadn't been facing moments earlier.

Woozy, Dominick blinked several times while his hand massaged his forehead.

"What the hell was that?" He was about to comment further on it when he opened his eyes to a new surprise.

Terrance, wide-eyed, was backing away from him.

"What are you...?" Dominick started to ask. Terrance, his eyes now avoiding Dominick altogether, turned and headed towards the front door. •

Incredulous, Dominick called out. "Terrance?"

The reply was the thud of the door closing behind Terrance.

The stillness of the moment felt eternal, even oppressive.

He could scarcely breathe. A Tribe Called Quest continued to play in the other room, but the shock of the moment had robbed the music of its power.

How long he stood in silence, he wouldn't know. Every time his mind began to emerge from the shock, the reality of what he had just experienced

—*unmask, unmask*—

dumbfounded him once again.

Had not circumstance intervened, Dominick thought he could have stood there for an age. The ringing of his phone cut through the fog and somehow reminded him that he was still a part of this world. He crossed the room in long strides. It was probably Terrance calling to explain himself. Or maybe Sherrill McKinnen again. Or perhaps Linda with an update. Or the hospital with news of Mr. Wellington's improvement! He got to the phone on the fourth ring.

Unrecognized number. Dammit.

"This is Dominick."

"Mr. Dominick Reinhart?"

"This is."

"Good evening Mr. Reinhart, my name is Kenneth Sato and I am a senior partner with the Ryu Law Group. Is now a good time for you to speak?"

It took Dominick a moment, but then he remembered.

"Yes. Of course."

"We reviewed the material your office submitted, and I apologize for the delay in responding. The second set of bylaws from your office was a significant departure from the original, so there was considerable time invested in making certain that our understanding of both documents was accurate."

*Linda sent them the rewritten by-laws*, Dominick thought.

For a moment he almost swooned with gratitude.

*Praise Jesus,* Grandma said in his head.    He shrugged. Praising Jesus was always a good idea, yes?

"What did you find?" Dominick replied.

"If at all possible, these are matters best discussed in person or over a secure line.  Given the absence of the latter, is it possible that I can come to you to meet?"

\*                            \*                            \*

He was tall for a Japanese man, 50s with sharp eyes and an impeccable suit even at the day's end.  They walked into Dominick's massive study with its mahogany wood paneling and recessed lighting, and Mr. Sato opened his briefcase upon sitting.

Terrance, whom Dominick had called moments earlier, had not answered his phone.

"I appreciate you seeing me on such short notice," Mr. Sato said as he gathered papers.  "I also wish to express my condolences to you on the recent passing of Mr. Silvers.  I am honored to assist you in his place."

"That's kind of you." Dominick could pretend to be sane, he realized. "What have you found?"

"The team who devised these documents did an excellent job.  They are both meticulously crafted, and the differences between them are nuanced." He'd put on reading glasses, and something in the smile playing at the corners of his mouth as he spoke struck Dominick.

"You sound impressed."

"It is true, I appreciate exceptional legal work." Sato pulled out a stack of documents. "And I also appreciate a worthy legal challenge. It is, if I may admit, one of my defects."

Within seconds, Dominick felt like he'd stumbled upon a worthwhile ally in Sato. *Praise Jesus indeed*, he thought.

"Something stroked your competitive edge?" Dominick felt himself easing into his executive persona as if it were a hot bath. The familiarity of leadership comforted him, if only for a moment.

"Would you prefer details or the high-level summary?"

"The high-level summary."

"The rewording of the second version of the bylaws is considerable. The ideas expressed are elegantly articulated and the nuances are well-covered. However," he said with a smile, "it is not without an important flaw, the exploitation of which could be significant."

"Explain."

"By virtue of your absence and non-participation as the heir apparent to the existing Chief Executive, as was explained to me by your office, that this document was ever generated at all represents leverage. Because of the specificity of the initial document as to the importance of the interim CEO satisfying clear and specific criterion, the fact that no pre-existing consideration to the original interim chief executive was included in the exhaustive rewrite makes the whole document itself challengeable by law."

He smiled triumphantly. Dominick was attempting to be cautious, and yet he could feel his excitement beginning to build.

"You're saying that because the original document was extensively re-written without the presence of the party aimed to benefit from the first version, that there's a case?"

"In the most basic terms, that is accurate," Sato said, "Unless there were either of two factors which would seriously undermine this position."

"Those are?"

"The first is that the board could prove that the affected party, in this case you, had willfully chosen not to participate in these proceedings. If they could prove that efforts of inclusion had been made and had been either ignored or rebuffed, that would erode the position's strength."

"That would require forgery on their part," Dominick said. "What is the second factor?"

"The second factor would be if, under the new context dictated by the revised set of bylaws, you were offered and accepted an equal or reasonably comparable position to the one that was written out of the original bylaws."

Dominick's blood went cold.

"Reasonably comparable position," Dominick repeated.

"Yes. If you'd been offered and accepted a position in the vein of the interim CEO, which is actually spelled out in the new set of bylaws, then the position loses its power as well." Dominick started to speak, but Sato beat him to it. "It bears mentioning that such a position, albeit differently named, is spelled out in the second iteration of the bylaws. But this other position is at the behest of the acting Chairman of the Board and must act in accordance with the will of the Board at large. These stipulations do not exist in the early incarnation of the bylaws. The interim CEO wasn't given totalitarian control, but the executive freedoms featured in the first set of bylaws is effectively thrown out in the second set of bylaws."

Thoughts that Dominick was dreaming left him. This was

all-too-real. Sato continued.

"This brings me the third item of business. As it would happen, your office also sent this over, before close of business."

Sato reached into his briefcase and unearthed a third stack of papers.

"It is an offer of employment, made out to you, for a position that in substance bears a striking resemblance to the very reasonably comparable position spelled out in the second set of the bylaws."

"What a coincidence."

Sato might have smiled, but professionalism won out. He again consulted his notes.

"While the compensation package is significant—well into eight figures with stock options—the duties, roles, and responsibilities fall directly in line with the curtailed version of the second iteration of the bylaws. The title of this position is that of 'world-wide chief operations officer.'

"Given that, I find it curious that there is a section that, if agreed to, indirectly indicates that this chief operations officer is only allowed to alter or in any way interfere with the *named* holdings and their subsidiaries and new business holdings generated by exploratory ventures. And yet—and this is key— certain *unnamed* holdings are, by implication, prohibited from alteration. 'Worldwide' or not there are company holdings, which painstakingly go unnamed here, which would be outside of the purview of the so-called 'Worldwide Chief Operations Officer.'"

"Show me."

Expecting this, Sato slid over a highlighted document without another word. Dominick grabbed it.

The language was clear in naming what fell under his

jurisdiction and only what fell under his jurisdiction. That there were exceptions and exemptions from this would have been something another attorney, much less Dominick himself, could have easily missed. With everything else being carefully laid out, there was no doubt the true nature of this position.

There was also no doubt about the existence of company assets the board was committed to protecting.

Like a supply-chain that finances murderers in the Congo, he thought.

"If you will, please notice how obscure the wordings for the references to these unnamed holdings. This is truly exceptional work."

Dominick thought in silence. When he spoke again it was with a confidence he'd almost forgotten he had.

"Mr. Sato, I am learning the incredible lengths these people will go to achieve their ends. Examples of that are well-represented in this document. So I would be remiss to not say this directly." He leaned forward. "They will fight with everything they have, and what they have is considerable. Nor will they fight with either fairness or honesty. I need to know right here, right now, that you and your team are up to meeting this challenge."

Sato didn't hesitate.

"Meeting worthy challenges is why I practice law. My staff stands with me."

With a smile that felt two days overdue, Dominick rose from his seat and extended his hand. The two men shook.

"Prepare the lawsuit," he said. This time Sato smiled.

*          *          *

He saw Sato out and felt a twinge of excitement at the possibilities. But the moment he closed the door the world changed again.

This time it wasn't with a flash of light or a shudder of vision. The unremarkable trigger was a simple click of a door jamb finding its indifferent way home. The empty silence that followed brought forth a striking revelation: he was alone.

No Arthur Wellington. No Antoinette. No Dai. No Terrance. Not even Sherrill McKinnen. No one. Only silence, only stillness.

*You should close your eyes now* Roger said in his mind.

The *bang* that followed made Dominick jump. Then he remembered the blood—there was so much blood.

He marched towards the kitchen, the bottle of Johnny Walker Black Label firmly in mind, and then thought of Roger's cold body lying on a table. His hands shook as his traitorous mind reminded him that Roger's head was a few ounces lighter than when he awoke this morning, thanks to the bullet that tore through it. Roger was stiff, dead, gone—like Vincent.

As if in slow motion, Dominick's legs gave way; he sank to his knees, eyes lit with tears. How could it be? How could his boy now be a pile of ashes buried in a hillside? How could it be that all he had of his own flesh and blood was pictures and videos and memories?

*Uneasy lies the head that wears a crown*, Mr. Wellington had once told him. *Hold your family close. It's desperately lonely at the top.*

"I tried that." The tears flowed freely. "I swear I tried."

*You sure you want to marry a white woman?* Grandma had

asked him.

"For God's sake." Exasperation—even recollected exasperation now twenty years old—was fuel enough to get him to his feet. "Antoinette was incredible."

*You just married me to be his son.*

"That's not fair," he said, wiping tears away as he again focused on the bottle of amber liquid in the kitchen. "Things changed. Doesn't take away from what was. She was a queen."

He got moving. Approaching the kitchen, he recalled when they picked out the kitchen cabinets upon building the house. They'd compromised; Antoinette chose the honey blonde color, he picked the fixtures. Their interior decorator, a charming Frenchman also named Vincent, called their teamwork delightful.

She was pregnant with their own Vincent then—not even showing, so new was their little miracle. Meanwhile Violet ran around the house scouting for tea party locations. That was a lifetime ago.

Dominick grabbed a glass, opened the seal on the bottle, and poured about as much alcohol as the glass could hold.

*Drink, drink, drink* the voice inside him panted. Already he was seeing a night ahead of indulgent food, on-demand pornography, and a great big middle finger to the pressures of life.

He hoisted the glass, but then a new thought bloomed.

The anticipatory excitement in his chest lingered; the fumes from the whiskey quickened his heart rate. The moments, dry and heavy, ticked by.

*What are you waiting for?* the voice demanded.

His eyes found the nearby cordless phone. He lowered the glass and a few steps later he grabbed the telephone.

His mind empty but heart throbbing, he dialed. It soon rang in its dull, impersonal, vacuous way. Then the voice he'd not dared hope to hear spoke.

"What is it, Dad?" Violet said.

Dominick closed his eyes to the tears.

\*                    \*                    \*

# CHAPTER TEN

## Monday Evening

"Dad? Hello?"

Astonishment finally released him.

"Pumpkin, yes, I'm here."

"Oh my god."

"I'm sorry. Violet."

"Why are you and mom both calling me today?"

His free hand went to his chest at the spike of gratitude. Sometimes it was indeed better to be lucky than good.

"Your grandfather. He's in the hospital."

"What happened?"

"Heart attack. He's in a coma."

"Oh my god!"

"I know." Dominick's mind raced over how to conduct this conversation. Improvisation seemed to be working. "It was a complete surprise. But there's a lot more going on that we should discuss. In person."

A moment of silence followed.

"'A lot more going on,'" she repeated. "Is that code for mom is finally leaving you?" So unexpected was the blow that it stunned him. "Granddaddy might be on his death-bed and you two are fighting? Are you serious right now? Can you two be any more pathetic?"

"Violet—"

"I don't need to be in your divorce. I'm sure your lawyers can figure it out. I have to—"

"His last words were about you." Dominick prayed his pounding heart wasn't audible through the phone. "About you. And about Vincent."

Silence was her reply. He breathed through the ache in his chest; he wasn't going to get a second chance like this.

"Twenty minutes," he added with fabricated calm. "That's all I ask."

Her silence stretched into eternity, but he didn't dare break it. *Come to daddy*, he mouthed.

He heard a *click*, and then a dial tone.

Even as his heart erupted he allowed his eyes to close and he forced his thoughts into silence. But the voice in his head spoke anyway.

*Improvisation my ass*, it screamed. *Goddamn ingrate!*

Before he knew it, he banged his free hand on the kitchen counter. Catching himself, he dialed Baxter's number.

"Yes, sir?"

"Status."

"Mrs. Reinhart is with the Kelleys. Café Gratitude in Larchmont Village. I have eyes on."

"I need your information on Violet verified, immediately. The moment you have a man with eyes on her I get notified.

224

Understood?"

"Priority action, verify Violet's location and notify. Understood."

"Confirmed." Dominick disconnected.

He stood ramrod straight as his heart hammered blood through his body. He visualized a team of workers standing around the shattered remains of the optimism he'd enjoyed sixty seconds earlier. Their confusion was his own.

His cell phone rang again. Dr. Lockhart, his phone screen informed him. He should answer. But he couldn't bear hearing that his blood was free from psychoactive substances; after meeting a talking snake, witnessing a suicide, then having a psychedelic time-traveling experience that corroborated the death of his attorney, he didn't have it in him to hear that he was "fine."

He answered anyway.

"This is Dominick."

"Mr. Reinhart, this is Dr. Lockhart. I have those test results you requested. Your blood count, metabolic panel, and lipid panel all show normal."

Dominick closed his eyes. "Very good."

"The toxicology report will take more time. I'll update as soon as I hear."

"Thank you, doctor." Dominick disconnected. Why had he thought there was an easy, chemical-based explanation to all this?

*Is that code for mom is finally leaving you?*

He nodded. Yes, the women in his world had gotten quite vicious.

*You only married me to be his son.*

*Back off, Dominick!*

Emboldened, the voice in his head joined the chorus of memories.

*Call an escort. Hell, call two. Blondes, young Antoinette look-a-likes.*

Dominick snarled. Why not order two prostitutes? *Menage-a-trois* action was in fashion—ask Antoinette. Hell, ask Roger.

Roger's last words floated into his mind: *you should close your eyes now.*

Dominick jolted at the remembered *bang.*

Shooting pain in his hand made him look down. He was gripping the phone so tightly his fingers were turning colors. He let the phone drop. Like a spent weapon

(*or Roger's body*)

it thumped onto the floor.

In less than a breath, he had the glass of whiskey.

\*          \*          \*

*Clair de lune* was a fitting soundtrack for many reasons.

One, it was the only song he'd ever studied to impress a woman. Two, because he'd succeeded in charming her that splendid spring day in her father's piano room, the song itself became a kind of love anthem for their early years. Three, the cascade of notes on page two sounded like Debussy's rays of moonlight dancing upon the sea; how perfect, then, for it to play the first time her body joined his.

Insecure in the way that beautiful women often are, she insisted their passion be shrouded by the darkness. But as hesitancy gave way to intensity, their colliding bodies found their rhythm. After a rustle of satin fabric and a sweating and tumbling embrace, he lay on his back and beheld a vision of art in which he was happily participating: there she was, his queen-to-be, with her movements driven by pleasure, her form silhouetted by the moonlight, her face lost in passion. He could have died from joy.

Then, something wasn't right.

Her moaning—rhythmic and breathy—continued as before. But now the music changed; gone was Clair de lune, and its place was something...Eastern. Women sang a droning chant. Candles flickered, but here there was no moonlight. Incense burned. The sheets were different and the bed was low to the floor.

The movements were wrong as well. Antoinette was beneath him now, not straddling him. Her body was as lovely as ever, but her head was turned away from him...and someone else's hand caressed her cheek!

The hand belonged to another woman; but even as she stroked Antoinette's face the woman was staring into Dominick's eyes. She was familiar in a distant, loathsome way. Her free hand then went to her wavy brown hair, which she brushed aside to free her mouth for a kiss she then planted on Dominick's lips.

Her tongue slipped into his mouth like a wet serpent. Instead of recoiling in disgust, he felt himself grab her face roughly as if encouraged by the snake's invasion. The serpent retracted and the woman he knew but didn't know then bent down and kissed Antoinette.

*That's MY queen!* Dominick screamed inside himself.

"So lovely," he heard himself say with a voice that wasn't

his. He thrust himself into her more quickly. Antoinette's moans intensified. Dominick, unheard, shrieked in silent rage.

"The word is choice," a new voice said to him. Its tone was slow, ponderous, arrogant. "He will have one. The outcome of his choice will be either beneficial. Or consequential."

The new scene was saturated with orange; it was like sitting at the rim of the world and being bathed in an unobstructed sunset. Dominick now sat on a bench near a river whilst people speaking Japanese, Dutch, and Spanish passed by. Nearby were ancient windmills that turned their wooden blades in a measured, tortoiselike fashion.

"He needs time. This can't be rushed," Dominick heard himself say. His voice was familiar, but not his own. It was also constricted—drawn tight like piano wire in the hands of an assassin.

"You've had twenty years," the first man snorted. Higgins, Dominick thought. The man before him was Gerald Higgins. But the face was wrong; it was inhuman, almost demonic. It shifted and pulsed as though dark currents cascaded beneath his skin.

The Higgins-demon rose from the bench and looked out at the river. Its choppy water, now a brilliant orange in the setting sun, mimicked the distortions in his face.

"Get him in line," Higgins said. "Haven't you lost enough already?"

Without turning, he moved away. His silhouette disappeared into the orange haze and the scene morphed. The color deepened, as if burning. Soon black smoke blotted out the view altogether; all that remained was the powerful scent of tobacco mixed with pepper and eucalyptus.

"It's falling apart," Dominick said. The voice still wasn't

his, and now its tone was even tighter; perhaps the piano wire had found its victim. "They know."

He was now behind the steering wheel of an aging SUV. Someone new was beside him, but his face was obscured by billows of smoke.

An orange ember burned in the haze beside him, and then a new blast of heavy smoke filled the air. It smelled of sunlight and earthworms, of machetes and sweat. Impossibly it whispered *Vuelta Abajo* into the darkness.

"They don't know everything," said the man beside him. His voice was as thick as an untouched forest. Leftwich, Dominick realized.

When the smoke cleared Leftwich handed him an envelope.

"This is?" Dominick heard himself ask.

"The cavalry."

A puff of smoke obscured the envelope as Dominick's lined hands opened it. When the air cleared a picture of a disheveled red-headed woman was now visible—a mugshot.

"You can't be serious."

"Serious as the heart attack we're both about to have." Leftwich cackled humorlessly before succumbing to a coughing fit. Once the coughing subsided, he continued. "What other choice is there? They know about me, about you, even the *santera*. This is completely off their radar."

Leftwich pointed a finger at the mugshot and his cigar hovered above her menacingly. The woman in the photo began to weep. Dominick protested.

"But her? Of all people?"

"Mentally ill and homeless. No one's going to miss her. Perfect vessel."

"That's not what I mean!" Dominick screamed. "He has history with her! History they're going to use against him. This could ruin everything!"

"If you're right about him, he'll keep his shit together." Leftwich took another puff. "Besides, I had to move fast. She arrives tomorrow and she'll be set up with everything we discussed. Hope those trinkets you got from that freak in the desert actually work."

Dominick released a frustrated sigh—and then beat his fist onto the steering wheel repeatedly. It carried on for several moments. Indifferent, the smoke pulsed on.

When silence fell again Dominick's voice sounded defeated.

"Kidnapping the mentally ill." It sounded more like a confession than a protest. Another thick swirl of smoke followed. It smelled of blackened fields and crying children.

"Seven thousand," Leftwich's sandpaper voice responded. "Know what that is? That's the number of people murdered in the streets by a government we fund. Seven thousand people *in six months*. So yes. Kidnapping the mentally ill."

The smoke came in a series of rings, each thicker than the last.

"Any chance that freak with no face will give you any more info?" Leftwich asked after several moments.

Dominick's eyes lingered on the woman's photo as she wept; her muddy red hair fell into her face like a thin curtain incapable of protecting her. Dominick felt himself shake his head.

"I think he's just along for the ride." His eyes hadn't moved from the photo. Within moments a reassuring hand clapped him on his shoulder.

"She's perfect," Leftwich said again. "And he can handle it."

Dominick put a lined hand on the steering wheel, but this time didn't beat it. "Fine." He sounded exhausted. "Are you ready for your close-up?"

Leftwich laughed thickly; it was like trees shuddering in a night wind. "You want to shoot it now?"

"How much longer do you think we have?"

"You're not worried about obstructing the contract too soon?"

"She's en route. We're past that."

Leftwich nodded grimly from behind the smoke.

"Let me finish this," was his reply.

The smoke thickened and the stench grew more powerful. Somehow it consumed the darkness.

Sensations joined the stench. Dominick's heart rate accelerated—but that's because he couldn't breathe. He couldn't breathe!

He twitched in the suffocating darkness. His stomach cramped as if unseen knives stabbed him. His clothes, moist with hot sweat, clung to his body like leeches.

In a daze, he reached out for the bottle of painkillers he'd left on the nearby nightstand. A stab of pain above the elbow suspended the effort. His dim world came into focus. No more painkillers, he suddenly remembered. He'd traded his last two pills for a nickel bag. That too was gone.

The stench was him—he'd soiled himself. He'd have to clean himself in the bathroom.

Using his good arm, he pushed himself upright on the cot and tried to stand. His feet got tangled somehow when a fresh blaze of pain shot up both legs.

He cried out and fell forward, landing heavily on the scratched wood floor. He blinked away stars as two cockroaches skittered away from an open bottle of ketchup that lay on the floor beside him.

Blood and saliva streamed from his mouth. His pants were by his ankles, he realized. That's why he fell. He must have pulled them off in his sleep.

Or someone had pulled them off him.

His swelling lips quivered as his teeth chattered. The chills were on him. After that would come the pain.

"Help" he tried to say. His swelling lips made clear speech impossible. He could taste the dirt on the floor mixing with his blood.

*Please help me,* he tried to say. But the shakes, the fear, and the pain rendered him silent.

\*    \*    \*

# Monday Night

The world spiraled. Yet when Dominick's eyes blinked open they told him that he was lying on a stationary floor. His head insisted otherwise.

He was face-down—with his mouth open and a good amount of drool running out of it—but he was lying on the plush carpet of his TV room and not on a vomit and blood-stained wooden floor. Even with his head circling like a plane in a holding pattern, the pain and dizziness were barely a shade of what he'd just experienced. The shivering agony that gripped him then was a special kind of hell.

"No more whiskey," he muttered into the carpet. His lips were puffy; he wondered if they were bleeding.

With the world cartwheeling, his neck immobile, and his head an angry stroke of pain, he could have lay face-down on the carpet for a while longer. But biology had its demands.

He flopped one palm to the floor, then the other. As he fingered the carpet's surface and prepared for a push, he tried to count the number of times he'd recently risen from a surface meant for walking. When he got to three he pushed.

The world spiraled faster. With effort, he managed to get upright and staggered towards the hall bathroom.

"That's four, not three." He lost his balance and steadied himself against the wall. "Forgot the hospital floor."

He put a finger to the drool running out the corner of his mouth and checked the color. No, it wasn't blood. God, that had been so real.

*True fracturing respects neither time, nor space, nor even identity.* Sherrill McKinnen had said that.

"No shit." Dominick ambled toward the bathroom.

After relieving himself (and resisting the urge to vomit yet again), he staggered back through the hallway towards the TV room. Even in the haze of inebriation, he knew he needed his phone.

"Violet. Baxter's confirming intel on Violet," he told the TV room as he searched. He tried to reach into his memory for their conversation, but the dreams

*(fracturing)*

kept getting in the way.

"As serious as the heart attack we're both about to have," he said as he pulled cushions from the couch. The floor pitched about him, but he was determined to navigate its movement and keep his balance.

"Fucking my wife," he lamented. "Hippies fucking my wife." His saliva glands again went into heavy production.

He spied the phone under the coffee table. With a gasp his eyes found the surprise it held.

He'd gotten a text message from Violet.

*Outside Griffith Park Observatory. Tomorrow. 11 AM. 10 mins.*

His face went cold—and then he threw up anyway.

*Not on the phone, not on the phone!* he thought wildly, but he'd already dropped the phone to his side. He retched with surprising force.

*Barfing again,* he thought as he gripped his stomach. This room would smell awful; he'd need to pay Ms. Hernandez and her assistant extra for this.

In moments he finished. He blinked and took a few breaths. His throat had been ravaged and he had the unpleasant feeling of stomach acid up his nose, but he did feel a little better.

He surveyed the damage. He'd just redecorated the carpet and also added a new splash of color to the coffee table. It was of Italian design, made from walnut, shipped from Palermo, and had cost him four grand. Now it was a puke-stand.

"Horizontal puke canvas, maybe? New medium, Dai." He found his phone again, and once the world stopped spinning again he dialed.

Nearly three rings this time.

"Yes, sir." Baxter's voice was colored by grogginess.

"Sorry to wake you. New developments. New

developments." Dominick squinted against the headache. "Griffith Park. Or rather, the Observatory. Griffith Observatory. Outside it. I'm meeting Violet there tomorrow. Eleven AM. I need the area checked beforehand. See if someone's already got to her and they chose that location to stake us out. You follow me?"

"You're asking for a counter-surveillance stance outside the Observatory?"

"Yes, exactly. Confirmed." Dominick would need to pay Baxter extra as well. Good thing he was wealthy. "But not just that. I need her followed afterward. And I need to know if someone else follows her as well. Call in as many men as you need, I know it's a lot. I know it's a lot. But it's important."

"Anything you say, sir. I'll have her followed and counter-surveil her exit. I'll have you covered as well."

"Yes. That would be great. But listen. Eyes only. No ears. You understand? Absolutely no ears on. I'm holding you personally responsible for that."

"I understand, sir. Visual surveillance only, no mics on site."

"You're the best. You're doing a fantastic job. I know it's a lot, but you're doing a fantastic job."

"Thank you, sir."

"Okay, that's all. Bye. Wait, Baxter? Who's outside right now? Who's on me? Parker, right?"

"Yes, sir."

"Good. He's good. Okay, have him stay on Violet. I want the best we have on her and Antoinette."

"Of course, sir."

"Great. Thanks. Fantastic job, like I said."

"My pleasure, sir."

Dominick hung up. He dropped the phone and again his hand went to his head. God, did it hurt. He needed water.

"Violet," he told himself as he walked to the kitchen. "I need to plan for Violet. Where is Terrance? Where the hell is my best friend?"

Should he call him? No, no more drunk dialing. He called Terrance a few hours ago and got no answer.

He grabbed the phone again anyway. Seconds later, it rang through to Terrance's line.

No answer.

"Dammit, Terrance." He hung up and then typed a text message: a single question mark. He wanted to type "WTF" alongside it but refrained.

"Water." He needed to sober up and get to planning. He had a daughter to protect. An empire to reclaim.

He again dropped the phone and went to the kitchen. En route he was struck by a random memory. His kitchen was nearly the size of the one-bedroom apartment that had once housed him and his mother. How had he never noticed that before?

He went to the sink and poured himself a tall glass of triple-filtered reverse osmosis water, and he couldn't help but remember the sink of his youth. It was half this size, no double-basin affair, with no garbage disposal and certainly no triple-filtered reverse osmosis spigot nearby. The hot water often didn't work, so he was tasked with heating water on the stove in a pot, then he would place that pot into the sink and use that as the basin with which to wash the dishes.

He smiled. What strange times those were. He enjoyed washing the dishes because it meant his hands would find warm water regularly; drying the dishes meant holding a cold damp towel and wiping even colder wet dishes. During the winter that could mean numb fingers by the end of the job. But washing was a joy. To this day Dominick sometimes washed dishes by hand because it helped him think.

"No dishes now. But you can clean some puke if you want." He'd been puking a lot lately. That couldn't be healthy. He wondered if Mr. Wellington's condition had improved.

Then, again as if from nowhere, were Leftwich's words: *as serious as the heart attack we're both about to have.*

This time it landed. He dropped his cup and bumbled out of the kitchen so quickly that he slipped and had to catch himself on the doorway. Once into the TV room he fell to his knees and scooped up his phone. Heart again pumping, he dialed Leftwich's number.

He got voicemail.

"Fucking ass fuck." He dialed again. No answer. Again he dialed. Again no answer. "Motherfucker."

*His accomplice Leftwich is not far behind.* Sherrill McKinnen's words haunted him. He resisted the impulse to throw the phone into the wall. He dialed again.

Someone answered.

"Dominick?" It was a female voice, cautious and thin.

Dominick's mouth worked in surprise.

"Katherine? Where's Christian?" There was silence, then muffled sobbing. "Katherine?"

"He's gone," she moaned. "He's gone."

"Gone?"

Her reply was a grief-struck moan.

*Good luck,* Leftwich had said. She cried on.

There was a fumbling *thump* through the phone, then three beeps as the line disconnected.

Normally he would race to Christian's home in the Palisades. He would make calls to colleagues and associates; he would consult his (new) attorney; he would even call the police.

"Normally."

His heart in his throat, he walked as steadily as he could to one of the cabinets lining the TV room walls. He pulled out a drawer and retrieved a writing pad and a pen. Almost every room in the house was stocked with a pad and pen somewhere. One never knew when inspiration would strike.

Or tragedy, in this case.

He sat in the loveseat, the puke across the room momentarily forgotten. The empty white page stared back at him.

*You'll regret this,* the voice in his head warned. He ignored it.

He started with the dreams he'd just had. He wrote every detail he could remember. His mind, feeling cluttered from alcohol and distracted by shock, worked slowly. But he persisted.

Once he exhausted that line of memory he shifted his focus to all the details he could recall about Sherrill McKinnen. He wrote everything he remembered her saying as well as everything he could piece together from all the

*(fracturing)*

dreams he'd been having. A puzzle emerged, and he circled words and drew lines between pieces that seemed to connect.

He noted other details: the surveillance photos he received of him and Dai; the bizarre encounters with the drug-addled man outside the hospital; the subsequent experience with the snake. He added bits about Dai, Antoinette, and the Kelleys.

Then he covered the board meeting, and Leftwich's goodbye and Rebecca Tisdale's evasion, plus the position of "worldwide operations officer" that smelled of a sham. He wrote of Lawrence Silver's abrupt demise—a demise that the snake had predicted to a tee.

He wrote of Roger. His heart hurt at the association.

(*Vincent was my fault.*)

But again he persisted.

The time passed and the pages piled up. He had to pee again. His head hurt, he was thirsty, his fingers cramped. His phone beeped with an incoming text message. He ignored all and pushed on.

Two hours later he had eight pages of notes. Each of them now lay before him at various angles. They reminded him of dead fish he once saw floating in a lake. It was not lost upon him that such dead fish often pointed to poison lingering below the surface. There was poison here too.

He rose, drank some water, and again visited the bathroom before returning.

When he returned his eyes then went to four statements:

*Serious as the heart attack we're both about to have. - CL*

*Good luck. - CL*

*The company is a liar and a killer. It killed me. In two days it'll kill you too. - AW*

*Now you've begun to understand how much of a lie 'what is' really is. Be careful. - AW*

He drew lines connecting them, then added a single word that he underlined three times: "murdered?"

"Terrance had mentioned that."

He wrote "motive" and added a question mark. He then wrote what seemed preposterous, but also stated the obvious:

"they knew it was coming."

*You're going to think your way through this?* The voice in his head laughed at him.

Nonetheless, he gathered the papers and descended into his basement study; this was the informal study, without the impressive credenza and over-priced Italian furniture. This one had only a simple desk, and much more importantly, two large whiteboards.

He spent the next hour transferring his ideas from the pages onto the whiteboards. He utilized different colors—green for seeming allies like Sato and Terrance and their items, red for Wallace Purdie, the board, Rebecca Tisdale, and blue for Sherrill McKinnen and all things wacky.

His stomach cramped and the night sky was giving way to gray, but still he fixated on what had emerged on his whiteboards—and what hadn't.

"Even dead fish have something to say."

Finally, he wrote two words: *Why now?*

This whirlwind of impossibility, with all its bizarre players and permutations, had one epicenter: right now. Why? He didn't know—but he knew who did.

He listed each remaining member of the board. Individually or collectively, they had answers.

An idea bloomed in his mind. He'd have to run it by Sato, but the small smile on his face let him know that his efforts tonight had borne fruit.

His eyes found a clock: almost 7 AM. He was meeting Violet in a few hours, and Baxter was likely mobilizing his men in preparation. Dominick sighed. He needed to prepare his plan, but he also needed to keep his baby girl safe.

*You can't keep yourself safe,* the voice in his head accused.

He snorted, circled the board members' names, and then left the whiteboard.

He ascended back to the TV to retrieve his cell phone. He expected it to reveal an array of missed calls and a flurry of messages about Christian Leftwich. To his surprise, there were no missed calls and only one text message. It was from Violet.

*Can't make tomorrow. Call U 2 resked.*

He hung his head. Then, after a sigh, he called Baxter once again.

*                    *                    *

# CHAPTER ELEVEN
## Tuesday Morning

An hour after his second call to Baxter, Dominick was in the bathroom holding tissue paper to his bleeding jaw. Distraction had dealt him a blow while shaving.

He considered it a warning. Now was a dangerous time to be careless, sleep-deprived or not.

His phone rang. It was barely 7 AM, so he assumed this was the call about Christian. But after he re-entered the bedroom he was given immediate pause by the name and face on the phone. Apprehension, that bastard of a grinning devil, danced in his stomach.

"Hey," he answered, attempting neutrality.

"Hey," Antoinette said. "Is it true? About Christian?"

"How did you hear?" he blurted out. *Before me*, he wanted to add.

"Why can't you just answer me?"

Thump, thump, thump went his chest.

"I'm sorry. It's been a long night. I don't have details. But Katherine said he was gone."

She was silent, doubtlessly with her hand on her chest in her particular way of expressing surprise. He considered the next path of conversation but was interrupted by the image of Bill Kelley's smiling face leaning in for a kiss. He gagged.

*Cheating druggy bitch!* the voice shouted.

Distraction having felled him once again, Antoinette spoke.

"I'm sorry about Christian, but I need to ask you something else. Have you gotten a divorce lawyer yet?"

His heart sank like a boulder hitting the Pacific.

"You're calling me to ask which lawyer to have your lawyer contact? Now?"

"I was calling you to see if Christian had passed away, if you were okay, and yes, to ask who my lawyer should contact. How else am I supposed to know? Would you rather my lawyer ask you instead?"

*She considers this a FAVOR?* the voice in his head screamed. *Asking which lawyer she should inform that she's leaving you is her idea of a FAVOR?*

For once, he and the voice were of one accord.

"How long have you been sleeping with Bill and Elizabeth Kelley?" That crossed a line, but anger had him now.

"Excuse me? My personal life is none of your—"

*"Who my wife is sleeping with is absolutely my business!"*

"Do NOT raise your voice at me! As much as you wish you were you are NOT my father!"

"How *could* you? He's in a coma, maybe on his death-bed, and you use him to MOCK ME? You despicable—"

Three beeps.

He screamed and threw the phone to the floor.

"*God-damn you!*" He pounded his hand on the nightstand and then kicked it for good measure. Pain immediately shot through his foot, which angered him further.

His phone, which survived the impact to the floor thanks only to thick carpeting, rang once again. Disbelieving her gall he scooped it back up.

It was Linda.

He retracted from his battle stance and took a breath. "Yes?"

"Good morning, sir. I'm very sorry to say this, but Mr. Leftwich passed away in his sleep last night. Congestive heart failure. His office is notifying the executive team as we speak."

Dominick was silent for a moment. Linda was being her usual sharp-as-a-whip self, ensuring that he had critical information as it became available.

"Thank you. Contact all C-level executives and schedule a meeting to discuss today. Ideal time frame is early afternoon, after the team has digested the news. I'll be in office."

"Yes, sir."

"Thank you. That will be all."

He hung up and stared into the mirror on the other side of their bedroom. The man staring back at him didn't appear unsettled, but only because the contorting demon in his belly was hidden from view. Lingering rage now mixed with mounting dread; it was a nauseating combination.

He took a series of deep breaths. Why did he let things with Antoinette spiral down so quickly? Now he'd have to apologize, goddamn her.

His mind returned to the board. Yes, the shady-ass board, he mused—they were the bigger problem. Just ask Christian.

*Good luck,* the old man had said to him.

So as much as the Detroit Ghetto Boy inside of him wanted to keep swearing about Antoinette, he still had a high-stakes corporate assault to mount. People were dying. And while it should have been simple drunken hogwash, dreaming of Leftwich mentioning a "heart attack we're both about to have" was now a hell of a coincidence given that it *just happened.*

There was no denying it; for both Leftwich and Mr. Wellington to anticipate their futures meant foul play was a certainty. He didn't need a toxicology report to tell him that.

*The company is a liar and a killer.* Mr. Wellington's words had been the pinnacle of absurdity on Sunday night. By Tuesday morning it had become a dire warning. *It killed me. In two days it'll kill you too.*

He paused. Today was day two. Was he also in danger?

It should have been a ridiculous thought. This still wasn't a Martin Scorsese movie with gangsters and dirty cops and tommy guns. This was one of the largest privately-owned corporations on the planet. This was business.

But people were dying.

Yes, far better to be safe than sorry. The same held true for Violet and for

*(bitch!)*

Antoinette, regardless of what's going on between them. He needed to keep them safe. And his own safety?

He tapped his fingertips together. He'd keep Parker near him. But he also needed to make some moves before any other bombshells landed. This was his company now, by god. He'd find out what the board was trying to do with it come hell or high-water.

*Don't be hankerin' for a fight, boy. You'll find one.*

"Why do I keep forgetting Grandma's in there now too?" He threw up his hands in exasperation.

His phone, still in hand, rang once again. Sato's office.

"Dominick Reinhart."

"Good morning, Mr. Reinhart. This is Ken Sato from the Ryu Law Firm."

"Good morning, Mr. Sato."

"My team prepared the brief we discussed. I have reviewed it, made the necessary refinements, and I am now ready to present it to you at your earliest convenience. There are several points I'd like to discuss with you before we proceed."

Dominick blinked. "I like your speed."

"Given the circumstances the more quickly we move without sacrificing our effectiveness, the more successful this venture is likely to be."

Dominick felt a tiny smile within him. "I have an idea I'd like to share as well." Grandma's admonition again drifted in his awareness, but his desire for offensive action silenced it. "Why don't we meet for breakfast near your office?"

"Of course. Shall I await your call?"

"That would be perfect."

Dominick disconnected the line. Yes, it was good to get moving. There was a lot of mess to tend to.

He closed his eyes. Speaking of mess, there was still Antoinette to deal with as well. Even thinking her name made his heart throb. How could such a brief conversation get his blood boiling? They were on the phone for what, ninety seconds?

The memory of the wet serpent invading his mouth made him grimace. It hurt his heart to admit it, but that part of the dream likely wasn't drunken hogwash either.

"She's going to remember the name-calling." He muttered. He should've mentioned Violet. That he'd made contact with Violet was a point that, if played well, could have been used to bring Antoinette closer.

*You don't need her,* the voice hissed. *You don't need either of them.*

"Good Christ." He rolled his eyes as he moved towards his closet.

By the time he donned his cuff links he had succeeded in getting his mind back to its familiar winning groove. He would win this important day. This was the turning point.

He would launch his offensive while the board thought he was off considering the "promotion" and reeling from Leftwich's passing. While they thought him occupied he would sift through their dirty laundry and find his advantage.

Then maybe, just maybe, he'd also shift some good momentum back to Antoinette. Anything was possible.

\*           \*           \*

He left home ten minutes later, dressed in one of his favorite Canali suits, and felt almost like himself again. He took the Bentley coupe. Beautiful but impractical, it was among his most senseless material indulgences. Even though he'd chosen the "more sensible" V-8 version of the Continental GT, the lease payments were four times the rent of his first LA apartment. Further, he suspected that there were tractors with better fuel efficiency, and the car's sexy lines created a blind spot that could almost accommodate a school bus.

Yet it was irresistible. It said, in emphatic terms, that he had Made It; to the part of him that remembered being cold, poor, and hungry, that was reason enough to buy it. His inner Detroit Ghetto Boy certainly approved.

Besides, he'd explained to Antoinette, it was less stereotypical than him buying a Cadillac.

Feeling focused and strong, he blew through the city streets. Parker, in a dark sedan, trailed behind him. This was a beautiful day to conduct a strike.

His meeting with Sato went well; Sato's legal meticulousness continued to impress. He informed Sato of his plan and its intent, and the appropriate documents were drawn up. He left Sato with a palpable feeling of excitement. (What assisted this feeling were the two red-eyes he'd consumed in lieu of sleep last night.)

His plan required going into the office. He guided the Bentley from 4th street down onto Hope and into the underground garage of the massive US Bank Tower, but instead of being greeted by the exuberant valet Francois, a new forty-something man appeared out of the kiosk.

"Good morning, Mr. Reinhart." He gave Dominick a bright smile. "Francois has fallen ill, but he specifically mentioned you as one of his favorite staff members to serve. I am Jacob."

Was he enthusiastic? Friendly? Absolutely. But Francois hadn't been absent, ill, on-vacation, or even late in one instance Dominick could recall in twelve years.

"Ill?" Dominick asked. "What happened?"

"Food poisoning. His spirits are good, but his stomach, far less so. Hopefully his recovery will be swift." He opened Dominick's door. "I understand your car is usually washed and waxed on Tuesdays. Would you like me to see to that?"

Dominick exited the car and considered. It didn't particularly need it, but Bentleys were made to shine.

"Sure. Thanks."

Jacob got into his car as Dominick made his way towards the elevators. A few moments and sixty-four floors later he strode into his bustling office.

Several 'good morning, sirs' were handed out, and many a head was nodded his way. When he went to his own office Linda practically leaped to her feet.

"I'm so sorry about Mr. Leftwich."

He went to her and held her plump, smooth hands.

"As am I. But I'm supremely grateful that I have you. I can't thank you enough for your clear head and proactivity these last two days."

"You're very kind, sir."

"I'm serious. You've been amazing through this storm and the difference it has made is difficult to overstate. Your bonus is coming early this year."

"Thank you, sir." She blushed.

"I have a new task for you and you alone." He almost smiled to himself in anticipation. "I'm conducting an audit of our all holdings. I want you to contact legal and obtain detailed information on all of our corporate assets. Let them know that this request is coming directly from me. Once you have a full report, forward a secure copy to Mr. Sato at the Ryu Law Group."

"Yes, sir."

"You are to discuss this with no one but me and Mr. Sato personally. Not Derrick, not anyone else in Mr. Sato's office, nor anyone else here. Is this clear?"

"Absolutely. What is this about, if I may ask?"

"I don't know yet. But I intend to find out."

"I'll get right on it, sir."

"Thank you."

He went into his office, closed the door behind him, and pulled out his cell phone with a sigh. He dialed Antoinette's number. His heart rate began to elevate once again, but he breathed through it. Keeping his cool this time was imperative.

Unsurprisingly, she didn't answer.

He didn't leave a voicemail. She didn't quickly listen to her messages, and she may not listen to his at all after their exchange this morning.

"Send a text message to Antoinette," he told his phone. "I'm sorry about earlier. And we need to talk. Immediately, and in-person if at all possible. And not about our relationship. Send."

He replaced his phone and sat at his desk. He had three hours before he'd meet with the other executives. He waded through company emails. But his mind remained on the power play he was enacting and on Antoinette. He prayed he would talk to her again. He wasn't sorry for taking exception to her framing her call as though it was for him. But if apologizing would get her to listen to what mattered, he would do it anyway.

His phone rang immediately, surprising him. He checked it—Antoinette. He gulped down whatever had just spiked in his chest.

"Thank you for calling back," he answered.

"You made it sound important." Annoyance sprouted at her dull tone, but he beat it back down.

"It is. Are you somewhere we can meet?"

"Why can't this be handled over the phone?"

He looked around his office. Maybe he was being paranoid, but given the circumstance taking chances would be foolish. "It's better if we meet. I can explain why when I see you."

She huffed. Again he breathed through the irritation. Who knew that meeting one's husband was an arduous task?

"Where are you?" she asked.

"The downtown office. And you?"

"I can meet you downtown," she evaded.

"Good." He said, his jaw tight. "And please don't take this the wrong way, but it's important we're alone."

"I thought this wasn't about us?"

*Don't bite, don't bite, don't bite* he told himself.

"It isn't. Hopefully you'll understand the logic when I explain it. Please trust me. I know I was an asshole this morning, but this isn't about that."

His heart throbbed so hard he felt it in the tips of his fingers. But he knew enough about sales to keep his mouth shut when he was on the verge of getting a "yes." Moments hung in the silence.

"Okay," she said. "Where do you want to meet?"

He breathed a sigh of relief.

\*　　　　　　　\*　　　　　　　\*

Twenty minutes later he entered a nearby vodka bar that he'd heard referenced by one of the younger executives. He'd slipped out alone, without Parker, and took a cab—all of which was unusual for him. He thought that by going to a place he didn't normally go and by a mode of transportation that he didn't normally take, he'd be more likely to disguise his intentions and go unnoticed by any interested parties.

To his surprise she was already there. She was generally late for everything, but also beautiful enough and important enough for her habitual tardiness to be tolerated nonetheless. Yet there she was, waiting for him. If only that meant something.

She was dressed simply in a long, loose, neutral-colored dress and flat sandals. Her hair was pulled into a pony-tail and her wrists jangled with silver jewelry. Her face was devoid of make-up save lip-gloss. She was a touch red from sun exposure. Yoga at the beach was the culprit, if he were a betting man.

She didn't see him enter, so for a moment he watched her from afar. Adorned as she was in the hippy-chic style she'd picked up in recent months—since her time with Mr. and Mrs. You-Know-Who—in some ways she didn't look much like the woman he'd married almost twenty years ago. Still, sizing her up from across a room as might any man upon seeing a beautiful woman in a bar, he couldn't help but be stung by a strange nostalgia.

Why wouldn't he? He still remembered every line kissing her eyes when she smiled; he knew every curve of her body; he knew which cousins she hated growing up; he knew which wine she drank when happy and which she drank when stressed. He knew her almost as well as he knew himself—or so he'd thought.

They were like strangers now. How had they gone so wrong?

"This isn't about that," he reminded himself as he stepped forward and raised his hand to get her attention. She turned his way and no smile came to her face. He felt a bite of sadness. This wasn't ten years ago in San Francisco; this wasn't Alioto's at the Fisherman's Wharf; there was no succulent dinner to be had and even more succulent sex to follow it.

This was his emotionally-vacated estranged wife, and if he didn't remember that he'd be lost. If he made this meeting about their relationship after promising not to do so she would never trust him again.

"Hey," he said simply as he sat across from her. He could feel the barrier between them, high and wide like a concrete blast wall.

*Stay focused,* he thought.

She looked at him but didn't reply. Instead she opened the menu.

"Curious place you chose," she said. "Did you already know about their first signature drink?"

She pointed to the cocktails. In large print at the top of the list was their version of a Salty Dog—which they had dubbed "Future Ex-Husband."

He almost smiled.

"No," he said. "In fact, I hadn't."

The cocktail server came over.

"Hey there, can I start you guys off with something?"

"Pellegrino, flat" Antoinette said.

"Cranberry and lemon please."

"Right away." The server flitted away.

Antoinette looked at him, her face as blank as a cloudless sky. He started to speak when he suddenly recalled that same beautiful face bouncing rhythmically as someone else had sex with her.

He fake-coughed to cover his disgust. Once again, thanks

to his distraction, she filled the silence.

"I know you have something to share," she said, "but since we probably won't be meeting like this again for a while there are a few things I need to say too." She took a breath and put her palms on the table. "First I need to apologize. For a couple things." Her voice was low. That happened when she was nervous. "I'm sorry I hit you. That was unacceptable, and I'm a little ashamed of myself." She broke eye-contact to shake her head. "And the way I handled that conversation. After he collapsed, I mean. I blindsided you. I could have handled that better."

From a distance he was aware that his mouth had opened. She snorted.

"That look, really?" She almost smiled at him.

"I'm sorry, it's just..." he trailed off. "Where is this coming from?"

"You were out of line this morning. Way out of line. That's not like you."

"I'm sorry."

She gave the server a thin smile as she returned with their drinks. When the server departed she continued.

"It made me realize I could be better about this."

Both her tone and her gaze held steady, even as he watched her squirm under the vulnerability. An ache bloomed in his chest at seeing her transform, as if by sorcery, back into a version of the woman he'd loved for half his life. His eyes stung in acknowledgment.

"I need you to be who you're going to be," he babbled, as if the adrenaline running through him was now laced with truth serum. "I can't handle you switching back and forth, not now, I can't—"

*She got some this morning*, the voice in his head spat. *She's in a good mood because another man gave it to her! YOUR WIFE.*

"I'm not done," she interrupted. "And it's not good news. But in a way I was trying to help you."

She broke eye contact and her ring-less left hand fidgeted. He held up his now-sweating palms to halt the proceedings.

"Listen, if this is about the Kelleys—"

"It isn't."

She again looked down to gather herself, which stoked the fires of his angst. She needed silence, but he was desperate to avoid more pain.

*Boy, take your whuppins like a man*, Grandma admonished him.

Right then, on the blade of rising panic and exasperation of his well-planned meeting going extraordinarily off-script— right then is when he felt it: the vague but unmistakable feeling of his head beginning to swim and his awareness drifting up, up, up and away.

*No, no, no*, he said to himself and shook his head in a vain attempt to focus. Unawares, her eyes were still off to the side.

"It was last year, right after you and Dai." Her voice sounded far away. "I was...exploring. You were in Montreal. And I attended a gathering."

Her words floated around him like fireflies on a Kansas summer night. They were distinct, yet she seemed to retreat into the distance. The room was now brighter, and quieter, than before.

The light around him then shuddered, as if rocked by thunder. In a flash he saw them again: the throng of masked dancers moving about each other like silky shadows.

*Unmask, unmask!*

The electronic music, the splashy rich colors, the smell of incense touched with marijuana, all bombarded him in an instant. And there she was again—that masked angel in white. Lavender flowers encircling her head and familiar diamonds shimmering from her neck, she lingered by the statue of a winged god's embrace with masked eyes pointed his way.

Dominick gasped.

"You were the unicorn!" he panted as the vision fled from his view. Gone again were the dancers, replaced by a hazy vision of Antoinette in the vodka bar.

Regardless of the haze, he saw her eyes widen.

"He told you?"

"What? No. No. I mean..." Dominick, dizzy, grabbed the table with both hands as if tactile sensation might re-ground him into reality. "I'm sorry to interrupt. What are we talking about?"

"Terrance tried to have sex with me at a party," she said. "I didn't. But I played along to see if he would go through with it. He would have."

This time he didn't realize his mouth had dropped open.

"At first he didn't know it was me," she continued. "I had on a mask. But when I took it off it didn't stop him for long."

Dominick's awareness was returning to his body, but now his head was swimming for a different reason.

"I'm sorry I didn't tell you before," she continued. "I didn't know how, not with everything that was going on between us. But he came to me over the weekend and begged me to never tell you. So I knew it was time."

Dominick's head throbbed. His wife, *his* wife, was the lonely angel? At a masked sex party? What the hell?

"I know he cares about you," she said. "But you two still

have that high school jealousy-envy thing too. I thought you should know."

"How far did you go with him?" Saying it nauseated him, but he needed to know.

"No details."

"Humor me."

"No," she said. "But there was no, you know—he didn't..."

"He didn't put it in you."

"No."

"Any part of you?"

An exasperated look from her. He held firm.

"No," she said.

He took another breath, but all he inhaled was more shock. Silence.

"What do unicorns have to do with anything?" he asked.

"It's a party expression for bisexual women. You call them unicorns because they don't really exist. How do you know about that?"

He shook his head. "I don't know. A dream, I think."

Her expression was one of doubt, but he barely noticed.

"Well, the main thing I want you to know is that he would have. If I hadn't stopped him." She took a sip of her water. "I did consider it. For a moment I did. But sleeping with your spouse's friend is a little shitty."

She took another sip, but this one with a spiteful smile.

"You and Dai were never really friends," he said with a rueful smirk. "But touché. Not that we're talking about us."

"Oh, I never said I wasn't going to talk about us. Double-standards are one of a woman's privileges." Her almost-smile got a shade wider.

He thought the surrealism of their conversation would

make Salvador Dali proud. Of all the topics about which they'd be civil, even connect in some strange way, this one? But even as pillars of trust and friendship toppled around him, another puzzle piece fell into place.

"You told her about Terrance."

She looked at him with surprise. "I asked her if he'd come sniffing around her too. He hadn't."

Dominick said nothing. If Terrance ever suggested sex to Dai she would reach for the nearest sharp object.

"I also told her about the Kelleys," Antoinette continued. "I knew she wouldn't touch you again if there was a chance of us working out. She's a good soul, and I want you to be happy if you can be. I meant that."

He resisted the urge to search for the cameras recording the joke being played on him. *My wife told me that my mistress is a good soul.*

He had no idea how to respond, but before he could he was taken hold again by that unmistakable feeling of his head beginning to elevate.

"For the love of God," he said.

"I'm sorry, but it's true."

"No, I was thinking of something else."

He stared at her with all the focus he had remaining. If he was going to continue to get high without notice then he'd find a way to operate despite it.

"There's something I need to tell you," he began. He was thankful to get on-script. He could put the pounding of his heart behind him for a moment, light-headed or not.

A hawkish-looking young man with dark hair and tight clothing abruptly came to their table and stood next to Antoinette. He stared at Dominick but said nothing.

"Can I help you?" Dominick said with as much irritation as his floating head would allow.

It was Antoinette's confused expression that informed him—even before she said a word.

"What are you—?" she said with a confused look over her shoulder.

The young man, motionless, stood all of six inches to her right.

"I thought someone was about to interrupt us," he said to Antoinette. "You didn't see him?"

He motioned to the grim-faced young man, who only continued to stare. Antoinette turned his way, looked at where the young man stood and beyond, and then turned to Dominick with a shake of her head.

*You have got to be kidding me,* Dominick thought.

"Never mind." Dominick met the young man's gaze for a moment and shot him an annoyed look. He then tried to focus solely on her; with the young man standing so close it was almost impossible.

"Anyway, thank you for coming," Dominick started. Then the young man began to speak.

"Have you considered how Bill and Elizabeth Kelley make you more vulnerable?" the young man asked.

Dominick gasped in spite of himself. As if what he said wasn't startling enough, the young man's voice was distorted and far deeper than it should be.

"You okay?" Antoinette asked.

"Yes." He was breathless. "I'm trying to say I'm sorry for this morning. Name-calling is unacceptable."

"I appreciate the apology but more than the name-calling was out of line. Not that we're talking about us."

"You can't control what she does, it's true," the young man said. "But your father was accurate when he said that the woman you love also wields the greatest weapon with which to hurt you. He was accurate in more ways than either of you realized."

"Something's going on with the company," Dominick spat out. He was already off-script and his composure was deserting him. *The snake spoke true*, he reminded his sprinting heart. *He's not really there. But listen.*

"What do you mean?" She looked confused.

Dominick shook his head. *Focus, focus, focus* he told himself.

"Well—" Dominick began.

"She isn't going to understand how much she can hurt you," the young man boomed. "Nor is she going to ever understand the danger that her vulnerability poses to you. Your enemies are already examining ways to exploit that."

"Well, what I mean is...I mean that something us up. The company, with the company." Dominick's words were halting, hesitant.

"You just said that. What's going on with you?"

"I'm fine. I just mean that you can't trust them either," Dominick said. "The board. That's what I'm trying to say. Tisdale told me you asked her about the Hamptons house. I don't know how she was to your face, but what she said to me was that she didn't know if you were trying to hurt me or embarrass me and that she didn't care."

"What does this have to do with me?"

"What you should ask yourself," the young man said, "is what you would do if you had massive financial resources, no moral restraint, and a would-be puppet turned-pest in your midst? Who is heading into divorce proceedings with a newly-bisexual wife that's dating a couple that uses recreational drugs?"

Tears were in Dominick's eyes now, but still he fought.

"I'm saying you need to be careful," he said as evenly as he could. "They might try to use our problems, or even you directly, to get to me."

"That's crazy talk," she said with a shake of her head. Under other circumstances he would have smiled at her using his expression. "They're the Board of Directors, not the mob. My father's known some of them longer than I've been alive."

Dominick noticed that the young man's face was changing. It grew darker and began to contort. His brown eyes began shifting position and his nose and face began to elongate. Wings sprouted from his back.

*He's becoming a hawk,* Dominick thought.

"Even now you're strengthening their position," the fearsome-looking hawk monster said. Despite that his mouth-turned-beak could not possibly produce human speech, as with the snake no sound emanated until he opened his mouth. "Did you think that because you took a cab you could not be followed? Or that because you're in a bar you cannot be overheard?"

"If you'd said that before now—" Dominick snapped, then clamped his mouth shut. *Goddammit to hell.*

"Huh?" Antoinette said.

"Never mind." He wanted to pound on the table like never before.

He now had her full attention. She looked at him, her mineral water forgotten, and he could feel the wall between them had slimmed. Her bright green eyes were now open and present.

"What happened?" she asked. "What are you afraid of?"

Her tone was so unaffected, so clean, so unguarded that he could have wept with the release on cue. She was there with him, if only in that moment. It was an inkling of the reunion that his heart desperately wanted.

The hawk-beast beside her leaned in closer to Dominick, fixed him with a giant, piercingly clear brown eye, opened his beak, and said deeply:

"If you tell her what you fear, and your enemies are listening right now, what will you have told them as well?"

Dominick's eyes closed in dismay.

*Exactly how to best squeeze me,* Dominick moaned within himself.

Feeling lost, he hung his head and let a tear fall. When he saw it drop onto a napkin an idea dawned on him. His face relaxed with sudden, cautious hope and as he tilted his head up—and in so doing he found himself staring into the intense face of the hawk.

The hawk winked at him and backed away. Within moments it faded into thin air.

Dominick looked back to Antoinette, who now eyed him with real concern. He pulled a pen from his vest pocket and started writing on the napkin.

"You know what? Never mind," he said with some hostility. "Why am I even talking to you?"

Her face contorted in anger but he tapped on the napkin with the pen and widened his eyes at her. Within moments she got it and looked down.

*Someone is listening to us,* he'd written.

She looked up with alarm.

*Pretend to fight,* he wrote.

"Dominick, you're being stupid," she said, not sounding convincing. He continued writing.

*The board is unpredictable. Even dangerous. Leave town & take the Kelleys & Baxter with you. Immediately. Christian was poisoned, maybe your dad too."*

"Whatever. I don't care anymore." He pleaded with her with his eyes. "Have your lawyer contact mine. Let's get it over with."

She took the pen and wrote.

*How do u know ur not paranoid?*

He frowned. Paranoia was the least of his concerns. He wrote quickly.

*Please trust me. I'm begging you.*

She sat back and considered. Her confusion was clear, but he was gratified to see her taking it seriously.

"I'll see what I can do," she said. He nodded.

She drank her mineral water, fished out a few bills, and then left them on the table. She rose, but then stopped beside him.

"Get some more sleep," she said.

With her standing so close, his love for her almost betrayed him; he had to stifle the impulse to reach out to touch her.

Surprising him, she put a hand on his shoulder for a brief moment and then walked away. He exhaled and ripped up the napkin into tiny pieces. Too late he remembered Violet. He turned—but Antoinette was already gone.

He then remembered that he'd ordered a drink, and he started sipping the cranberry juice.

That didn't go as expected. But perhaps the overall objective still had a chance at fulfillment. He hoped that the man-turned-bird was as altruistically-intended as the snake had been earlier.

He shook his head about Terrance. If the board was listening, they'd have that too. Could they use that against him? What the hell would he do with that himself?

His phone rang. Curiously, he pulled it from his pocket. Higgins.

With a more-than-casual look around himself, Dominick answered.

"Hello, Gerald."

"Hello, Dominick." His words were as snail-slow as ever. "Did I catch you at a good time?"

He's not even trying anymore, Dominick thought.

"I'm inclined to say yes, but I get the impression that you already knew that.

"How could I know that?" Higgins said, the smile in his voice evident.

"How indeed? But you weren't calling to discuss my availability."

"This is correct." Gerald managed to milk three syllables out of 'correct.' "I'm calling about the offer recently extended your way. You are familiar with Napoleon Hill's first meeting with Andrew Carnegie, no doubt?"

"We all are, as you well know."

"The part I find of interest here is the timer Carnegie held under the table set to 60 seconds after he'd extended his offer to Hill."

"You're rescinding yesterday's offer because I'm taking too long to accept it? Even though you said take a couple days off to consider it? Is that the eventual point you're arriving at here?"

"Feeling impatient, are we? Well, who can blame you?

With your father-in-law's sudden illness, the untimely death of your personal attorney, the suicide of that poor fellow in front of you, and now Christian's passing I expect you've had quite a time the last day or so."

Dominick waited without answering. Eventually Higgins continued.

"And true, I happen to agree with Carnegie in that if a man is given ample opportunity to evaluate an offer and yet refuses to accept it, then it is proof that he's not the man for the position. But what I find of particular interest right now is that legal informs me of your sudden research into the company's holdings."

Ah, Dominick thought.

"I'm conducting an internally-focused audit of our assets worldwide," he said. "I've retained contractually-bound legal services to assist in that endeavor, as is my right as an existing senior executive of the company and an internal candidate for its position of chief operating officer of worldwide operation."

Dominick had prepared for this exchange with Sato that morning. Granted, he'd expected the conversation a little later in the ballgame, but their planning was sound and he remained confident.

"It's part of my evaluation of the aforementioned offer," Dominick continued. "Since there is such specificity regarding company holdings under my purview, I'm doing my due diligence of researching the company holdings in general."

"Understandable, very understandable," Higgins responded. "But as your services are no longer needed by the company effective immediately, you are no longer privy to private company information and thus must cease your 'audit' immediately."

In a breath, Dominick was on his feet.

"Come again?"

"You're fired. As of right now."

"On what grounds?"

"It is the opinion of the board that given the extraordinary events of yesterday you do not currently possess the mental and emotional health and stability to adequately serve in a high-level capacity. The board convened an emergency session this morning and voted in this regard. Your severance will be befitting a man with your history of service, of course. And your recommendation will be glowing."

Dominick was lit with rage.

"Are you out of your mind?" His voice was tight. "The wrongful termination suit alone will cost the company tens of millions in legal fees and damages. Add that to lost market share, weakened stock price, and missed opportunities due to corporate distraction. You'll set the company back years!"

Higgins' tone remained unconcerned.

"Litigation is, of course, your right. What is no longer your right is access to private company information. The Ryu Law Group has been notified. You or your representative will be allowed into the building if you'd like to collect your personal effects, under security escort. Or we can ship them to you. And your car is outside if you'd like to take possession of it."

Aghast, Dominick turned towards the entrance. Sure enough, through the floor-to-ceiling window he spotted his Continental GT idling outside. Jacob stood beside it attentively.

It did indeed appear freshly waxed.

It was another moment where time froze. Everyone and everything seemed more there than they'd been moments ago;

the overly-smiling cocktail server, all the other patrons, and his large, panther-like car with its added shine all felt hyper-present.

The bird-man had not only been right, but Dominick had been even more wrong about the board than he'd dared to conjecture. They were willing to bleed the company in a wrongful termination suit that they couldn't win and would ultimately cost the company for perhaps years to come—all to protect their hidden corporate interests.

How had Higgins had gotten the others to vote with him? The "emergency meeting" would have been recorded, and that recording would be shown in the court. So when they cast their votes they all knew that they would be held responsible—and they *still* did it.

Although he wasn't saying a word, he could almost feel Higgins smiling.

"Gerald. You amaze me."

"I'll take that as a compliment."

"Don't." Dominick hung up the phone.

\*     \*     \*

Moments later he was in the car and on the phone with Sato.

"This is highly irregular," Sato was saying. "It is clear that what they value most is not bound by the parameters of conventional wisdom or corporate appropriateness. This makes them dangerous indeed. However, you are correct about the wrongful termination suit. Perhaps this gives us an opening."

Dominick was guiding his behemoth car down Figueroa en route to the freeway.

"Tell me."

"They cannot hope to win the lawful termination suit, so the true goal is likely to stall and obscure whatever it is they most wish to protect. This knowledge gives us leverage. We dictate the terms of the wrongful termination suit and legally compel them to reveal the holdings in the counter-suit retroactively."

"Get it started. And keep me updated."

He disconnected and swerved onto the 110 south freeway. He could go to Mr. Wellington's bedside and perhaps find some solace or inspiration there. Or maybe call Antoinette and let her know 1) the threat of the board is real and 2) leave town today and take the Kelleys with her as they were doubtlessly on the board's radar as well. They'd followed him to the bar—they had someone tail the cab. They had a meeting to fire him *this morning!* Before he'd put anything into play. What was everyone still doing in town? How were they able to pull that together?

Maybe they'd planned it from the outset and the job offer was always a smokescreen, he thought.

Thank God the bird warned him. Given that they were probably being monitored it was a very good thing that he hadn't bared his soul about his fears. His latest hallucination had, like the last, actually done him a solid.

"And since we're evaluating, it's time to admit that these hallucinations can't actually be hallucinations. Granted, they don't seem to really be there, which is why no one else sees them, but they tell me things that I couldn't possibly know."

His train of thought stopped—why had he just said that? Why now, of all times, would he bring into sharp focus something that could easily drive away what little sanity remained in his head?

He shook the thoughts away and barreled onto the I-10 west. Lack of traffic and large gaps of no thought (due to shock, he imagined) carried him home in record time. What should he do? Eat? Make more phone calls? Calm himself and then visualize the best outcome for himself so that he could then make it real?

By the time he'd pulled the car into the garage under his home, he'd forgotten he'd even asked this question. Things had spun so far, so quickly, that when he'd stopped to think of it he could barely breathe.

Soon he found himself standing again in his bedroom. His bed, large and comfortable, beckoned. No, he wasn't tired. He was, in fact, still fully dressed. Still, he laid down on his bed, shoes and all. His eyes were wide open, as if he'd drank a gallon of coffee, but maybe laying there relaxing his body would clear his head.

Then heard it.

*Tap. Tap. Tap.*

The sound went into his ears, not his brain, so he didn't move.

*Tap. Tap. Tap. Tap. Tap.*

He blinked. That was nearby. He turned around. Was that his window? He looked at the window, rubbed his eyes, and then looked again.

Outside of his bedroom window, to his disbelief, was a large, majestic brown bird tapping its beak on the glass.

To Dominick's uneducated eyes, it looked remarkably like a hawk.

He went to the window and began to open it. Somewhere

within him was a protest; a bird of prey, especially one that size, could badly injure him if it wanted to. He opened it anyway.

The bird beat its mighty wings and flew off. Within moments it landed on his front lawn, atop his lion face fountain. The hawk then turned its head towards Dominick and screeched in a single piercing tone.

Confused, Dominick stared at it. It screeched twice more, then waited. It moved its head in jerky movements but continued to look at him. Still he stared. Then it began screeching repeatedly, even more loudly, and began to beat its wings, even as it didn't take to the sky.

Still his mind hadn't put it together, but his body got moving anyway. He left the window and headed for the stairs. Fear rose within him and he walked faster. He took the stairs down two at a time. By the time he'd gotten downstairs, the fear had snowballed and he broke out into a full sprint.

He had just opened his front door when a thunderous roar vibrated through the length of his body. The air punched him from behind, hoisted him up, and flung him forward. He had enough time to realize he was flying when he hit something hard and the world went black.

*      *      *

# CHAPTER TWELVE

## (no time)

When Dominick opened his eyes he was already standing. Surrounding him, as far as the eye could see, was a field of flowers in resplendent bloom. Blood reds and bright yellows, fresh blues and regal purples, pinks and whites and oranges all swayed about him in a dazzling array. It was as if he stood in a sea of living, singing color.

And they *were* singing; a faint chorus of millions of tiny voices was joined in a harmony that kissed the skin of his bare arms. It was a welcoming serenade; he knew

*(Dominick)*

that the song was written for him, arranged for him, sung for him. It was the truest instance of a "love song" that could be.

Warmth in his heart urged him forward. He had no fear of stepping on his love singers; they swayed in concert with his movements like dancers on a breezy day. How alive he felt!

He knew only sky, sun, color, and love; it seemed as though the world contained nothing else.

*(Dominick)*

Then there was something else—*someone* else. He glanced to his right, and walking in step with him a few feet away was Mr. Wellington. He was bright and vibrant; his face was alive in a way that Dominick hadn't seen in years.

Dominick stopped. Something tugged at his chest. The chorus continued to sing, but now off-key.

"You lied to me," Dominick said. "Why didn't you tell me the truth?"

Mr. Wellington continued to walk but looked at Dominick as he moved through the dancing flowers. He smiled, as warm and pure as a child's embrace. It was a smile that spoke silent volumes; it spoke of the complexities of love and the fragility of humanity. It was a smile of hope and frustration, of discouragement and pride, of greed and gratitude.

While still walking, Mr. Wellington slowly faded away; as the sky and flowers and sunlight replaced his still-moving figure, his green eyes didn't leave Dominick's.

Nor did his smile ever fade.

Then he was gone, and Dominick felt a release as the chorus swelled around him.

*(Dominick)*

He turned again. Now to his left was a thunderous roar that could only be the sea. The field of flowers sang on, but they were joined by a bass note that resonated throughout his body. There, a bit ahead—how had he not seen it before? He spotted where the field of flowers gave way to the brilliant blue expanse; it must be a great cliff, where the sea beat against the rocks far below and made its booming song. The smell of spray joined the floral aroma surrounding him. The water and earth, it seemed, had already found an easy harmony.

*(Dominick)*

He moved, as though floating, towards the cliffside, towards where color and song gave way to water and sky. As he drew closer to the cliff the light intensified, but it didn't seem to bother his eyes. If anything, it beckoned him further into its embrace.

Ahead, facing the endless expanse of blue, was a small figure. The sight of the silhouette froze him. Could it be? *Could it be?*

Desire shot through him; he darted forward. The closer he got, the more certain he became and his heart threatened to burst from joy.

He could make out the familiar sandy-colored curls on the figure's small head, and his beloved name was about to leap from Dominick's mouth—but then the boy spoke.

"Wait." His voice was clear and strong.

Dominick, feeling like a passenger in his own body, halted. The chorus of flowers now felt like a supporting ensemble to the solo being roared by the bass of the ocean. The boy, standing with his back towards Dominick, seemed poised to conduct it all.

"I'm not your son," the silhouette said in Vincent's voice. Yet Dominick knew it was the truth. The voice exuded confidence and ease that belied the youthful frame before him. "You can go to him. At some point you must. But not today."

"What?" Disappointment sloshed around within him.

The silhouette before him was suddenly larger; it was no longer the outline of a boy's body, but a man's.

"It would be a waste," the silhouette said in Roger's voice.

He turned, and Dominick could almost see his face. "You know that. You're a fighter."

Dominick noticed movement in his peripheral vision. Two small contorting figures, writhing in pain, were at his feet.

"The voices that have haunted you. The voices of fear and anger," the Roger-like silhouette said. "Silenced. I doubt you will miss them."

They looked like small imps from a forgotten underworld, ashen in the sunlight, whispering obscenities to no one. They wilted before his eyes.

The Roger-like silhouette motioned Dominick closer and turned towards the sea. "Come."

Feeling lighter, Dominick stepped over the writhing imps as they too faded away. He walked alongside the Roger-like figure, and together they approached the infinite expanse. The colors were richer than anything he'd ever beheld. Sun, sky, earth, and water mingled together as if the sole purpose of their creation was to partner for eternity.

Lights danced in the air. Dominick's smile widened; he could feel them. In fact, he *knew* them. They weren't lights at all, but slices of his own life, out there soaring in these magic skies.

He closed his eyes and focused his mind. He felt his awareness, like outstretched arms, extend out to those dancing lights. There, high and to his left, he felt his mother's rich contralto voice; she sang along with Mahalia Jackson from one of those old 45s that had been stuffed in a box under the living room table. He felt Grandma's sweet potato pie out there too—pie he often buried beneath a mountain of whipped cream when the adults weren't looking. Dominick's smile widened. There was Vincent's single-toothed grin as he took his first chubby-legged steps with arms outstretched and tiny fingers splayed to their limit. Oh, the richness! It was as though God had reached down to the sky and painted Dominick his own portrait of joy.

He opened his eyes with a grin. He half expected the Roger-like silhouette to give a speech, if not a full elaborate oration, to explain the bounty dancing before them. But nothing needed to be said. The lights, the colors, the song, the feelings, all surpassed words. So when he turned towards the silhouette, unsurprised to see that it was now a younger version of Mr. Wellington, Dominick didn't say a word.

The Mr. Wellington-like shade offered him a single purple flower. It was a violet; Dominick accepted it in silence. Fragile and beautiful, at its center was a small star that burned with vitality. Understanding, like a lover once lost, embraced him. When he looked back up at the silhouette it was Dominick who smiled.

Dominick turned his gaze to the sea and breathed in the dancing lights of love, the singing flowers, the booming surf, the endless sky. He threw open the doors of his heart and welcomed it all into his being; he continued until he thought he might burst, and then continued for a few moments longer.

Filled beyond capacity, he now stood alone on the magical cliff at the edge of eternity. The shade of many faces had left him. He was given space to claim the moment for himself, he was certain of that. It was time. With a quiet peace that almost surprised him, he turned away from the sea, glanced once more at the violet in his hand, and retraced his steps.

The flowers, ever embracing, rejoiced his return. He felt himself becoming lighter; with each step the world got brighter and his footsteps became more weightless. Within moments he no longer felt among the flowers but above them. He continued, and the separation between himself and the light became more and more difficult to distinguish. He soon lost sight of his hands, his feet, and the singing flowers beneath him. But the smile on his face and determination in his heart lingered. He soon disappeared into brilliance, and the joyous flowers sang on.

\*        \*        \*

It was black again, but his first awareness was of the weight. The heaviness of it was incredible; it felt like steel dumbbells had been hooked into every square inch of his skin and then thrown downward. He felt pulled by his head, by his back, by every inch of his arms and legs, by the tips of his feet. Pulling, pulling, as insistent as starving prisoners clawing from their cages—everything pulled him down.

Tension twitched in his face. The black became gray, then a pallid white, then a blinding mash of colors as his eyes flicked open. His chest, impossibly heavy, heaved in air. He breathed in again, heavily, as if for the first time in ages. Then he had an odd yet amusing recognition: for once he was not awakening on a surface intended for walking.

Instead, he was on a metal table.

Fighting a stiffness that shocked him, he sat upright—and then noticed he was nude. He froze. His mind made a futile attempt at understanding the information his senses now fed him. He now sat naked on what looked like a lab table. Everything around him was fluorescent light and bare sterility.

He had just noticed a tin platter of surgical instruments beside him when the door opened and a man in a white lab coat walked in.

Upon seeing Dominick the man froze.

He was mid-fifties, with a thick salt-and-pepper mustache that quivered as he stared at Dominick with wide eyes. He wore yellow surgical gloves, and one of his gloved hands had yet to part company with the door he'd just opened.

Finally, the quivering mustache and the mouth beneath it produced sound.

"You were dead," the man said.

Dominick heard the man's words and yet could not immediately make sense of them; so he continued to stare at him in silence.

"You were dead," he repeated. "You had no pulse. You weren't breathing. You suffered a catastrophic cranial trauma. You were dead."

Dominick's face remained expressionless, but his mind surged forward. Something—everything—was *different*. He touched his head as if checking for this mysterious catastrophic cranial trauma, but it was a strange ruse. Even as he acted like a man trying to figure out why he was naked on an examining table, he was simultaneously aware of answers beyond explanation.

Like the memories dancing in the sky, he could *feel* the man before him. Beyond the blank stare and quivering mustache was a terrified confusion that would soon send the man sprinting for help. Without knowing how he knew, Dominick accepted this as fact. He also accepted his newest objective: produce a different outcome.

"How long was I out?" Dominick asked.

"You weren't out, you were dead."

"But how long?"

The man stared at him with an empty face. Dominick waited.

"You were DOA four hours ago."

Dominick blinked. *In two days it'll kill you too.* It was Tuesday night; they were right on schedule.

He reflected for a moment. Four hours was plenty of time for word to spread.

"What part of town is this?" Dominick asked.

"Mission Junction. Three miles northeast of downtown."

Dominick didn't smile because he knew it would invite questions, even arouse suspicion. So instead of outwardly rejoicing this information and the opportunity it provided, he simply nodded.

"What's your name?" Dominick asked him. The man still hadn't moved from the doorway, nor had his gloved hand come off the door. His eyes looked mesmerized. "You probably already know mine," Dominick smirked.

The lip beneath the mustache relaxed—marginally.

"Brian. Brian Calden. I'm a medical examiner."

Dominick smiled thinly and donned a "pleasant-but-focused" expression.

"Mr. Calden, something extraordinary has happened. I can't explain it, much less do justice to what I just experienced. If you'd like to hear it, I'd be happy to have coffee with you and share it." The mustache quivered and the man blinked, but the slightest of nods followed. "But right now I need your help."

It was still a moment before the mustache stopped quivering. But when Brian Calden, medical examiner, finally took his hand off the open door and entered the room,

Dominick knew he'd succeeded.

*　　　　　　　*　　　　　　　*

# Tuesday Night

Twenty minutes later Dominick was in a cab—a relative rarity in Los Angeles, and since the advent of ride-sharing they were nearly extinct altogether.

Nonetheless, he was in his second cab of the day. His once-favorite Canali suit had been reduced to shreds and then cut from his body in preparation for his autopsy. Luckily for him, fortune had intervened; Brian Calden kept a fresh set of clothing to change into when examining corpses was a particularly smelly affair. They were ill-fitting on Dominick, but they would do for the evening. Dominick's keys and wallet had been in his pocket and thus had escaped obliteration when his house exploded; his phone had not been so lucky.

He doubted he'd need it for the night's endgame. With the proper resolve and commitment, all things would fall into place.

"I'm an atheist," his cab driver was telling him. His English had the unmistakable sing-songy cadence of Mexican Spanish. "I read a lot on secular humanism. But I also believe that beings from outside of Earth are responsible for life here. So every night I study the stars."

Dominick, amused, allowed him to speak. Why not? Of

all the cabbies he could get after being dead for four hours, was it not perfect that he'd get a chatty atheist who subscribed to the "Life by Aliens" creation theory?

The cabbie explained his nightly skyward meditations, and Dominick recalled how everything had felt so clear in the field of singing flowers. The dank smell of the cab and the feel of the cheap seat beneath him felt less "real" than the memory of that endless field of color and song. He wondered how his story would fit into the cabbie's cosmology.

"Here we go." The cabbie said as he parked in front of the Short Stop bar. Dominick paid him and then offered his hand.

"Thanks for the ride," Dominick said as they shook. "You're on the right track with the stars. There's more out there than we can possibly imagine."

The cabbie grinned, and Dominick felt the man's glee at his beliefs being affirmed. Dominick himself smiled as he remembered the singing flowers and got out of the cab.

By bar standards, it was a slow night. Given that it was Tuesday and the Dodgers weren't playing in their stadium a half-mile away, only the die-hards were likely in attendance. A chunky bouncer in black stood just outside the doorway, a young couple smoked nearby, and a chopper-style motorcycle was parked on the sidewalk. Nothing of particular interest met his eye, and there was no outward indication that Dominick was correct about coming to this particular bar at this particular time. But his easy confidence remained.

Out of place in his ill-fitting clothes, Dominick gave his ID to the towering bouncer and entered.

Two steps into the bar Dominick saw he was right. Why wouldn't he be? Of all the places to be taken to after dying, he was taken to a coroner's office bare minutes from the place that would contain the one person he needed to see most urgently under these incredible circumstances.

A man sat alone at the end of the bar, and Dominick joined him. Dominick gestured to the three empty beer bottles nearby.

"Four-dollar beer? That's all my memory's worth?" Dominick said.

Terrance leaped off of his stool with a panicked cry. He gaped at Dominick and stared in mute horror.

It was almost like watching a long-running sitcom; Dominick knew what glib lines were to follow—some joke around not punching Terrance for his betrayal, as it were—and he knew they'd have the effect of acknowledging Terrance's crime and absolving him of it in neat and clever fashion. Their sitcom was nothing if not crisply-written.

The sight of Terrance's stunned, transfixed face, full of shock and fear and grief and guilt, told Dominick that their old show had been canceled. The witty one-liners and familiar storylines had no place in the brave new world of his rebirth.

So when Terrance, eyes wide, slapped himself, Dominick wasn't surprised. He didn't roll his eyes or make a teasing joke intended to reassure Terrance of his sanity. Instead, Dominick gave his friend a small smile and the barest hint of a shrug.

"I know." He motioned for Terrance to sit.

Terrance, moving like a man haunted, came forward with hands outstretched; when he touched Dominick's shoulders he gasped as if the solid flesh was more shocking than whatever he'd expected. Terrance then grabbed Dominick's face, as if needing skin-to-skin affirmation. Moments later Terrance withdrew his hands looked at him again with new eyes.

Then he burst into tears.

His shaking head fell onto Dominick's shoulder with a thud. Dominick hugged him. Between the sobs Dominick could make out something approximating "I'm sorry."

"Hey, hey," Dominick said. "I know. Just think of it like a miracle."

"I ID'ed you! I ID'ed your body! You were..."

"Yeah."

"I saw you! I *saw* you! You were, I mean, you were—"

"Yeah," Dominick said again. "I know." Dominick paused, and let his silence be filled with throbbing house music and the cathartic sobbing of his friend. "But I wasn't really...I didn't go..."

He trailed off and let Terrance cry a few moments longer. When he spoke it was with a rueful smile.

"I didn't go to where Vincent is," Dominick finished. "Not all the way."

Terrance, his face overwrought with emotion, again stared at Dominick like a man unwilling to believe his sanity. Dominick placed both hands on his best friend's shoulders.

"Listen," Dominick continued. "There's a lot going on. I still don't understand all of it. But I need your help to finish it."

"My help?" Terrance was aghast. "Negro, you just rose from the dead! The fuck kind of help you need from me?"

Dominick smiled in spite of himself.

"That wasn't me. If it had been up to me I probably would have run to my boy as fast as I could." He felt the prick of disappointment, but also the relief of admitting the truth. "I need your car and your phone. For the night. And I need you to let me stay dead for now."

He held out his hand. Terrance stared at him with a blank,

disbelieving face.

"Like you'll be using them tonight anyway," Dominick groaned. "You're drunk."

Terrance handed over his car keys and phone with a grimace.

"I mean, what the fuck, man?"

*What the fuck indeed,* Dominick thought.

There was no time to explain, of course; not that Terrance would believe it. Dominick didn't believe his own life, so he wouldn't expect anyone else to do so either. He opened his mouth to promise answers later anyway when something entered his mind that stole his thoughts away.

"Oh god," Dominick blurted out. Concerned, Terrance looked at him. "Do you remember me talking about Sherrill McKinnen? White girl, red hair?"

"What are you talking ab—"

"Sherrill McKinnen. She was in elementary school with me. Took Carlos Bautista's pencil box and blamed it on a kindergartener. I had a whole thing with her stepfather in front of her house when we were kids, remember?"

"Why the hell would I remember—"

Dominick waved it off.

"Then just go with this next part." He looked towards the door.

On cue, the slender redhead in an off-the-shoulder top and snug designer jeans entered the bar. Without a pause, she turned in their direction and came their way.

Terrance turned in time to see Sherrill McKinnen fling her fiery mane aside and assume the seat next to Dominick.

"You can't possibly have ID," Dominick said. She cocked her head playfully but didn't reply.

"Who is this? Who are you?" Terrance's Cop Voice was greatly diminished. *Bless him for trying*, Dominick thought.

"This is Sherrill McKinnen. Who's not really Sherrill McKinnen. It's complicated." Dominick turned to her. "He's already drunk and in shock, so how are you not making things worse?"

"Necessary risk." Her voice was as intoxicating as angel-song. "May we speak for a moment?"

Without waiting for an answer she slid off the stool and strutted across the bar floor.

"Hang tight for a second," Dominick said. "And drink some water."

"That doesn't help—" Terrance was drowned out by the music as Dominick moved to catch up with her. She walked to a far corner before turning to face him.

"We need his help," she said. A furrowed brow was Dominick's response. "This is the end, and someone gets to make certain Sherrill McKinnen returns to her loved ones."

Dominick blinked. For all his new-found knowledge and insight, he hadn't considered that.

He also recognized the implications of her words. He remembered Mr. Wellington walking among the chorus of flowers and then fading into the light. It brought a spike of emotion into his throat.

"So it's true." He wasn't asking. "They're both..."

"Gone."

He swallowed the finality of that. Sherrill McKinnen, eyes patient, allowed him.

"And you can't get her home either," he said. "Because you're not really..."

"Exactly."

"Who are you?"

She smiled. It was brilliant.

"Have we not tried that conversation already?"

"Can't you just tell me without the dancing and the levitating and the—"

She put a finger to his lips.

"What matters are the choices we make," she cooed. "I chose to see this through. It is now time for you to choose the same. If you dare." He answered with a hard smile that almost surprised him. Her eyes softened. "You are everything I'd hoped you'd be."

Her voice, clear and lyrical, cut through the loud music and pierced him. He might miss Sherrill McKinnen.

"I should warn you." Her eyes, two icy halos, were dazzling. "The next time you die will be the last time you die."

Again he let his eyes do the talking. She responded with a sigh, and then put a cool hand on his cheek.

"Help me understand one other thing," he said. She donned an expression that was at once both playful and patronizing. He ignored it. "What's in this for you?"

"Ah."

With a mischievous smirk, she edged closer to him. Not for the first time, her beauty struck him as preternatural. He suddenly felt less supernaturally knowledgeable and more predictably male.

"I'm serious," he persisted. "The gorgeous fairy godmother thing is a nice act and all..."

She was almost upon him, nodding with fake understanding, even as she draped her arms around his neck.

"...but I know this isn't charity, so what—"

She kissed him—and the world disappeared.

Exhilaration washed over him like a tsunami; it wiped clear his thoughts. He knew only the softness of her lips, the eventual dance of their tongues, and the sensation of his fingertips gliding down her back like rainfall.

Yet somewhere, buried beneath the sensuality and sweetness, was a whisper of a covenant that transcended time, space, even mortality itself.

In a flash he saw them: the stag in the road with its majestic horns, the impossibly large snake atop Lawrence's desk, the fearsome hawk who had tried to save his life. He saw each of them, and yet he saw beyond them; he glimpsed into their essence, into their world. He saw courage, pain, turmoil, desperation, hope. He saw a war that spanned a generation; he saw greed and bloodshed. He saw the determination of the brave; he saw the grim resolve of those standing firm in the face of possible destruction.

There, in the carnage, as a tie between two realities, was a blood contract. Silent as granite, it was a pact outside of time. It said nothing, yet it meant everything.

Like a tale lovingly told, Sherrill McKinnen drew the kiss to a close. When she withdrew her lips from his and backed away, it was with a sly yet loving smile.

Yes, he would miss her.

"Go in peace, Dominick Osiris Reinhart."

Her eyes fell closed and her body listed off to the right; Dominick reached out and caught her arm. Impossibly, the tautness he'd felt in her figure seconds ago was already gone; her arm, while still slender, was now pliant to the touch.

"What? Who are..." she slurred in a raspy voice. Her eyes, now a muddy brown, looked confused. She closed her eyes again and wilted, and Dominick had to hold her upright even as he motioned to Terrance to join them. By the time Terrance made it over she was unconscious.

"Have them call you a cab and get her to your place." Dominick handed her to Terrance. "She'll be out for a while. And when she wakes she won't remember anything from before."

He knew this without a doubt. Even before the kiss he'd felt like a sponge of fresh insights and impossible awarenesses; that feeling had already accelerated.

Dominick continued. "Her name is Sherrill McKinnen. Contact DPD back home about her. She's a missing person."

Terrance took her limp figure in his arms, but upon looking at her face he nearly dropped her. Already she was a different person; there was more weight in her face, and she looked haggard, worn.

He stared at Dominick with wide eyes. Dominick knew that no explanation would satisfy.

"Go home and take her with you," he repeated. Again, he got an eventual nod.

This was it. This bizarre moment, in a dark, loud bar in the shadow of downtown Los Angeles, was likely the last time he'd see his imperfect best friend.

He was touched with gratitude for almost four decades of friendship. There was anger as well, and with it was righteousness and disappointment. His emotions were a jigsaw puzzle of shocking intricacy. What could he say?

Dominick put his hands on Terrance's shoulders and tried to soften his face with a smile.

"Get some rest."

Terrance, who still stared at him with eyes ragged from the last four hours of grief, confusion, and guilt, managed another nod.

Dominick lingered. He could almost hear Dai quoting Brutus and Cassius as they exchanged their last goodbyes. With a supportive squeeze, he released Terrance and looked at Sherrill McKinnen one last time. Her face, luminous minutes ago, was now pallid and wan. His gorgeous fairy godmother was gone; he was on his own.

Or was he? He looked at Terrance.

"Where did you park?"

*        *        *

The world had transformed before his eyes. Darting through Echo Park and merging onto the 110 south, he noticed that the downtown towers looming overhead now had shapes and colors emanating from them. He blew by them in an instant, but like lonely spirits they whispered to him as he passed.

"...so excited..."

"...fucking bullshit.."

"...please, oh please just..."

Their words—sad, lonely, hopeful, scared—echoed behind him as he barreled down the freeway; it was like passing through a mist that had something to say.

*Welcome to my new life,* he thought.

He headed west onto the 10-freeway where he received his next surprise. As with Brian Calden (medical examiner), he could feel the drivers around him. In a silver Subaru ahead of him a distressed young woman was in mid-text argument with someone close to her heart; in a tan Camry, two cars back, a man was in silent terror about a recent diagnosis; in a silver Lexus, to his right, an exhausted man contemplated suicide.

*You should close your eyes now.*

Dominick squinted his eyes against the memory and focused on the road. True, the perplexing voices that haunted him at his journey's beginning had been silenced by the field of singing flowers. But what had replaced them in his second life was far more distracting—or perhaps worse.

"Enough to drive a dead man crazy." He was now convinced that most people with sight beyond the five senses ended up on heavy medication—prescription or otherwise.

All the more appropriate, then, that his current destination housed an exception. For all the uncertainties that lie ahead this night, the next sequence of events held no mystery. He knew there would be a parking space out front; he knew that his keys had survived his death experience so that he could use them this final time; he knew that as he entered her yard he'd see her on the porch. That she leaped to her feet upon seeing him with her mouth a small circle of shock was also expected.

"I knew you wouldn't change the locks," he said.

Like Terrance, Dai gasped. It appeared that visual information alone wasn't sufficient proof that the dead had risen. Secondary input—in this case a smart-assed comment—seemed required.

She crossed herself. Given that she called herself a recovering Catholic he took that as an involuntary action and further proof of her shock.

"You didn't feel me coming this time." He mounted the porch and stood in front of her. Eyes moist, she shook her head. "I'm having the opposite experience. I'm feeling, seeing, hearing everything. It's like the whole city's talking to me." He tried to smile, but even Reincarnated Dominick had difficulty being anything but honest in her presence. In truth, he was frightened by the increasing amount of information that life was hell-bent on giving him.

He saw the dam of her doubt giving way. Unlike the others, he had no sense from her directly. He found the silence around her reassuring.

Like Terrance, she raised a hand as if to lay a finger on his face. Amused, he grabbed her hand and lay it on his cheek. She exhaled and began to both laugh and cry as she buried her head into his chest.

A lifetime had passed since he'd last held her and stroked her hair. He wished it was under better circumstances; as with Terrance, odds were strong they wouldn't be meeting again.

*Focus,* he told himself.

"I don't have much time," he told her. "But I need your help."

She held him a moment longer, then withdrew and studied his face. Something inside him, unseen and silent, stirred around under her scrutiny.

"Walk with me," she said.

She took his arm and they left the porch and headed towards the street. Upon reaching the sidewalk his feet turned west—towards the beach.

"It's all over you," she said as they strolled into the Venice night.

"What?"

"The other side. The darkness and the light, and their fighting. And death. It's dripping off you."

Somehow, this wasn't surprising.

"What about all the things I'm seeing and hearing? Is this what you psychic types normally walk around with?"

"You're between worlds and you've tasted death. There's nothing normal in that."

A wave of emotion surged through him—so strong was it that he fought the sting of tears. He felt the pieces come together with almost mechanical precision, and the picture revealing itself was worse than he'd feared.

"The board," he said. "With me and Mr. Wellington out of the way, they're going to target Antoinette. And Violet. Beneficiaries of our stakes in the company." He ground his teeth in frustration. How had he not realized this before? "I'll warn Antoinette. But I need you to find Violet. Help her."

Dai stopped. She turned to him and ran her hand through her hair. She only did that in times of great stress.

"If you don't end this tonight, it won't matter. They'll never be safe." Her eyes were hard, despairing things. "And that's not the worst of it."

He looked at the black sky and breathed down his quickening heart-rate. How many times had that happened over the last two days?

Again she took his arm and they continued. The sound of the surf amplified with each step.

He kept silent as they approached the black expanse of the Pacific. They crossed the boardwalk in deliberate steps and came to a halt where the concrete walkway gave way to ancient sand. A homeless man—Jeremy Woods, Dominick somehow knew—quivered on the concrete nearby as he relived his platoon taking fire in an ambush outside of Kabul.

"Tell me the worst," Dominick finally said. They gazed into the darkness together for several moments.

"I can't see it." Her voice cracked. "But you can. It's a part of you now."

He should have been frustrated with her Delphian non-answer. But what he felt was growing apprehension in his stomach; he'd lost the luxury of impatience.

They stood side by side and faced the darkness; the mighty pacific tossed about like a restless beast. Dominick realized two things simultaneously.

One, he was losing sense of himself in the swirl of feelings and awarenesses that bombarded him like the RPGs that haunted the nearby Corporal Jeremy Woods, USMC; Dominick was aware of his own consciousness, but the line between himself and the tumult around him grew thinner by the moment.

Two, Dai was right. Buried within the cacophony was crucial information. Deadly information. It was in the darkness, unseen now but heading his way like the harbingers of the apocalypse. Like those four ghastly riders, the truth was dangerous, wicked, and his first impulse was to turn and sprint in the opposite direction. He took a frightened step backward, and then she spoke again.

"Say it out loud." Her voice serene, she faced the ocean. "Don't keep it inside. It's not personal. It's not you. It doesn't have to be you."

Her last line didn't make sense, but it echoed in his head nonetheless.

*It doesn't have to be you.*

His retreating foot came forward.

*It doesn't have to be you.*

The black ocean thrashed against the shore; the sand, relentless, beat it back. Jeremy's whimpers drifted into

Dominick's ears like frightened prayers unheard.

*It doesn't have to be you.*

No, it didn't. It didn't have to be him, not the *real* him. He didn't have to face the dire truth galloping towards him as if hell burned close behind it. He could pass that responsibility to another part of himself. He had someone close by indeed who was calloused and more acclimated to the dangers of life.

This someone once grew tired of tasting his own blood and learned to give as well as he got; at seventeen this someone stared down the double barrels of a sawed-off shotgun and considered throwing a punch over giving up his coat; this someone stood his ground and fought six others in a hopelessly bloody fistfight rather than run.

This was the someone he'd tried to leave on the violent streets of his youth, but who'd lingered inside his head all these years. Once, when set free by alcohol, this someone shocked Antoinette by taking her from behind, grabbing her hair, and demanding she scream his name like she meant it. This someone recently tried to punch a member of the board of directors.

The someone he usually dismissed as his Detroit Ghetto Boy might be useful after all.

Dominick smiled without knowing it. It was easy; it was like passing a microphone. *Okay*, he thought. *Just this once.*

Within moments the words slipped from his lips without interruption.

"The board," he said. "They're feeling themselves. They got me, they got Mr. Wellington, they got Leftwich. They think they're running shit. But they're nothing. They're pawns. They're just too stupid to realize it." He smiled. He was afraid, sure. But fuck backing down. "It's the other side.

The darkness. They have the power. And they're going to fuck us all. Sherrill McKinnen, all her people, you, me, the company, this whole planet. They'll kill us all and have a damn good time doing it."

His teeth remained in the snarl that his Detroit Ghetto Boy favored. But Dominick felt that his alter ego had done his job. He started to relax his face and ease himself back into the spotlight; it was his turn to re-assume the microphone.

"Wait." Dai sounded far away. "There's something else." The fear in her voice caused him to pause inside himself. "Something's there. Don't let them hide it from you."

Dominick was halfway between himself and his other self when he was struck by the hint of something terrible. Both halves of him had separate reactions, but even that schism of consciousness was eclipsed by the enormity of the whispered secret.

"The fuck?" he heard himself say.

"No. Can't be." Dominick moaned.

Horrifying. Unspeakable.

"The *fuck?*" he heard himself say again.

"No, God no."

*Get him in line. Have you not lost enough already?*

A stream of denials couldn't change his dawning realization: that line wasn't from a drunken dream. That was a glimpse into the secret past.

That was a statement made by Higgins and directed to Mr. Wellington—about Dominick. About the darkness.

And about Vincent.

*Find my granddaughter, tell her I'm sorry. Vincent was my fault.*

It was sickening, appalling, heartbreaking—but it was

true.

"Motherfucker," he heard himself say.

"No. It was an accident, a terrible, terrible—"

Dominick lost his words as the world disappeared. The beach, the ocean, the sand, Dai all vanished; he saw only a swirl of darkness as he spun downwards. Down, down, down he descended into a pit of pain that set fire to his soul.

He fell at an impossible pace. It was his version of the drug-induced journey spoken of by the Kelleys to Antoinette; except his discovery was of the horrors of hell. Scenes, like vignettes, spiraled past him on his way down. Taken together, they told the nightmare of his life and added a brutal twist.

He saw the riverside bench in the Netherlands where Higgins and Mr. Wellington once sat bathed by the blood-red setting sun; those ancient windmills bore witness to the warning Higgins delivered that day: *get him in line. Haven't you lost enough already?*

He spiraled further into the past. Dominick saw the sun again, high and bright, as it burned down on Redwood National Park that fateful, wretched day his sweet-faced boy was rushed to the hospital. He saw the hospital room, bright with indifferent fluorescent white light, where his young prince slipped from his grasp forever.

Dominick screamed even as he wept.

His dark descent ended with a sudden, violent, painful collision with the truth.

*Vincent was my fault;* Mr. Wellington's final declaration was an accurate confession.

The realization wasn't a whisper, it wasn't a feeling, and yet it was both.

"They killed my boy." Dominick's mouth was dry as

Saharan sand.

*Vincent was my fault.*

"THEY FUCKING KILLED MY BOY!"

Rage, deep as the cosmos, exploded inside of him. It went everywhere, it went nowhere. Fury propelled him deeper into the dark truth; he spiraled further. How could he fail to protect the life of his beautiful little boy? How could he fail this most basic father's responsibility? His mind tore apart as the rage and the regret careened in separate directions.

Then—he saw movement! Something like smoke, there but not, flitted away from him. Rage, having found a target, ignited him. He shot after it.

Unaware of how he was moving or even of where he was, he chased it with a fury that grew hotter with each impossible stride. Or was he flying?

He didn't know or care.

He barreled through a maze of living, moving darkness. Unseen claws tore at him and voices shrieked in his ears, but he ignored it all. His remaining shred of sanity begged for a pause of the madness, begged for him to wake up, begged for this nightmare to end.

But he heard nothing, felt nothing, saw nothing—other than the fleeing dark sprite just beyond his grasp.

He felt its fear, and even that fed his rage. It had been right there, hiding, even as he'd re-visited that cold, indifferent hospital room. It had been hiding in the truth that he was never supposed to see. It had been hiding in the greatest pain of his life—that shady little *motherfucker...*

A surge of anger and a moment's hesitation by his prey brought the chase to an abrupt end. Dominick—or some shade of him existing in the dark maze—slammed into the creature at full speed. It shrieked.

Dominick's blood rage became battle rage. Pain shot through him as the beast fought back, but the harder it fought the more infuriated Dominick became. Thrashing and screaming, they tumbled until Dominick felt it wriggling in his hands. Pain cascaded across his face as he squeezed with all his strength. A cry ushered forth from everywhere—from within him, from the beast in his hands, from the contorting maze around him.

The symphony of screaming was pierced by a calm, steady, familiar voice.

"It's simple," the unhurried voice said. "But extraordinary. An exchange, as with all commerce. They get what they want, we get what we want. We can do virtually anything we want with them behind us. They keep us invisible to scrutiny, immune to prosecution. And they arrange accidents for those in our way. Permanent accidents."

With an ear-splitting cry, the unseen beast collapsed in Dominick's hands. The world shattered in an explosion of darkness.

Silent stillness reigned.

Then, like refugees returning to a devastated homeland, sensations emerged from the darkness.

First came a smell; it was a pungent scent of spiced incense, thick as the darkness itself. The air felt hot, wet. Then came sounds; heavy, irregular breathing, punctuated by grunts, and a rhythmic wet click of saliva keeping time in an obscene melody.

Then, as if by magic, the lighting director raised the house lights and the unholy scene came into view. There was Wallace Purdie, nude, with his swollen whale-like body lying atop a massage table. The dark head of a far-too-young brown girl bobbed at his groin. Atop a second massage table lie Higgins, face down, as a shirtless Asian boy of twelve slathered oil onto his back. The opulence of the room—a gilded feat of golden light and polished surfaces—stood in mute contrast with the scene it hosted.

"Our weak link is weakening further," Higgins said. "And I fear his affirmative action protege may never come on board."

Wallace grunted.

"Indonesian talent, my god," Wallace Purdie sighed. "Let him learn the hard way."

"I thought similarly, but we still need him."

"Maybe a warning shot," Wallace Purdie offered. "Sambo's got two kids, conveniently related to the weak link. Say our friends go after one of them. Might break Sambo, solve two problems. He quits, we get somebody more aligned. I like Miller." Wallace spasmed as a deep moan escaped him.

"Yes," Higgins said in a slow hiss. "They'll need to be marked. At least one of them."

"Daughter has a birthday party coming up. Janice and I will be there. I'll mark the boy. His little girl's quite a number, hate to waste that." Wallace spasmed again. "That's really good, hon."

The scene darkened as the recessed golden light faded, and with it went Dominick's strength.

He was swept along in a stream of sorrow. The metaphorical became one with the literal; he tasted the sorrow around him as it mixed with his own. The stream, possessing its own agenda, took him along a route of its choosing.

The stream of sorrow flowed to a crumbling village in Colombia where industrial waste poisons the air, soil, water, and people; it flowed to ancient communities in Somalia

Cedi Ali Rajah

shattered by tribal warfare fought with modern firearms. It flowed through the silent pain of an Albanian girl trafficked into the international sex trade; it flowed through a mother in the Philippines whose teenage daughter was killed in the streets by a state-sanctioned death squad.

And there, drinking deep of the misery—at every assault, rape, murder—was the darkness.

"The price is blood." The measured, laconic voice of Higgins was clear. "But it doesn't have to be yours or mine. They don't care who bleeds. So like any good vendor, we provide a medium by which the customer is connected with the product they desire."

Vincent, his vibrant, beautiful Vincent, tripped while they'd been hiking amongst the Redwoods. Kids by the millions fell every day. But Vincent hit his head against a nearby tree, and while the blow was a glancing one, it nonetheless created a blood clot in his brain that stole his life away. What happened to Vincent was a tragic, awful, ill-fated accident.

Except for a little invisible push.

"If you fail to honor your sworn agreement," Higgins lectured Mr. Wellington, "the proverbial chickens will come home to roost. I doubt that you want that. I doubt that your family wants that."

Witnessing this, Dominick had no words. Even his blood rage had seeped away. All that remained was him and the truth, united at last. They were like old friends brought together by the death of a loved one.

In this case, Vincent's.

"Dominick!"

The ocean roared. Dominick didn't hear it. His ears, his heart, were too full of the truth.

299

"Dominick! Can you hear me?"

The truth and the sea, adversaries for his fractured attention, battled one another. Dominick and his Detroit Ghetto Boy stood within each other and gaped in silence. What else could they do in the face of the bald, uncaring truth?

"Dominick!"

Eyes—yet another set of them—opened. The haze of the physical world came into focus. His first recognizable sight was that of the round, frightened face of Dai hanging overhead.

"Dios, dios," she gushed as she held his face in her hands. He was on the sand, face-up. The sound of the sea was loud and wild.

He wanted to scream. He wanted to melt into the earth. He wanted to cry.

But all he could do was bring two sand-encrusted hands to his aching face.

\*                    \*                    \*

# CHAPTER THIRTEEN

## Tuesday Night

Dominick settled behind the wheel of Terrance's Challenger. The car's color struck him as oddly appropriate: black, the color ascribed to the many facets of death. When a man dies, black is the hearse that carries him to his resting place; black is worn by those gathered to grieve him; black is wrapped around that most grim of reapers who, with scythe in hand, collects the dead man's soul and ferries him into eternity.

Ironically, it is also the color used to describe his race...and the color of the darkness that he'd unknowingly served the last twenty years of his life.

Black was also a convenient color within which to hide the truth.

"If you let the rage take you, they will win," Dai had said.

He could feel her as clearly as the ill-fitting shirt on his back. She was on her couch, seated before an array of candles, channeling strength and clarity his way. He could hear the staccato Spanish of her near-constant prayer to the *Orisha* for his protection.

She would hold the light for him, she said. He didn't know what that meant, but it sounded like an excellent idea.

With a throaty V-8 engine roar he headed west, towards the beach. He would take his borrowed chariot-of-death up the scenic Pacific Coast Highway (alongside the black ocean, as it were), connect to the 10 East, and then the 405 North. From there he'd head to his final destination—no hearse required.

"Anger, hatred, violence. That's their lifeblood." Her bottomless eyes, flickering in the candlelight, had danced with concern. "You give them that and they'll destroy you."

"They can't manipulate me. I'm my own man."

In truth, her admonition was a wise one. Given what he'd learned, only the sweetness of her support stood between him and blinding fury that made Godzilla Mode look like a hissy fit.

Nonetheless, that would have to wait. This night held a specific window of opportunity—he could feel it as clearly as he could his own beating heart—and if he wasted time in righteous fury that window could close forever. So while he would have loved hours to digest what he'd experienced at the beach, there wasn't time. He and Dai had only the short walk back to the car to plan, and then it was time to go.

These few minutes in the car was therefore critical. How well he prepared would determine the future of their multi-billion dollar empire, the fate of thousands of exploited employees, the outcome of his life, the existence of Sherrill McKinnen and those on the other side fighting the darkness, and the safety of those he loved—roughly in that order.

"No pressure."

He headed north on PCH and glanced at the car's in-dash clock. He had about twenty-five minutes.

He called Antoinette first. It went straight to voicemail.

"It's me." He kept his voice steady and clear. "No, this isn't a prank. There's no answer I can give on a voicemail that's going to explain what's happened. There's certainly nothing I can say that's going to do justice to nineteen years of marriage. But I can say this: I do love you. And I thank you for giving me two beautiful children. I wish things had gone differently for us and our family. And I'm sorry for my part in that. But that doesn't take away from the pieces that have made my life worth living."

He paused and considered what more to add. A glance at the clock convinced him to instead tap the phone's red circle and end the call.

He then typed in Violet's number and initiated his next call.

But with surprise he saw her phone number was already in Terrance's contacts under the name "Maureen."

"Why are you calling me?" Violet's voice, emotional, screamed into his ear.

Time slowed. Assumptions, theories, and possibilities flooded into his awareness, and most of them quickened his pulse. But he refused to abandon his calm.

"Pumpkin, it's me." Dumbstruck silence was his reply. "I don't know why your number is in Terrance's phone under a different name. But that's not what matters right now. What matters is—"

"Dad?"

"Yes."

"I heard you were, I thought you were..."

"I was. And then I wasn't. But that's not important right now either." The patter of his heart insisted otherwise, but he wouldn't let adrenaline run this conversation. "I don't have much time. But your grandfather, I want to tell you what he said. He wanted me to tell you that he was sorry. He was sorry he didn't protect you and your brother. Like I'm sorry. I wish I could change everything. I can't. But I still love you to pieces."

A pause, and then sob was her reply. Emotions, powerful as the ocean outside his window, swirled in his chest.

"Uncle Terrance found me six months ago," she said through tears. "He said you were worried sick about me. I made him promise to not tell you yet. But he's been super supportive. I'm sorting some things out, and Uncle Terrance has been looking out for me and my boyfriend."

His poppa bear instinct perked up at the mention of a boyfriend, but then he heard a sound that erased all other thoughts.

In the background a newborn baby cried out.

"I'm sorry Dad, I need to go. Call me later. I love you."

The phone beeped as she ended the call, but the baby's cry continued to echo in Dominick's mind. Could it be?

The possibility, like a fresh match, struck an impromptu blaze inside of him. A grandchild? That would mean that his little pumpkin was now a teenage mother, on her own, without any of the assistance of the fortune that he'd worked his entire life to create for his loved ones.

It would mean there was an invaluable little soul out there that was a piece of him, a piece of Antoinette, a piece of Violet—vulnerable and dependent.

But most of all it would mean that the baby, like he and Mr. Wellington's other close blood relatives, was in danger.

*Sambo's got two kids, conveniently related to the weak link. Say our friends go after one of them. Might break Sambo, solve two problems.*

Dominick's eyes narrowed at the memory. Yes, such men would have no difficulty murdering an infant. To them it would be cleaning up loose ends; wouldn't want any pesky beneficiaries impeding their plans. And what plans they were—sowing seeds of discord across an entire planet! Such a task required focus. That it also empowered a savage dark army was secondary.

He merged onto the 10 Eastbound and drove faster. He again felt the drivers around him—someone was excited about a party, someone else was tired from work, another was concerned about a news radio story, and yet another was intoxicated. How many more people were in this city? How many people inhabited cities across the globe where the company had offices, holdings, interests, influence? How many human lives were impacted daily by company activities? Market research had the number in the tens of millions. They spanned all ages, genders, ethnic groups, and ideologies; they pursued their hopes and dreams, tended to their families, enjoyed their friends and their hobbies and their personal pursuits. They lived out their lives, all the while oblivious of unseen malicious forces directing them as might a puppeteer.

*The company is a liar and a killer.*

Arthur Wellington knew that first hand; he protected Dominick from that knowledge, shielded his naivete, and allowed him to believe the company's sanctimonious stance of service and excellence. As a result, Dominick served his entire career as an unwitting accomplice to the innumerable crimes the company committed around the world.

Included on that list was the murder of his own son.

*'What is' is the grandest lie of all creation. It is the greatest shame of my life.*

"You goddamn sons of bitches."

There was Dai again, in his mind. He could feel her concern for him rising; he was broadcasting strongly now, so she could feel his mounting ire.

*I'll keep it together,* he told her with his mind. Rather than hear the words verbatim, she more felt their meaning and the energy behind them. Lying on this particular line, therefore, was impossible; he should be thankful the board hadn't put a telepath on retainer.

Under other circumstances, he would have been amused. Two nights ago Mr. Wellington complained about Dominick's lack of "faith in things unseen." How things had changed. Dominick's grasp of the unseen had grown exponentially, thanks in large part to his own recent and unfortunate passing.

"I didn't just die, I was murdered," he told the Challenger. "They put a bomb in my Bentley and blew up my house. Details."

He was snarling. He commanded his face to relax because Dai was right—everything was at stake so a cooler head had to prevail. As much as he wanted to brutalize all of them, he couldn't lose his temper.

At least not on accident.

He took the exit for the 405 North and accelerated onto the sweeping curve of the merging ramp. From here it would be a short blast to Mulholland drive, and then to the gated luxury community of a similar name.

Then, come hell or high-water, he would end this.

There he was, a black man in a black car under a blackened

sky delivering death to an unholy contract with dark forces he'd unknowingly served his entire career. Plain to him again was the horror of this reality. Plain to him again was the danger to the countless lives hanging in the balance—and the outrage over the lives already lost.

"Vincent."

He banged on the steering wheel once, then twice. He stopped himself before the third strike and again commanded his face to relax. Jaw still tight, he depressed the gas pedal further and the speedometer inched past 85 mph.

*       *       *

Minutes later he pulled up to the security office for the luxury residential community the Mulholland Estates. He rolled down the window as the security man came over.

"Dominick Reinhart for Gerald Higgins, 14015 Aubrey Road," Dominick said in a clear, firm voice. The security man's name was Trent, Dominick realized. "He's not expecting me."

Trent-the-guard nodded, oblivious to the depth of Dominick's understatement, and returned to the security office. Dominick stared forward at the arched gate that helped keep the residents of the community safe from the outside world. The gate was a barred one, so it afforded a clear line of sight to the spectacular views that lay beyond. In some circles exclusivity was sweeter when outsiders could see but not touch.

Dominick closed his eyes and stretched his awareness forward. They were getting the call now. He could feel their initial reactions—disbelief, confusion, apprehension. He thought these were appropriate states of being when a man you murdered earlier that day checks in at your front gate and requests entry.

Trent-the-guard returned and Dominick took out his wallet.

"ID please?"

Dominick handed it to him. The man looked at it, then at Dominick, then to the picture, then back to Dominick. Dominick faced him, affording him the best view.

Taking his ID with him, the man again disappeared into the office. Moments later Dominick sensed their panic spike. He imagined them as roaches on a mad scramble after being caught unprepared by a kitchen light.

Dry minutes passed. Then Trent-the-guard reappeared with his ID and a sheet of paper—Dominick's parking pass.

"Keep this on your dashboard. Do you know where you're going?"

"I do."

"Have a great evening."

The gate swung wide and Dominick drove in.

*The name of the guard at the front gate is Trent Garrickson,* he shot out to Dai. *Address him by name if it comes to Plan B.*

He felt her understanding, even as she continued to pray. But he also noticed that her concern for him had risen. After eight months of silence between them, she still held him in her heart. Regret touched him. If only there was a way to do right by her; as Antoinette had said, Dai was a good soul.

But that ship had sailed. They had their one forbidden night, and now he had the virtue of her assistance if things went sideways. When tonight's dust settled, perhaps she would find another man worthy of her fierce brand of love.

He drove down the winding hill towards Higgins' mansion. Many of the homes in the community were situated to not obstruct another's tantalizing view; Higgins' was no exception. It was near the end of a long, winding street, the entire length of which commanded a view of the sprawling San Fernando Valley.

Wallace's giant S-Class Mercedes, the same bird of prey he'd parked outside Swingers, was now perched outside Higgins' home. Wallace's presence here had motivated Dominick's urgency in coming. Confronting them simultaneously was somehow the key to everything.

*I'm heading in,* he sent out to Dai. His mouth tightened and he said a single word.

"Vincent."

He whipped the wheel and jerked the car halfway into Higgins' driveway and stopped at a careless angle.

Knowing their eyes were on him, he left the car with a tight mouth and resolute eyes. He slammed the car door and made his way to the front door in stiff, purposeful steps. He let real anger bleed into his being as he pounded on the door far longer than needed.

Higgins' house cleaner—a small aging Brazilian woman named Luiza—cracked open the door.

He shoved it open stormed past her.

"Where are they? Downstairs?"

"Mr. Reinhart, I'm sorry but they—"

He strode down Higgins' main hallway, past his modern art collection, and descended the stairs. With each angry stride he stomped a little harder, but he kept the affected rage from clouding his sense of them. The first few moments between them would determine if he'd get a chance to enact Plan A—or if he'd be killed again on sight.

They were guarded, afraid, rattled, and now a few doors away. He tried to dial back the anger in his blood as he approached the library door, but already he could feel his control slipping. Their proximity was causing his rage to boil.

When he got to the double doors he shoved them open.

Gerald Higgins stood at his desk with his right hand near the drawer. Wallace Purdie stood across the room, far away from the door, with his left side hidden from view.

Dominick strode into the room with his heart in his throat.

"You assholes have been holding out on me!" he shouted. "And that stops right fucking now."

Their faces didn't change but their confusion deepened. Without waiting for a response he started towards Higgins. He flinched.

*Steady now,* Dominick told himself. *Don't get shot.*

"Is this room clean?" Dominick demanded as he came to stop.

"I don't know what you—"

"Don't jerk my chain, you pencil-dick bastard! Is this room clean, or do we need to go somewhere else to talk privately?"

Neither man spoke. Their indecision was thick enough to fill the room. Perfect.

"Fine. We'll do it here," Dominick sneered. "And the help will hear what they hear. It's not like you don't have friends on the other side that can make sure they stay quiet, right?"

"No, no, let's uh," Higgins said. He wasn't speaking in his usual slow fashion. This was going even better than Dominick had hoped. "Let's reconvene in my private study. Before we do, would you mind, um, removing your shirt for a—"

"You think I'm wearing a fucking wire?"

Dominick ripped off his shirt. Buttons popped, a sleeve tore. When finished he threw it at Higgins.

"You fucking guys. Can we do this now?"

Bare-chested, he glared at them. Higgins and Wallace traded the briefest of glances before Higgins motioned towards the door.

Without hesitation Dominick started that way, and Higgins and Wallace fell in step behind him.

*So far so good,* he sent out to Dai. Her concern had waned, but only by a shade. Now that he was there, with only discipline separating him from felony assault (if not first-degree murder), the feeling of her love and support was more comforting than he'd expected.

"Which way?" he asked as they came to the end of the hallway. Higgins moved in front of him and pushed a panel next to a bookcase. The bookcase slid aside to reveal a small doorway. Higgins then used three sets of keys to open the door, and thus revealed another descending staircase. Higgins then moved aside for Dominick to enter.

Remaining in character, Dominick started down without hesitation, but a subtle shift in Higgins raised an alarm. The moment the staircase was revealed Higgins was more sure of himself. Dominick also didn't love having them behind him as he descended into the darkness, but a certain amount of risk could not be avoided. Besides, he needed them to relax at some point for his plan to work.

They reached the bottom of the stairs and walked through a narrow tunnel. The energy of the environment changed with every step; he felt the ripple of goosebumps on his arms. They weren't headed to an ordinary room.

The hallway ended and Dominick stepped into a small,

octagonal space. Benches, low to the ground, were placed along the walls and formed a rough circle. At the room's center was a flat-topped block. It was covered by a black cloth, and sitting atop it was an ancient chalice and a jagged ceremonial blade covered in writing.

Dominick stepped towards the center of the room, and both Higgins and Wallace flanked out on either side of him. For the first time, a real sense of fear nibbled at his anger. The entire room was screaming. While the walls looked to be ordinary redwood paneling, they were cut from wood tens of thousands of years old; they emanated age-old savagery and their cries were deafening. Both the chalice and blade sang hundred-year songs of death by sacrifice.

The most frightening object was the one that appeared the most innocent; the innocuous black cloth draped over the block wasn't a cloth at all. Imperceptible to the eye, Dominick sensed it pulsing with life.

This isn't a room, Dominick thought. It's a gateway.

Higgins and Wallace, while still cautious and unsure, were calmer here. He was cornered in the one place that affirmed their dominion over the planet.

*We can do virtually anything we want. With them behind us we're gods.*

It was time to turn the tables on their smug reassurance. Dominick's eyes cut into Higgins.

"You think I don't know where I am?" Dominick's words were low, tight. "I'm going to let you in on something. I know why the FTC dropped the injunction against the NorCorp acquisition last year. I know why we've always been able to poach JL's best personnel. I know why the portfolio of every member of the board has seen unparalleled growth since coming on."

He walked to the flat-topped block—it was an altar, he knew—and he felt their anxiousness rise.

He dangled his hand over the unholy swath of darkness pretending to be a tablecloth. It wafted at his near-touch. Their fear notched-up exponentially.

"I know who the cavalry is, boys. And I want in." He looked up at them. "I want in right now."

Again they shifted with discomfort. It was working.

The ploy was simple. Channel his anger into righteous indignation that they'd kept him on the outside of the "real action." Demand inclusion into the inner circle. They'd long lost touch with honesty, character, or integrity, so they'd relate well to a blind lust for power. If he was willing to overlook them rigging his car with explosives and then detonating them in his home, well, then bygones were bygones, right?

Higgins and Wallace traded a look. They were still confused and unsure, but Wallace was sniffing at the bait. It was time to strengthen the value proposition; that was marketing 101.

"The depths of what you two don't know, don't realize, is beyond your imagining." Dominick spoke with passion and struggled to keep Vincent's face from coming to mind. "You're like Medieval kings, thinking you're living high on the hog but with no concept of running water, much less trans-continental flight or nanotechnology. There is so much more out there! You're missing out and you don't even know it. There's power that makes buying companies look like trading baseball cards. It's right under your noses. I can show you."

The hook was going in. Powerful people throughout human history all shared a trait that could be used to manipulate them, provided one was audacious enough to exploit it. It was a trait summed up beautifully in one of The Matrix films: "What do all men of power want? More power."

Wallace was sold; Dominick didn't need psychic ability to see that. The prospect of elevating his perversion to heretofore undreamed-of heights had him salivating.

The image of the young brown girl's head bobbing beneath Wallace's hairy, inflated stomach flashed into Dominick's mind and his mouth tightened further.

*Indonesian talent, my god.*

Dominick tried to will away the girl's age
*(15)*
but the truth was unrelenting. And then there was Vincent.

*Daughter has a birthday party coming up. Janice and I will be there. I'll mark the boy.*

Three years ago Wallace presented Violet a beautiful white DKNY dress for her 14th birthday; two weeks later Vincent was gone. Somehow, Wallace had marked him to die.

Fury vibrated throughout Dominick's body.

"What are you waiting for?" he screamed. "Limitless power calls and you stand around like idiots?"

Wallace looked to Higgins, as if for permission. Higgins, unsure but coming around, gave him a small nod.

"This is, um, not how we normally do this," Wallace said. Dominick started to relax. Wallace was about to share their initiation process. After which, he'd be in.

Once in, he'd bring it all crashing down.

Wallace came towards him and pointed at the altar.

"It sounds like the cat's out of the bag. But before we can speak on it directly we have to follow the code. It's one of those things."

Wallace shrugged with a chuckle; his excitement was palpable. Dominick's stomach twisted into angry knots.

"The code?"

Wallace went behind the altar. He picked up both the chalice and the knife, and took great care to not touch the cloth in the process, Dominick noticed.

"Yeah." Wallace presented both knife and chalice to Dominick. "The blood code."

"Yes." Higgins was back to his typical slowness. "With your blood, willingly given, you swear fealty to the code and consecrate the contract with the other side. It is a binding agreement."

Dominick's heart plummeted.

"Any attempt to discuss the contract with anyone who hasn't taken the oath is forbidden," Higgins enunciated. "Any attempt to obstruct the execution of the contract is forbidden. Violating either of these comes at the cost of your life."

"We usually have a lot more ritual around taking the oath." Wallace, excited, fidgeted like a child awaiting Christmas morning. "But like I said, your situation is a bit unique."

Realizations, like blades of truth, cascaded down upon Dominick.

He could never infiltrate their inner circle and tear it down from the inside; betrayal brought death, care of the darkness. That's what killed Mr. Wellington and Christian Leftwich. Sherrill McKinnen had tried to tell him that, but he'd been too busy foaming at the mouth while playing Chopin to hear her.

Plan A would never work. But now he was doomed because it was too late to back out.

Bitterness exploded in him as he looked at Wallace.

"Oh, and the knife is obsidian, so it's a lot sharper than it looks," Wallace said. "A little prick will do."

Heart throbbing and head swimming, Dominick glanced down at the chalice and blade in Wallace's outstretched hands. That's when he saw it.

There was a prominent bulge in Wallace's pants; he had an erection.

Dominick's Ghetto Boy screamed—and the rage-bomb erupted.

It was like the punch at Swingers, but far worse. And Terrance wasn't there to stop him.

Teeth bared, seeing only a red haze and Wallace's dumb, perverted, murderous smile, Dominick grabbed the obsidian blade. In a blink, he swiped it under Wallace's meaty chins.

An outpouring of crimson followed Dominick's hand, and Wallace's smile transformed into a look of choking astonishment. He dropped the chalice as his hands went to his blooming throat. Wet, impotent gasps escaped him.

A new madness seized Dominick, and with it came a new idea. Did he dare?

*You're motherfucking right I dare!* his Ghetto Boy screamed.

Dominick whirled on the wide-eyed Higgins and tossed the blade at his feet with disdain.

"I offer you eternity and you want to play games?" Dominick shrieked. "Is this a billion-dollar empire or girl's club?"

He scooped up the chalice, held it under the choking, staggering Wallace, and caught some of his blood.

He turned to Higgins, raised the chalice for a toast, then pretended to drink. He held his lips closed, dry swallowed, and allowed the blood to pour over his mouth and chin. He then threw the chalice at Higgins.

"Is that enough blood for you?" Dominick screamed. "Can we talk business now? Or do we eat s'mores and I braid what's left of your fucking hair?"

Undone, Higgins' eyes darted between Dominick and Wallace.

"You lunatic! Lunatic!" Higgins stammered. "What have you done?"

Dominick reached out with his mind and broadcast with as much power as he could muster.

*Dai I'm improvising! May need you to make that Plan B call anyway!*

Plan B was her calling the front gate security to alert the police of a murder, should Dominick get killed (again). It was a long-shot, but if the police responded and discovered his fresh body the resulting scandal would rock the board.

But he hadn't planned for this.

The light dimmed. An impossible wind blew. The walls and ceiling retreated before their eyes; the room was growing. Higgins, his eyes wild with fear, looked over Dominick's shoulder and abruptly backed away.

Dominick turned to see that Wallace, now on his knees with his back towards them, had stopped gasping. The black cloth on the altar, now dripping with Wallace's blood, rippled and pulsed.

*Dai, something's up! Dai? Dai!*

Silence—he was losing touch with her. The room continued to expand, and Dominick could also feel it filling up as well. Something unseen was being poured into the room, and it choked out all connection to the world outside.

The source seemed to be Wallace.

"Lunatic! Lunatic!" Higgins continued to scream. He ran

to the wall where the door had been—now more than twenty feet away—but the door had vanished.

*Well shit*, Dominick thought.

He turned to face Wallace.

Wallace, still with his back to them, removed his hands from his throat and stood. He turned. His face was a horrifying mask of death; it was devoid of blood, his mouth was askew as if in mid-gasp, and his vacant eyes had rolled into his head. Nonetheless, he took two steps to the altar and reached out.

The black cloth flew into his hands.

The unnatural wind blew harder as Wallace brought the cloth to his face. It spread out over his face and then liquefied. He stood, palms raised to the ceiling, and it stretched itself over his entire head and torso. Within moments he was covered in a living, liquid, oozing darkness.

The jaw worked up and down as if to stretch. Then the head turned towards Dominick.

"You have our attention," it thundered in a thousand voices. "What do you propose?"

"He doesn't speak for us!" Higgins shouted from across the room. His usual slow manner of speech was now abandoned. "He's not one of us! This was all a mistake! Don't let—"

Higgins gasped as his hand went to his chest. His face contorted with pain.

Dominick, his heart beating so fast he feared he might faint, forced his words to remain calm.

"If he dies, explaining it will be inconvenient."

Higgins dropped to his hands and knees and started panting. But his spasms subsided. Dominick, stifling the impulse to tremble, looked again at the specter.

"Your proposal," it thundered again. "We are listening,"

Dominick took a breath. "Flesh is weak. Corruptible. Temporary. Look at them. They've grown ineffective under the weight of their greed. They can't see past manipulating stock futures and raping children."

Dominick, terrified but affecting intensity, took a step towards the ghastly creature with a face made of black. This was the most important sales pitch of his life; it had lives depending on it, even as Dominick made up every word on the spot.

*Please god guide me true*, he prayed.

"But why endeavor to control a few companies when you can control an entire planet?" Dominick continued. "Why stop at one planet when there are entire realities out there? Waiting to be leveraged, waiting to be conquered?"

He pointed to Higgins, still on the floor.

"They don't have the vision for that! Buying a seat on a federal commission is a major victory in their minds. They know nothing of eternity! They know nothing of true power! Power that can shape the cosmos itself. But I do."

Higgins, still panting, shouted. "You can't...you can't just..."

Dominick whirled around, stomped to Higgins, and hoisted him up by his throat. He squeezed and couldn't help but enjoy the look of terror in Higgins' eyes.

*Don't consider the cost. Consider the profit.* Higgins' words. Vincent was part of the cost. How many others?

"You thought you were a god? Feeling like a god now?" Dominick let the spittle fly from his mouth to Higgins' face.

As Higgins' struggles lessened, Dominick was tempted to keep squeezing. But he could feel the fear from Higgins being lapped up by the specter behind him. Dominick's eyes narrowed.

*Congrats, Higgins, you were right—they don't care who bleeds,* Dominick thought as he shoved Higgins away from him by his neck. He fell to the floor with a gasp. He then scurried to the ceremonial knife, now covered in blood, and scooped it up. Wild-eyed, he pointed it at Dominick.

This time the specter intervened.

"Enough," it roared. Higgins retreated like a frightened animal. He clutched the blade with both hands and held it before him like a shield.

Dominick turned again to the black specter of many voices. The air continued to swirl around them. Had he done enough? For that matter, what was he doing?

The specter opened its mouth and thundered again.

"We find your proposal...intriguing."

Dominick nodded. That had to be good, right?

It continued.

"True power requires imagination. Creativity. In this regard we agree that your predecessors have been limited." Its voice was terrible; it was the sound of anguish and death.

"You can't do this! We had a deal!" Higgins, unhinging, now screamed from across the room. He brandished the bloody blade with one hand and tore at his clothes with the other.

Dominick kept his eyes on the ghoul. After a moment it nodded.

"We wish to know more of your proposal," it said, "and verbal communication is limited."

The specter opened its arms as if to embrace. Dominick's fear surged.

"Show us your vision," it said.

It felt as though a freight train slammed into his mind at full speed. Dazed, he realized the truth. The board didn't have a telepath, but the darkness didn't need one. The moment they got into his mind, they'd know his true intentions.

He tried to shield himself, but their onslaught was swift and unstoppable. In less than a breath, they were through. An instant later, he was drowning in darkness.

"You are still their champion." The chorus of voices thundered from everywhere. "Clever. Resourceful. A pity."

It was over. He'd failed.

"Now you will die," it added. "Slowly."

"*God-fucking-dammit!*" he screamed. He didn't know if that was himself or his Ghetto Boy. It was too late to matter.

Down, down, down he spiraled again. He was spinning. Everything gyrated. Everything *hurt.* End over end, he tumbled. Pain exploded over every inch of his being. He couldn't thrash about, he couldn't fight. Was he even in his body anymore? He didn't think so. All he knew was darkness and agony.

Bitterness found a way through the pain. Dai, Antoinette, Violet, oh his Violet—they'd be lost. They'd be killed. He screamed in rage, and the darkness filled his mouth and choked him. Of course they wouldn't make it quick. This time there were no singing flowers or fuzzy memories. They would simply dish out pain—brutal and relentless.

"*Damn you!*" His taunt turned into a cry of agony as blows rained down on him. He tried to cry, tried to scream, but the blows beat even that from him.

*Dad?*

A glint of light, only a pin-prick, opened somewhere in the curtain of black. His boy! Yes, the agony would end at some point; maybe not soon, but at some point. Then he'd be with his boy again.

*"I'm sorry, buddy!"* He forced out the words, even as they were interspersed with his own tortured cries. *"I love you so much. I'm sorry!"*

Their assault intensified, but the pin-prick of light grew to the size of a marble, and then a baseball. His boy was there, his real, honest-to-god boy—not a shade wearing Vincent's face, but the little guy he'd missed every day since the accident.

Bitterness beat down his excitement. That wasn't an accident; his boy had been murdered. Dominick had failed to protect his little guy. With him gone, they'd now they target everyone else he loved.

Again rage surged within him, in defiance of the pain. But then he heard a whimper that wasn't his own.

He turned his attention to the light, but the whimper wasn't from there either. Who was that?

More screams, stereo with his own cries of pain, reached his awareness. Unlike Vincent's voice, which had almost lessened Dominick's level of agony, this new voice stoked the fires of his hatred.

He knew who it was. Upon that realization, for the briefest moment, even the pain was dulled by the surge of rage.

Wallace Purdie was out there screaming.

*"You goddamn pervert! You murdering motherfucker!"* Dominick, fighting through the pain, searched with renewed vigor to locate the source of Wallace's cries.

The blows to Dominick's being, which had been relentless, now dipped in frequency. Lost in rage, he didn't notice. His only focus was finding Wallace.

Once he found him, he would brutalize that fucker with every iota of strength he had left.

He sensed Wallace flailing in the darkness, his rotund form

drowning in the sea of black. As beaten as Dominick was, his anger intensified as he prepared to inflict even more violence upon the man who'd helped murder his son. He reached out with what passed for his hand and grabbed Wallace by the hair. He drew back his fist to pound Wallace's fat, blubbering face even deeper into oblivion.

But then he stopped. A new idea arrested him cold.

Wallace continued to scream and wave his arms in a desperate, agonized panic. But Dominick was riveted in place. This new idea, the ultimate tyrant, had not released him.

But could he do it?

As if to motivate the action, a hot knife stabbed into him. Once in, it was twisted. The pain was excruciating. But this unspeakable idea still gripped him.

Even with everything hanging in the balance, could he really?

Another knife plunged into him, even deeper than the last. Dominick's cry was long and desperate. He didn't know if his focus could withstand another.

Still, doubt hounded his resolve. Could he?

"I have to try, buddy. I have to try." Fresh tears in his eyes, he cast his view to the small hole of light. "Vincent, you're the best part of me! I love you!"

Two knives stabbed into him this time. Even as he cried out in agony, he turned to Wallace and did the unthinkable.

He put his arms around Wallace and hugged him tightly.

"It's almost over," Dominick screamed. "Just hold on!"

Everything exploded.

*       *       *

Before he opened his eyes, he knew pain. It gripped him, held him close like a desperate lover, and spread itself along the entire length of his body.

*Dad?*

There was a pull at the corners of his mouth—a smile? His bleeding lips, which currently were part of the chorus of pain, wouldn't quite cooperate. It didn't stop him from trying.

There was a sliding feeling as well. Subtle, but real. Yes, something fundamental, something central, something closer to him than breath itself, was making a slow, smooth, warm exit.

Still, the sound of a scream, high and shrill, pried open his eyes.

"I won't, you hear me? I will not!"

His head would only move bare inches, but his neck obliged just enough to offer him a view. Debris lie everywhere. Wood smoldered. In fact, he was beneath some of it right now—pinned. His leg was twisted at an obscene angle, and neither of his arms responded to his brain.

His eyes could move, and another screeching cry drew their interest. The screamer was Higgins. Yes, he knew Higgins; he was a weasel of a human being, but currently looking even more so on his knees with his shirt torn open, his face bleeding, and his eyes wild.

"It's mine! All this is mine!" Higgins shrieked. Up went his right hand, then down it came with force. "I deserve it! I earned it! And *we had a deal!*"

His hand flew up again, and a glob of blood was flung into the air. Down went his hand again. There was a knife in his hand; Dominick recognized it from somewhere. Higgins was stabbing someone. Dominick could see nothing else, as his neck would move no further. The pain, the incredible pain, squeezed tears from his eyes.

Then there was someone else.

Someone—or maybe some*thing*—emerged from a dark chasm in the shattered wall. Sure, it looked like a man, with legs and arms and a gangly way of moving through the wreckage as if dancing with it. But it had no face. No matter where it moved, no matter what fire light reached its way, its face remained in shadow. Instead of a nose, cheeks, facial features—it had only eyes.

And a glowing smile.

"Mine, mine, mine!" Higgins screamed as the figure danced towards him. When it was nearly upon him Higgins gasped and brandished the blade as if to attack.

The figure danced past him without a glance.

It was nearly out of Dominick's view when it stopped. It stooped, reached into the ash and dirt, and then stood again moments later. In its hand now dangled a black cloth. It was limp and tattered.

The figure inspected the cloth—and then it laughed. It was a wretched, nightmarish sound. The figure threw the cloth over its shoulder like a spent dishrag. Still laughing, it turned Dominick's way. Its eyes were amused—impressed maybe? It gave Dominick a laughing, nodding, thumbs-up acknowledgment.

Then it walked away and vanished into the darkness.

Higgins returned to his screaming assault. Dominick also heard the sounds of sirens. Everything seemed to be getting further and further away.

That's right—he was busy. He tried to chuckle, but it came out as a sputtering gasp. Yes, he was busy gliding away. It felt like being a lopsided dab of butter on a piping hot muffin— slowly sliding away. It was time to go; hasta la vista baby, bon voya-jee, don't forget to write.

Sirens now nearly drowned out Higgins' screams, but all of it was now disappearing behind the haze. Dominick tried to smile again. Good thing Higgins wasn't stabbing him like that. If so he'd be...

Dominick closed his eyes.

*      *      *

*White. Silent, eternal, motionless white.*

*No time. No thought. No presence. No awareness. Only white that spanned forever.*

*Until—a realization.*

*Murderer.*

*Heaviness now. He was aware of himself, aware of his being. He sank.*

*A voice whispered from the white.*

*"Dominick Reinhart."*

*Two lights, blue as the boundless sky, emerged from the white. But Dominick continued to fall.*

*"I didn't even blink," he said. He felt a hole inside himself growing larger by the moment. "I did it and I didn't even blink."*

*The voice whispered a reply.*

*"Still you doubt their power to incite? To corrupt?"*

*His descent slowed. The hole inside him froze in place. In moments he was no longer falling. The two blue lights settled before him.*

*"You are the champion of champions, Dominick Reinhart."*

*Puzzlement. Time stretched, even as nothing moved.*

*"What happens now?" he asked at last.*

*"You choose."*

*More silence. It permeated his indecision and took it afloat as might a mighty ocean. Again time stretched into nothingness.*

*"But the board," he said. "And the company, and justice! What about——?"*

*"You have won."*

*He could not dare believe it.*

*"It's over?"*

*"The darkness was broken. It can no longer protect the guilty."*

*Could it be true?*

*"It's really over?"*

*Brighter still, eternity glowed.*

*"Yes. Now you may go where you choose."*

*The light filled him. It was welcoming light, healing light, loving light.*

*"Wherever you go, go in peace, Dominick Reinhart," the blue lights sang. "We thank you."*

*The blue lights evaporated. Again the world was only white. Silent, eternal, motionless white.*

*He ached with a yearning so powerful he thought it could freeze time itself. His heart, his life, his dreams, his being, all cried out in a unified stance. God, how he wanted it.*

*And yet...it wasn't time.*

*"I love you so much," he said. He felt him out there; a smile of reassurance, a smile of understanding. Their time would come.*

*Dominick smiled. The world went still.*

*                         *                         *

With herculean effort, he got one eye open. The other, crusted over, was stuck; only a glint of a hazy world peeked through. Grey light stabbed into his eyes, and a series of blinks resulted. Both eyes eventually came free.

The world came into focus, and his first realization brought the beginnings of a smile. For once, thank God, he was waking up in a bed.

He was in a large hospital bed, in fact. There were tubes up his nose. Thick casts encased both his forearms, and another was wrapped around his left leg, which was elevated. Dull pain was in his hips; a glance downwards showed him a kind of metal harness protruding from his pelvis. He noticed all this without reaction.

It was a quick wiggle of his fingers and toes that convinced him that somehow, he was in fact, still alive. A full smile finally bloomed on his face.

He looked beyond his bed and noticed that there was much more to see. He was flanked by an array of flowers on both sides, but some had wilted. Discolored petals hung off a couple here and there. Some of the vases could accommodate more flowers than they held. He also wasn't alone; to his right, a sleeping Dai was curled up on a large love-seat. A tear welled up.

He noticed something else: next to his hip, in front of Dai, was an opened envelope. He saw both paper and something else peeking out of it.

With considerable effort, he willed his right shoulder to engage and reach for the envelope. After several attempts, he was able to snag it both between two of his fingers and bring it to his face.

From it he pulled a letter written in Violet's handwriting. His pulse quickened.

*Dear Dad,*

*I hope you can hear me, and even if you can't I hope you can feel my love for you. I'll come by to visit but I wanted to send this ahead of time. So I'll always be by your side. Dai is there a lot of the time, but I want to be there all the time. :-)*

*First I want to tell you my good news. I'm doing really well! I'm four months sober (yeah you read that right), yes, FOUR MONTHS SOBER, and I'm working a really strong program. I volunteer at a home for battered women and their children, so I spend a lot of time taking care of little ones so the moms can have breaks. I love it. These women are so strong, it's inspiring. Fills me up every day.*

*And the picture I'm sending you is <u>really</u> special, which is why I wanted it to be at your side. There's somebody that's been helping me so much in program. He spoke at a meeting when I first started coming around and I couldn't believe my eyes. I went up to him afterwards and that's when we both realized. He wants to come see you too. He's got a LOT of recovery, and I wouldn't be where I am already if not for him.*

*I love you Dad, and I will see you soon.*

*Pumpkin (but REALLY Violet)*

Dominick's hand quivered. With two fingers he extracted the photograph, brought it to his face, and then time froze.

It was a smiling photograph of his baby girl, except she was now a tall young woman with a bright smile and a huge mane of light-brown curls.

Next to her, sporting a broad smile of his own, was a handsome elderly brown man in a wheelchair. The lines in his face and the thinning gray hair did nothing to hide the resemblance; his face was a mirror of Dominick's own.

Dominick gasped.

Dai stirred in his peripheral vision, but Dominick's focus remained fixed on the implausible picture dangling before his eyes. It was like looking into an alternate reality even more impossible than the one he just left. But its reality was evidenced by the two smiling brown faces before him representing two generations of his family.

Even as Dai awakened, Dominick remained frozen. His mouth hung open even as hers broke out into a wide grin and she rushed to the bedside. She covered his face in laughing kisses, but he continued to clutch the impossible picture between his fingers. When he felt her tears on his face as she held him tight, his eyes closed. He remembered the words, clear as a summer night sky.

*Go in peace, Dominick Osiris Reinhart.*

Yes, as a matter of fact, he would. Regardless of what happened from now on, he would do just that.

His smile turned into a chuckle, the chuckle into a laugh. Dai hugged him as he laughed; with the picture still dangling between his fingers, he felt so full he thought he might burst.

*        *        *

# EPILOGUE

The far-flung TJ&D empire, with offices on four continents, tens of thousands of employees across the globe, and annual revenue in the billions, was undone by a fifty-dollar dashboard camera.

The company's downfall was initiated by the shocking run of events that preceded it; by itself, the sudden deaths of three board members would have doomed a lesser organization. The scandal of the story, however, lay in the details. When emergency personnel responded to the explosion at the estate of Gerald Higgins, they found him mutilating the body of Wallace Purdie. Shocking photos, captured by a member of his staff, depicted a bleeding, half-naked, wild-eyed Higgins attacking a first responder with a knife. It was later reported that the knife was a 2,000-year-old artifact listed as missing from the Metropolitan Museum of Art. Further intrigue was provided by the discovery of Dominick Reinhart amidst the rubble; pronounced dead one day earlier after his own home had exploded, he was found severely injured and in a coma. Questions of how, why, and what happened spread like wildfire across the airwaves.

The *coup de grace* came after Dominick awoke 14 days later. In what would be the final twist of the story, he obtained a video through the will of his late father-in-law Arthur Wellington. Dominick submitted the video to the authorities. It soon leaked to the media; within days, it was on screens across the world.

The video showed Wellington and Christian Leftwich seated in a vehicle discussing their company's lengthy criminal history. They'd recorded themselves with a dashboard camera.

*"Christian, what are we talking about here?"*

*"Well, Arthur, we're talking about a board that has overseen or committed virtually every corporate crime in existence. Fraud, tax evasion, bribery, embezzlement, money laundering, labor racketeering, insider trading, and we're only getting started."*

*"There's also the personal offenses. Human trafficking, child pornography, conspiracy to commit murder, sexual assault, and outright rape."*

*"Some of it's just business. Microprocessors need tin. Congolese warlords with tin mines need money."* Leftwich coughed loudly.

*"Some of it's personal. Opium fields in Afghanistan don't harvest themselves. So if you have a habit, may as well get some skin in the game."*

They concluded their astounding conversation by sharing the whereabouts of records of these activities; names, numbers, financial accounts, dates, notes, and several photographs were obtained from the estates of both men.

The reckoning was swift.

The estates of every board member, alive or dead, were raided. Assets were frozen, fines levied, and federal indictments handed out in bunches. Gerald Higgins was already confined to a mental institution, and the remaining members of the board of directors were taken into custody. A media spectacle ensued; as the new faces of corporate greed and corruption, they were paraded about, their hands cuffed and heads bowed, and lead from courtroom to courtroom by a swarm of federal agents. It was widely speculated that none of them would see the outside of a federal penitentiary.

The company's stock price tumbled. Days later, as the company lingered on financial life-support, it was acquired by an investment group; many assumed that its assets would then be sold off individually.

Yet the line of chauffeured vehicles assembled before Dominick's new Venice home implied something different. When Dominick saw the collection of businesspeople making their way to his front door, he knew his life's next chapter was about to begin.

\*             \*             \*

Carson Miller stubbed out his cigarette. It had been his tenth of the day, and as he prepared to light his eleventh the small jittery man sat across from him.

"Thank you for meeting me, Mr. Miller, I appreciate your time." Even seated he couldn't be still. Where the nerves ended and the cocaine began, Miller neither knew nor cared.

"What do you want?" Miller said from behind his sunglasses.

The jittery man glanced around himself as if the patio of Miller's villa contained spies.

"It isn't what I want that matters, it's what can be created. Mr. Purdie had certain proclivities I was charged with supporting, so I was indirectly privy to, uh, certain interests that protected Mr. Purdie and propelled him to success."

"A lot of good that did him." Miller took a long drag as the jittery man laughed nervously. Fuck this guy, Miller thought.

"Mr. Purdie was not like you. He was not a man of restraint. Frankly, I fear his lack of restraint may have endangered me, given the current investigation into his affairs. Someone may mistake me as complicit in his more extreme activities."

"And I should care about you or Wallace because why?"

The jittery man licked his lips and folded his hands. "Mr. Miller, you resigned before the company fell. You're respected. Your family name carries weight. You could secure investment and start a new enterprise tomorrow. And because you are more focused than Mr. Purdie, more disciplined, you can succeed where he failed; you can enjoy protection and support without exceeding its limits. You can have your own empire."

"And you can avoid prosecution by getting back under the umbrella of protection." Miller blew smoke at him.

Again the jittery man laughed nervously. He answered, but Miller had stopped listening. He thought of his father, that self-important prick who hadn't said a word to Miller since Dominick Reinhart out-maneuvered him. For Miller to be forced out was shameful enough; for him to be forced out by a low-bred, low-class *jigaboo* was indefensible.

Miller took another long drag. He would have his revenge; his father would be forced to extract the telephone pole from his ass. No one will ever laugh at Carson Miller again.

"Stop talking," Miller interrupted with a raised hand. "How do I get started?"

The jittery man beamed.

"I don't have the details, but I can connect you with someone who does. Have you ever traveled to the Sahara, Mr. Miller?"

\*             \*             \*

# About the Series

If only a city could confess of the horrors it harbors.

The City of Shadows is a series of interlocking thrillers set in Los Angeles. From the palmy beaches of Venice to the pristine mansions of Brentwood to the darkest depths of Skid Row, the forces of good and evil collide in a struggle for power that leaves none unscathed.

These stories follow a group of loosely-associated LA residents who step forward—or are forced—into the fray.

Made in the USA
Monee, IL
10 July 2021